Praise for Winona Sullivan's Sister Cecile mysteries

A SUDDEN DEATH AT THE NORFOLK CAFÉ

"The author has been a teacher and analyst for the CIA, and she has a devious mind. . . . The Boston scene, the teenager and the nun, and the dialogue are attractively written."
—*The Boston Globe*

"A smartly paced, alternately sweet and tough story that has all the moves of a gangbusting nun."
—*Kirkus Reviews*

DEAD SOUTH

"Solid prose, conniving characters, and an undercurrent of humor will leave readers eagerly awaiting Cecile's next adventure."
—*Library Journal*

"Equal doses of suspense and humor keep this tale of a kidnapped CIA agent hopping."
—*Mystery Lovers Bookshop*

By Winona Sullivan:

A SUDDEN DEATH AT THE NORFOLK CAFÉ
DEAD SOUTH
DEATH'S A BEACH
SAVING DEATH

SAVING DEATH

Winona Sullivan

FAWCETT • NEW YORK

1211223\

A Fawcett Book
Published by The Ballantine Publishing Group
Copyright © 2000 by Winona Sullivan

All rights reserved under International and Pan-American Copyright Conventions. Published in the United States by The Ballantine Publishing Group, a division of Random House, Inc., New York, and simultaneously in Canada by Random House of Canada Limited, Toronto.

Fawcett is a registered trademark and the Fawcett colophon is a trademark of Random House, Inc.

www.randomhouse.com/BB/

Library of Congress Catalog Card Number: 99-091099

ISBN 0-8041-1899-X

Manufactured in the United States of America

First Edition: January 2000

10 9 8 7 6 5 4 3 2 1

1

South Florida
January 1976

NINETEEN-YEAR-OLD Juan Caldo ran through the South Florida night under the dim light of a quarter moon. Thorny spikes gouged him. Grass with serrated edges and saw palmettos cut him. The things that didn't cut, oozed sticky, stinging fluids that burned his flesh as he raced by, dressed in a ragged prison uniform.

He kept running.

Juan finally stopped, gulping hot night air. Gradually his heartbeat slowed. He laughed out loud and spun, arms raised. Freedom. He felt it, tasted it on his salty lips, clutched it in the air with his arms held high. A wild sound from his throat cleared the slash pines and rose to heaven. He kicked off his remaining shoe and danced barefoot on raw earth. The other shoe was long gone, bitten off by a solution hole formed in the ancient oolitic limestone a thousand years ago.

Juan Caldo stood, gasping for breath, a good-looking young man whose father once made shoes in Cuba, a young man formerly headed for studies in civil engineering and a brilliant career. Juan stared down at his bare feet, struck with the irony of his life. Two escapes. Cuba first, and now the North Broward Maximum Security Prison in South Florida.

He pushed it out of his mind, how he and two other men had dug a thirty-foot tunnel and crawled through mud and dirt and razor-sharp coral rocks to freedom. He didn't know that the other convicts were captured within twenty-four hours. All he knew was that he was free and shoeless on the edge of the Everglades. It had been easier to leave Cuba on a raft.

The police said he killed Victor Torres. Victor, who had been in bed with Juan's woman. Juan pled not guilty.

"Now what do I do?" He addressed the trees, the grass, the dry earth. He had nowhere to go. He didn't trust a living soul anymore; not woman, not man. His girlfriend, Nubia? He'd found her naked under a man. She'd screamed rape when Juan burst into the room. Juan breathed heavily and saw Victor Torres's dark, naked body. The scene played over and over in his mind. Was it rape? Victor Torres was a friend. Had been a friend. But Victor loved women; that was a fact. One dead man and an unfaithful woman. Juan couldn't go home.

He skirted the edge of the Everglades, walking all night, sleeping during the day, covering his body with pine needles as he lay on the soft floor of the January woods. Winter was the dry season and few mosquitoes tormented him. He covered twelve miles the second night and found a change of clothes on a clothesline. On someone's back porch he found a pair of sneakers. His feet were raw, his entire body hurt from scrapes and cuts.

At midnight on the third night he found a Dumpster beside a restaurant and retrieved a meal of pepper pork chops, creamy gravy, and rice. He found an outdoor water faucet in the rear of the restaurant and an empty wine bottle.

"Mother of God, you look after me so well," Juan said. He could live off that Dumpster. The prison was far behind. He felt safe for the first time in months, and he fell into a peaceful sleep at the edge of dense, subtropical forestland.

The young man lay all the next day under some palmetto scrub and watched the sky through a green curtain. Birds sang to him. Crows flew overhead. He saw a roseate spoonbill and a bald eagle and countless egrets and ibises. Finally he ventured out and explored the bordering wetlands, coming upon a hammock, one of the raised islands of hardwoods found in the Everglades. The hammock was about a mile away from the Turnpike and his restaurant Dumpster. It looked like home.

Juan quickly discovered that this part of South Florida was a strange no-man's-land where people lived in shanties, trailers, even old cars. The depleted fields grew poor crops; pigs rutted in dirty acreage beside their squalid owners. Banana trees grew in dismal intensity. This strange landscape existed somewhere between Fort Lauderdale and Miami, hiding on the edge of the Everglades, a third world not that many miles from the mansions of Coral Gables.

Two big gumbo limbo trees set about ten feet apart provided the basis of Juan's house. He built a sleeping platform in the upper branches, structured like an Indian chickee, open-aired and high so the breeze would blow the mosquitoes away. "My home," he said as he dragged boards to his hammock. "I will live here."

He spoke English. He would be a new man. No more Juan Caldo, the smart kid who lived on Calle Ocho in Miami, the kid sent up for murder.

One night he found a rusty ax in someone's trash. Just as he pulled it out, a rottweiler appeared.

Juan froze, ax in hand. "Nice dog," he said quietly.

The beast snarled, teeth like white fangs, bared to the moonlight. The dog's neck muscles bulged.

Juan took half a step back. "I don't fight, dog. Nonaggressive type, that's me." He kept his words soft, peaceful, English.

A low growl answered Juan.

"Go home," Juan whispered, his voice nervous. He knew dogs could smell fear. Juan started to back away slowly, ax in hand. He held it low, nonthreatening.

Another growl, the rottweiler was poised to spring. The dog leaped, bared teeth aimed for Juan's throat. In deadly silence Juan wrestled the dog back, his arms up, his mouth set in a rictus of fear. Snapping, the dog moved in, moved out, jumped. Juan finally held the animal at bay, one hand clutching the dog's throat. Saliva dripped on Juan's arm. The rottweiler growled, edged back, snarled viciously. The dog leaped. Sharp teeth reached around Juan's arm like a steel trap. Pain rocketed up his shoulder. The beast began a slow twisting of his dark muzzle, gnawing. Horrible sounds came from the dark throat. Blood spread. Gleaming black eyes stared malevolently.

Juan clutched the ax with his free hand and swung. A dull thud sounded. The blade cut deeply into the beast's neck. Blood spurted out. The grinding teeth released their hold. Juan's mangled arm pained him beyond reason, but the dog

3

was dying. Red blood shot from a severed artery. The dog whimpered, its tongue lolled out. The rottweiler died as Juan gasped for breath.

Juan's throbbing arm brought him back to reality. He wiped the ax on his red-stained shirt, then thrust the ax handle through the belt hole in his pants. He had to hide the dog. He took a breath and picked up the dead animal. Juan was taller than the average man from his country, close to six feet, and a strong man, wiry, lean, but not even that made carrying the sixty-pound dog an easy job. Juan lugged him ten feet, a hundred feet, a hundred yards, stopping now and then to ascertain whether he was leaving a trail of blood behind.

Juan carried the dog until he was a mile away, near a long fence that surrounded a field of cows. There he dug a hole in the earth, using the ax to scrape a grave a foot deep and several feet long. He covered the dog completely. If the corpse were left out in the sun, it would be swollen to the size of a monster within twenty-four hours, and the vultures would swoop down for a good meal. He didn't want the dog to be found.

He patted the earth flat, gathered some loose grass and covered the area. From there he walked home.

In his shack, grown now into a miniature two-room dwelling, Juan used one of his three wine bottles of water and washed himself all over. Then he rinsed his chewed arm until it appeared clean and wrapped it tightly with a piece of his shirt. God help him if it became infected. When he was a child, he had seen a cane worker slashed; septicemia had set in and the man died. Juan didn't want to die.

The bleeding stopped, but his arm throbbed horribly. "I've got to clean it right," Juan muttered, staring at the arm in the moonlight. At four o'clock that morning he ran to the restaurant next to where he pillaged the Dumpster every night.

It didn't take much effort to get inside. He pulled out the fan in the window, climbed in, and found a bathroom with a serviceable medicine chest. Hydrogen peroxide, soap, hot water. In the kitchen he found some clean towels for bandages.

The only other thing Juan stole that night was a salt shaker full of salt, several fresh rolls that he ate on the way home, and a quart of cheap beer.

The dog was in the ground only a day and Juan's arm was

4

already healing. He was again working on his home, chopping a strangler fig with his new ax. The vine was like rope, good to use. He even had screens, ripped old things, but his home was taking shape. People threw out everything a man could ever want. He'd already collected a pile of old magazines: *Home and Garden,* and dozens of back copies of *The Cattle Breeder's Digest*. He began to amass a collection of books. Juan Caldo read during daylight hours, but today he was working to take his mind off the dead dog.

"I'm going nuts by myself," he mused aloud that afternoon, weaving a thick vine into the rough ceiling. The arm started to hurt again, and he stopped working. There was no urgency in his life now. He settled down on an old mat and began to read.

A day later he was out walking along the edge of the cow pasture, watching the animals chew their cud. The heat was stifling. Dust rose in little puffs from the dirt. He needed to get out of the shack and look for air, but here by the field was no better. In the forest, at least, the trees offered shade. The open field was airless and hot, but looking at the cows was better than nothing.

The animals drifted in a hazy torpor in the grass, bulging animals with bony shoulder blades, whose tails barely twitched to ward off the flies. Three of the cows were obviously pregnant, their big bodies swaying as they foraged for sustenance. A fourth animal, a very small, brindle animal, lay on her side, moaning softly in the dirt. She was in labor.

Fascinated, Juan watched as the animal's hindquarters swelled, contracted, and swelled again. Then, from between the legs, a head emerged, slick, wet, bloody, then an entire body, gangly legs black with water, then a gush of fluid and the afterbirth. The cow gave a last grunt.

She turned and stared at the creature she had delivered. Slowly she rose to her feet and nudged her baby, speckled like herself but still dark and wet.

The calf looked dead.

"Breathe," Juan whispered. "Breathe." He could feel his own breath grow short, his chest tighten up.

The calf didn't move.

Juan pounded his hands together. Even though it was broad daylight, he broke his number one rule and ran the distance from the safety zone at the edge of the forest and into the field. He stopped beside the motionless calf. Not a flicker. The mother cow turned her eyes on Juan. He shoved the calf with his foot.

No movement.

Juan fell to his knees and grabbed at the slippery baby, held the animal's head in his hands, pulled the mouth open and made a cup with his hands and blew into the still mouth. He stopped and blew again, then pressed on the fragile ribs and watched as air and fluid bubbled out of the calf's mouth.

"Come on, Pastele, get some life." Juan breathed for the animal again. "I'm a crazy man," he whispered. "Crazy." He pushed, breathed, and watched. Finally the little animal took a long, shuddering breath. "Hey, Pastele, you live! Come to your mama.".

The mother cow bobbed her big head and nudged the newborn calf again. The little animal rose unsteadily, blinking murky eyes at the new world.

Juan backed off.

He returned across the field and slipped over the fence just in time. From his safe spot, flat on his stomach in the saw grass at the edge of the field, he saw two men approaching. "I saved your calf," Juan whispered, "Don't you find me."

The men spoke loudly.

"Looka the runt. No good. Looks like veal chops," the tall one said.

"Good cooking, little runt." The second one slapped the mother cow on the rump. "Let the milk come in good, then we'll take her down. Mama gets two weeks, then we have that barbecue you been promising Angee."

"Angee's birthday. We can have a hell of a cookout," the tall one said and chuckled.

Juan heard the words and clenched his fists. That calf was his. His fingernails cut into the palms of his hands until they hurt, while his mind formed a plan. When the farmers left the field, Juan slipped away and began to make things ready.

2

Connecticut
February 1976

DURING the following week, as Juan plotted to steal Pastele, Cecile Buddenbrooks, almost fifteen hundred miles away in a wealthy town in Connecticut, attended dance classes in preparation for her life in the social whirl that many rich girls fell into. Thirteen years old and pretty, Cecile didn't show any of the gaucheness preteens frequently exhibit. Her mother took her to Lord & Taylor to buy clothes for the season's first dance.

"You're too young to date," Cecile's mother said firmly, tugging a dress down over Cecile's hips. The dress was not exactly demure. "This is an eighth grade dance where you practice the rudiments of proper behavior with young gentlemen in a well-supervised setting. I hope you learned some manners in Switzerland when you were at that school last semester."

"I did." Cecile smiled. She had loved the Swiss school.

"You're a lucky child. You have a wonderful boy to go to the dance with," her mother said, wetting a stray wisp of Cecile's wild hair with saliva and tucking it into place behind her daughter's ear.

"I want to go with Paul," Cecile said firmly. "Or not at all."

"That nice boy already asked you. Woods Grantly, right? His father is president of the bank. Mr. Grantly is an old friend of your father's."

"Woody? I like Paul. I don't like this dress, but I'll wear it if I can go with Paul."

"This dress costs six hundred dollars. It's lovely. And Paul

7

is the cook's son. It wouldn't be proper. He goes to the public high school." June shuddered. Sometimes her daughter went too far. Cecile attended the finest private school for young girls in the state. She had beautiful, long brown hair, no pimples, slim; the girl was usually a credit to her family. But Cecile held some very weird, egalitarian ideas.

"Really, Cecile, what can we do with you?"

A week later Cecile went to the eighth grade dance with Paul Dorys, her dearest, very best friend for life, and they actually danced. Paul was a junior in the local high school. He looked good, but his suit was cheap and didn't come close to what the other boys were wearing. Cecile didn't care, and she let him kiss her at the end of the night. "I've never been so happy, Paul," she whispered after the kiss.

"Me too," Paul murmured. One last hug and they parted. She to her room on the second floor of the huge house, he to the servants' quarters in the rear of the estate where he lived with his mother, the cook.

A week later Cecile's mother went to Italy to ski with friends. Two days after that June Buddenbrooks was killed in an accident when her car spun off a narrow road coming down through the Alps.

Cecile loved her mother. Now the tall, slender woman who would appear at critical moments to make pronouncements and buy her clothes, then go off on another world tour, was gone. No more postcards from Zanzibar, no fuzzy telephone calls from Tokyo. June Buddenbrooks was dead, and her daughter was totally bereft. Jerry Buddenbrooks, Cecile's father, didn't know what to do with the girl. He suffered from his own grief, and when it was suggested he send his daughter back to a boarding school she had attended briefly in Switzerland, he agreed. The fact that it was run by the Catholic Sisters of Our Lady of Good Counsel was unfortunate as far as Jerry was concerned. Jerry Buddenbrooks was not a Catholic. Jerry abhorred religion. But everyone knew that the nuns ran the best schools. He was too busy to raise a teenage girl.

Cecile didn't really care where she went or what she did. Her life was over, and by going to a faraway place, she would be like her mother, who had traveled. "I'll write every day,

Paul," she promised her best friend the night before she left. Paul was helping his mother in the kitchen of the Buddenbrookses', Connecticut estate, cutting carrots and nibbling leftover funeral food.

"I'll answer every letter," Paul assured her. "Don't forget, summer is only a few months away."

Cecile nodded, bright-eyed. Paul would wait for her. She would wait for him. Forever.

The worst part of Juan's plan to steal the calf was digging up the dead rottweiler. Juan went out late at night with his ax and a trash bag he had emptied earlier that day. He dug with the ax. The earth had shielded the body from the talons of vultures, but Florida sunshine still caused the flesh to ripen quickly. It smelled.

"Oh boy," Juan gulped, then gagged. How the hell was he going to do this? He couldn't touch this thing!

He stepped back and took off his shirt, then wrapped it around his face, leaving only his eyes showing. "For Pastele," he said into his shirt and he went to work, scooping, shoving, pushing the dog into the bag. He closed it up, finally, and staggered to one side and did nothing but breathe the sweet night air.

Five minutes later he carried the dog in the bag to the cow pasture, pushed it through the fence, climbed through himself, and deposited the dead animal a good distance from the small group of cows. He buried the bag. By tomorrow afternoon the sky would be thick with vultures and there would be evidence that a calf-sized creature had died.

Juan walked up to the dozing cows. "Come on, Pastele, come with papa," he urged.

The little calf took one look at Juan Caldo and ran behind her mother. She had grown swiftly in the ten days allowed her. Now she jumped at his approach and bounded out of reach.

Juan took out a small rope. He tiptoed around the mother cow. "Okay, baby, don't move." Juan whispered his words. The other cows were alert, staring dumbly in the darkness. He didn't want to disturb them.

The calf nodded her head up and down and pressed against

her mother. "Good, stay right there," Juan murmured, and he moved fast, slipping the rope over the calf's head. "Good baby. Good girl." He rubbed the calf's speckled forehead.

Together they began the long trek back into the woods, Juan dragging, enticing, pushing the sometimes recalcitrant animal. Juan had made a pen ready, a small enclosure made of junk. Ropes, boards, old logs, whatever it took to make an enclosure for the calf. When Juan and Pastele arrived there an hour later, the calf was trembling and balky from being stuffed under the fence and pulled through, then half dragged, half pushed, through a mile of rough land. Home at last, the little calf cried pitifully. Juan rubbed her down with an old rag, patted her, and produced the food he had laboriously prepared earlier.

Juan made a baby bottle of milk retrieved from the mother earlier that night: an empty soda bottle and an old glove. He stuffed it in her mouth, but she turned away from him. Her brown eyes looked at him accusingly.

"You gotta eat, Pastele. You gonna die if you don't."

The calf lowed mournfully and put her head down, balking at Juan's attempts to be a mother. Maybe the calf would die after all.

He tried again. He squeezed a few drops of milk onto his fingers and stuck them in the animal's mouth. Juan felt the rough tongue tasting his fingers, then he felt suction. He did it again with the same results. Quickly he slipped the rubber-glove nipple into her mouth. This time she took a few tentative sucks from the bottle. "That's a girl," Juan whispered. His hands shook. He was more rattled than the calf.

By the end of the long night the milk was gone. The calf slept quietly as Juan watched.

His exhausted body rested while his mind roamed the path he had taken to arrive at this peculiar point in his life. Juan Caldo had arrived in Miami when he was fifteen years old. He struggled through school, struggled to learn English. His career plans in Cuba vanished, his math skills forgotten.

Later, Juan began night school at Miami-Dade Community College, taking their program of vocational English classes. By the time he was arrested for first degree murder, his English was manageable. He'd reached level F, and was ready to study something besides language. A new career. He had never considered animals as a career. His soft laugh made the calf twitch in her sleep. An animal was all he had now.

Juan devoured the magazines in his shack, particularly the breeders' magazines. "Careful calf feeding," he read slowly, "is important in the development of a good breeding animal."

He took care of Pastele, exercised her, fed her conscientiously, and eventually weaned her to milk in a bucket, milk retrieved stealthily at night from the field where her mother still grazed. She ate grass that Juan gathered, often substandard cattle feed: things like saw grass, rough, almost inedible forage that Juan chopped finely for her. But Pastele thrived on the raspy grasses.

Juan spent hours lolling in the hot sun that filtered down among his trees. He learned to love the hum of the afternoon bugs and the soft sound of his animal chewing the rough grasses. He mulled over the dilemma of his existence. He was a hunted man, a man wanted for murder, an outcast. He could never be an American. The picture of his murdered friend haunted him. He wondered what became of Nubia. Meanwhile he discovered other trash receptacles filled with old magazines. People threw out everything. Juan collected a veritable library of books on animal husbandry. He learned as much as a man could about cattle breeding.

Every night he lugged gallons of water from his restaurant's outdoor faucet. He foraged along the side of the road for grass, and he read.

Meanwhile Pastele grew bigger. But not very big. Maybe it was the genes, maybe the food, but the small cow remained small. A year passed.

11

3

CECILE Buddenbrooks grew like a young calf herself during the first year she was away from her home in Connecticut. Much to her dismay, she never came home that next summer. She wrote Paul long letters, once a week.

Dear Paul,

My father is going to be traveling and he doesn't want me to be alone at home, so guess what! I'm stuck here. I'm thinking seriously of running away. The nuns are okay. They're all Catholic and I'm learning all this God stuff. Mere Sulpicia gave me a book on St. Augustine. He's pretty cool. He had a son before he got to be a saint, and he wasn't even married. But then he was really good. Anyway, he would have run away too. I just don't think it's fair to be stuck here. The only good thing is that I have a friend named Helene and she'll be here all summer too.

Maybe we can run away together. Why don't you come over and meet us in Paris?

How are you? I miss you a lot.

Love,

C

Paul wrote back:

Dear Cecile,

I can't come to Paris. Wish I could, but I can't even afford a bus ticket down to New York. So I hitched, last week. I want to go to Columbia University so I went into the city and checked it out. Your dad said he'd pay for any school I can get into, like maybe even all the way through law school. I told him that's what I really want to do. He said if I can get in, he'll pay. I think my mom has something to do with it, but I'm not sure, and I don't want to say. You know how it's always been between them. Well, enough of that.

Anyway, your dad is okay, but he doesn't look real well. He put on a lot of weight. Mom's cooking too much good stuff.

Me? I'm good. The place is dead without you. Nobody in that big house, you wouldn't believe how it is. You're lucky not to be here but I wish you were anyway. I miss you. I really miss you.

Love,
Paul

Cecile and her roommate, Helene Waite, lay on their beds and talked, oblivious to the Alps that rose majestically behind the convent school and the towering clouds visible from their big window. "Paul loves me. I think we'll get married someday."

"Married? You're crazy, Cecile. I mean, there's a lot of stuff to do. Like college. I want to be a teacher, so that means college for me."

"Teacher? Your mom will have a fit. She thinks you should study medicine or something," Cecile said. "Anyway, maybe I'll be a nun."

"A nun?" Helene laughed. "Now that's seriously crazy. You aren't even a Catholic."

"Yeah," Cecile said. "You wouldn't believe how my dad despises religion, but here I am." She laughed. "Nun schools are good, that's all he knows about this place. My mom took me to a church once."

"What kind?"

"Don't know. But I guess I'll marry Paul instead. I love Paul."

"You're lucky. What does he say about it?"

"That doesn't matter. I'll tell him."

"Right," Helene said. "Just tell him."

Pastele passed cow puberty and acted like a postadolescent. She mooed plaintively, rubbing her head against a tree as

13

though aching for something beyond her reach. Juan knew what was happening. "Pastele, you grew up on me," he said to the heifer. "What we gonna do, Pastele? You getting lonesome and all that. Maybe you should have a kid. You ready yet?"

In the course of his extensive reading, Juan studied how breeding was accomplished between animals. Not that he didn't already know, but with valuable animals, one had to be very careful. He needed a bull. Late at night Juan scoured the countryside and finally found an ideal mate for his baby, a small bull, brindled with similar spots, a bull who resembled Pastele. Juan didn't want any huge bull having sex with the small animal; besides, he was developing ideas about breeding.

Juan trained Pastele to lead, fashioning a halter out of soft rope. He continued to observe the bull he had located. There were two bulls in pens, several miles away. In studying the little bull, it occurred to Juan that this animal was probably his baby's father. The question in his mind haunted him. Should he inbreed? From his reading, Juan knew that inbreeding could bring out the worst characteristics, but occasionally it reinforced the best. What should he do?

Juan decided to take a chance. Late one night when he thought Pastele was ready, he haltered the young cow, and they made the long trek to the bull pen. He opened the gate and pushed Pastele in.

"Have a good time," he whispered, and settled back to watch.

Before dawn it was over. Pastele was exhausted and trembling, but the deed was done. Now all Juan had to do was wait.

He already knew about the animal's inordinate fondness for the rough palmetto leaves. It was strange, but she appeared to prefer the rough stuff to the tall African pampas grass, or even the softer grasses in the fields. Even more than the plundered, half-ripe hands of bananas Juan dragged home from backyards, Pastele loved the exotic junk like melaleuca leaves, air potato vines, and saw grasses. Now that she was pregnant, Juan worked harder at bringing in good food. The cow didn't even care, and continued to eat the scrub.

The months passed. Pastele gave birth to a female, and

14

Juan rejoiced like a father. He would have died for a good Cuban cigar to celebrate. Juan named the midget Yuca.

The baby grew. Juan was astounded by the milk Pastele produced. From his readings he knew that quantity and butterfat content were important in gauging a cow's worth. He measured everything carefully, keeping exact records, comparing his figures with ideal figures. Pastele was above average on every count.

Two years later Pastele produced a small male calf and Yuca was pregnant. Slowly life continued: summers, winters, so different yet so similar. Days and nights and seasons formed a familiar pattern until one tragic day Pastele escaped from the pen and wandered down to the state road. In a late night accident, she was struck by a car and died. "My God in heaven, how can you do this to me?" Juan mourned. But somehow, his mourning was a prayer and his tiny herd of small cows prospered. He would never forget Pastele. Perhaps God was angry at him for his casual disregard of his old friend, for Victor's death. Juan was still sure of his own innocence, but how innocent could a man be for pistol-whipping another man? For leaving him to die at the hands of another?

One questioned haunted Juan. Who did kill Victor? And why?

Pastele's descendants grew. Juan's days and nights were spent madly foraging for food. The deep woods resembled a cultivated park now, although the cattle became progressively smaller with each breeding. In only three generations Juan had created a lilliputian cow with a gargantuan milk output. Any spare time he had, he used for reading. People's trash continuously supplied a ready source of reading matter. Juan Caldo was becoming an educated man.

One day from his penthouse roof, the top of the gumbo limbo tree, Juan saw some trucks drive to the edge of a distant field. He saw surveyors' instruments appear and lines being drawn. Next he saw a bulldozer. The land developers were coming.

"Paul's going to Columbia Law School," Cecile said to Helene. "And we're graduating from this place. Do you believe it?"

Helene grinned. "What I don't believe is that you want to be a nun. I think you're crazy."

The two girls were outside, walking along a small botanical trail within the school grounds. Edelweiss grew beside the edge of a sheer wall of stone that ended half a mile up in one of the Alps. The air was crisp and cool while the sun warmed their faces. Cecile stooped to pick a leaf and held it against her cheek. "The crazy thing is my father. He didn't mind I skied with the Swiss champion. Daddy thought it was great I almost broke my neck. He'd love it if I told him I worked with that CIA person. But mention God and the poor man freaks out."

"He's going to disown you, Cecile."

"Well, when I became a Catholic he almost did. He made me promise I'd go to Columbia for prelaw studies. He thinks that will make me marry Paul, a nice Jewish atheist, then I'll forget all this Catholic stuff. That's how Daddy thinks. Besides, he likes Paul now. I suppose it's a relative thing, Paul being an ungodly sort himself. Daddy likes that."

"Why don't you just marry him? I mean, you told me all about you and Paul."

Cecile tossed her head, surprised that her hair didn't sway in the cool breeze. She had cut it short a week ago. "Well, I do love Paul. But, I don't know, Helene. I mean, Paul and I, we saw each other during vacations. I can't change the past, but I've come to terms with the reality of it. I'll love Paul forever. He knows that. On the other hand . . ."

"On the other hand, you still have four years in New York City with Paul right down the street."

"And Daddy standing by with the shotgun, hoping I make a mistake." Cecile laughed. "What a crazy life."

The Florida sun darkened Juan's complexion. The endless work of carrying feed for his cows hardened his body. He spoke English every day to his animals and his vocabulary was extensive, although he pronounced some words strangely. For a while he had a radio that worked on batteries. Before the batteries died, he worked on his pronunciation. He had to prepare himself. The cows needed more forage than he could handle. The day Juan first observed the tractor two miles away, pushing dirt, he saw the writing on the wall. It was time to go.

"I am cleaning myself up," Juan said to Papaya the next morning. "I need work, I need money. We're leaving. You haven't seen people, Papaya. Don't be frightened."

Juan was the one who was frightened. He hadn't spoken to a human being in years. His voice was familiar to his animals, but it was not the voice he had started with. Now it was soft, kind, placating. His mind no longer belonged to a young man ready to pistol-whip another. His mind was filled with new words, new ideas. He understood suffering and pain and solitude.

He shaved himself carefully with an antique razor, looking in a piece of broken mirror. He was almost twenty-seven years old, and he was well-educated by countless magazines and books retrieved from the trash cans of northern Dade County. He had a set of identification papers from a Cuban named Juan Calderon. Like everything else, the papers came from the trash. Juan Calderon was probably dead somewhere. There were fights, people died, Cubans came unregistered, unknown. Even the picture on Juan Calderon's driver's license showed a face that could be his own, a dark face with shiny brown eyes and a moustache.

Juan Calderon walked into the restaurant, the very restaurant whose food he had been retrieving from the Dumpster for the past years. He suggested a new recipe, something from *Gourmet* magazine. His hands shook but his voice was calm. "I am the best cook. I know Cuban food. I know French

17

food. I can put this place on the map." He didn't so much exemplify confidence as certitude.

"Cook something tonight." The manager was dissatisfied with the current cook. Food had been getting bad. Juan already knew this, because the quality of Dumpster food had dropped dramatically. Juan had observed the clientele slacking off. He knew if he did well, he had a job.

The first night he cooked Palomilla steak. It was a big hit.

The second night Juan's baked yuca served with shredded beef was a success. He offered *bistec en rollo* the third night and people loved it. Juan had a job.

Juan was paid in cash. He bought an old truck cheap, taking a chance that the Juan Calderon of the driver's license was real and not in trouble. Now he could buy real hay for his cows. A month later he rented a decrepit mobile home with some land and moved his little herd in, one cow at a time, in the back of his truck. A year later he introduced himself to a lawyer. "I am from Cuba. I need a green card." He used a different name this time. It was easy to get an ID. Another Juan emerged.

4

April 1998

"AFTER you went to college, you still wanted to be a nun?" Leonie Drail asked.

"I wanted to be a nun since I was fifteen. My father hated the idea," Sister Cecile replied. Her elbows were propped on her big desk, her usually serene face earnest. "It really made me unhappy that he felt that way, so I didn't talk about it much. I completed college, just like he asked. And then he died."

"You were glad, I bet," Leonie said.

"Oh, no, very unhappy. I loved him. I still pray for him. He was my father and he loved me in his way. He really just couldn't understand my loving God more than his money. Of course, he spent his entire life making money, and I rejected it. That made him feel terrible." Cecile shrugged and smiled at her almost-thirteen-year-old ward. "God chose me," she said. "It was a calling."

Sister Cecile looked carefully at the girl draped over her client chair, the place where people looking to hire Sister Cecile, Private Detective, usually sat. Leonie had been growing again. Her stringy blond hair had been brushed carefully that morning and for once it looked presentable. "Your mother understood. Helene, my best friend all those years. I wish she could be here to see you now." Cecile blinked. She could never think of Leonie's mom without a huge surge of emotion.

"Stupid cancer," Leonie muttered. "Does that mean I'll get cancer too, like Mom?"

"No. Just eat lots of broccoli and don't smoke. You have a wonderful father, don't forget. He's very healthy."

"Broccoli. Sure. I get to choose between broccoli and cancer. And Dad's in Japan now."

"Japanese food is very healthy."

"Tofu. I wish Dad were back. Dumb CIA. Don't they know he has a kid? All this government stuff about parenting and they send him all over the Far East."

"Your father's a brilliant officer. He's doing very important work. And he knows we take good care of you."

Leonie's thin face wrinkled up, making all the freckles come closer together. She had never had freckles before. Pre-pubescent freckle syndrome, Sister Cecile thought, although she had never heard of such a thing. Maybe her ward should stay out of the Florida sun.

"Like being a dad isn't important," Leonie said, still stuck on the subject.

"It's a very important thing. Besides, you'll be leaving for Japan in a few weeks to spend the whole summer with him."

Sunshine spilled over Leonie's face. "I can't wait."

Sister Cecile's buzzer sounded twice. That was Sister Raphael's signal from the outer desk, and it meant Cecile had a client. Cecile and Leonie were in the nun's office. Today was "Bring Your Child to Work Day" in Dade County, and Sister Cecile was theoretically at work. The nun had two jobs. One was as manager of the Maria Concilia Retirement Community for old nuns on Miami Beach, the other was as a private investigator. The sisters in the Order of Our Lady of Good Counsel needed to support themselves, and while most of those young enough to work were teachers, some pursued other means of earning money for the order.

"You had better leave, Leonie. I must have a client."

"I'm supposed to observe you at work today," Leonie said.

"Clients like privacy." Cecile's voice was firm. "Please leave."

"No. It defeats the whole purpose of 'Bring Your Child to Work Day,' " Leonie said stubbornly. Then, "Please?"

The "please" sounded so good. Sister Cecile stared at the girl, a girl giving hints of becoming a woman. She sighed and

20

nodded. "Take that chair in the back and don't say a single word. Pretend you're invisible."

Leonie jumped out of the big chair and settled into the small chair against the back wall.

Seconds later a knock sounded on the office door. Sister Raphael opened it a foot. "Sister, Mr. Cruz would like to speak with you."

"Please come in."

The man who entered looked around the office carefully. His dark brown eyes swept the nun, staring at her oval face, short, curly brown hair, gray eyes, the white veil and modified white habit she wore. He seemed to reflect for a moment on her youth and her face. Men always looked twice at the face, an unusual face that some thought quite attractive. Then he looked at the office. He had an air of quiet patience as he studied the walls, the art deco picture of the Madonna, the Private Detective license, the photograph of the pope. Then he stared at Leonie and smiled, just slightly as though it were nothing out of the ordinary to find a skinny youngster in a private detective—nun's office.

In turn, Sister Cecile looked at him. He was close to six feet tall, thin and wiry, and his face was clearly aged by hours spent in the sun, yet it was light, as though much of the tan had worn off. Close to forty, she thought, and still quite good-looking. He was dressed well in an expensive suit that didn't hide his lean strength. The partial smile that appeared when he spotted Leonie faded away. His face became serious.

"My name is John Cruz," he said, and held out a hand. They shook. He had a firm, hard grip.

"Please sit down. Thank you, Sister Raphael." Cecile nodded at the older nun who had brought in the client and stood by the door. Sister Raphael looked perplexed, probably because Leonie was there and shouldn't be. The septuagenarian nun glanced at the girl.

Cecile nodded. "It's fine."

Sister Raphael left. Cecile knew she would be hearing about this. Meanwhile she had a client.

"How can I help you, Mr. Cruz?"

John Cruz sat quietly for a moment. Time, in the ordinary

21

sense, was not pushing this man. When he spoke, it was with a slight accent.

"I would like you to investigate something in the past. I have a cousin. Had a cousin," he corrected with the same half smile he had reserved for Leonie. "Many years ago this man, Juan Caldo, was tried and convicted of murder. We were from the same town in Cuba, my father's sister's son. I knew Juan, and one thing I know, he did not kill another man. I want his name cleared. I need to tell his family that Juan was not a killer."

The words came out in a slow staccato, as though he had thought them all out ahead of time.

"Is your cousin still alive?" Cecile asked.

John shrugged. "Who knows? He escaped from the jail many years ago. I want only to prove his innocence. Not find him."

"Why?"

The man looked down, his brow furrowed, and Cecile was sure his mind flickered back to the past, Cuba maybe, a sandy beach on a tropical island hung with tall palms and blown by warm trade winds, childhood with a close cousin. "Family," he said. "Always they are sad. And justice. He should not be remembered as a killer."

"I understand. How long ago was he convicted of this crime?"

"November 1975 he was remanded to the correctional institute. To be corrected perhaps?" He smiled wryly.

"Mr. Cruz, that's over twenty years ago!"

"Yes. This may be very difficult. You understand I am able to pay."

Sister Cecile took a deep breath. From the first word, this was a hopeless case. She should refuse it. "It may be impossible. Such a search could prove futile. Everyone involved may be dead, or moved far away. Twenty years. You may be wasting your money."

"I am ready for that chance. But I want you to try. That I owe my cousin, his family." The potential client pulled himself up straight in the chair. He stared at Leonie for a moment. "When you are young," he said, his eyes moving back to Sister Cecile, "the things that are important are things of the

22

moment, your own wants mostly. Later, things outside yourself take over. Twenty years is not much time to learn this."

"No," the nun agreed.

"Also, it has occurred to me more than once that the man who really murdered, the real killer, wasn't found. The Cuban community here in South Florida is very big. In twenty years this killer may be an important man; or maybe he is dead. I want you to find him if he is still alive. My instinct says he is here."

"You don't know who he is, do you? The real killer? I mean, any suspicions?"

"If I knew, I wouldn't be here. A Cuban who has been here twenty years? Maybe even an Anglo. I have names of many people back then. You can discover where they are now."

"Not a lot to go on, Mr. Cruz."

"Not a lot. Will you do it?"

Cecile thought about their dwindling finances. Repairs on the old motel the nuns converted into this community came high. Maybe she could help this man. "I will take the case, but I can make no promises."

John cleared his throat. "Certainly."

"And you must be open with me, tell me everything you know. Still, we may fail. You must understand this."

"I understand that you will try. We shake hands on this?" He stood up and approached her desk. Cecile rose and reached across the flat mahogany surface, meeting the brown eyes that, up close, she could see were flecked with deep green, like reflecting pools of an ancient forest. They shook hands for the second time, this time in agreement.

They both sat down. "And now we talk," the man said.

He talked. Sister Cecile wrote, taking careful notes, asking an occasional question. She forgot Leonie was in the room. True to her word, the twelve-year-old kept totally silent.

"Juan's girlfriend was raped by a man named Victor Torres. The accused, Juan Caldo, came into the room that he shared with the woman, Nubia. Juan caught Victor with Nubia. Juan was young, impetuous, a little drunk, angry. He had a gun, a very unusual gun that he had just purchased from a friend. He pistol-whipped Victor, could have killed him, but no, Victor was barely conscious, but still fighting. Suddenly things

23

changed. Juan Caldo himself was struck on the head from behind, because another person entered the room."

"Another man? You know this for sure?"

John Cruz nodded. "Juan told me this. He told me he did not shoot Torres."

"You believed him?" Cecile stared at her client.

"Yes. I believe him."

"Juan hit Victor Torres. Torres fell, Juan was struck from behind, and then?" Cecile asked.

"Juan blacked out. The rapist, Torres, was shot with Juan's gun. Juan regained consciousness. Torres was dead. The police arrived. The gun was gone. Nubia left long before, when the fight began, and called the police from another house. She didn't see the real killer. Neither did Juan."

"What happened to the gun?"

"The police assumed Juan hid it. The gun was never found. Witnesses saw Juan with the murder weapon earlier that night. Several months later Juan was convicted of murder."

"This gun. How could they tell the crime was committed with a particular gun unless they actually had the gun?" the nun asked.

"It was an antique dueling pistol. One of a pair. Special bullets, not modern, but round balls of lead, propelled by a special mix of gunpowder. Another friend, Nestor Lezo, the collector who owned the guns, he made the bullets himself."

Cecile was silent for a long time, running over the story in her mind. "And the woman who was raped, she never saw a strange man come in? So there was no witness to this? Juan never saw the man who hit him?"

"He said he saw a shadow, heard a sound, then was hit from behind. He never saw the man. Police said the bump on his head could have happened before. They didn't believe Caldo."

Cecile looked at her notes. "What happened to Nubia?"

"Nubia saw Juan hit Victor with the gun. She was forced to testify to this because she wasn't Juan's wife. She could not say what happened later. She never saw Victor being shot. She ran away when the fight began."

"Where is Nubia now?" Cecile wrote the name down.

"Nubia Quinjano is dead." The electric brown eyes flickered then closed for a moment. "Complications from AIDS, seven years ago."

Cecile felt a pit open in her stomach. This was not a light case. It was heavy and difficult. "Why did this young man have a gun?"

John waved a hand in the air. "Nestor Lezo had a big collection of old guns. Beautiful things, some from America a hundred years ago. Juan Caldo admired these guns, and Nestor sold him one the day before it all happened. One of a pair. A very beautiful dueling pistol. He should not have sold it."

"Nestor Lezo." Cecile wrote the name alongside the other names in the case, and made a note. "Where is he now?"

"Dead."

"When?"

John shrugged. "Very soon after. Less than a month later, I recall. Nestor was shot by a thief who stole the gun collection. These things happen, you know? Hear of a person who has guns, there is a break-in, guns are stolen."

Sister Cecile made a final note. What an impossible case! She stood up from her chair and began to pace the room, noticing, finally, Leonie, sitting still as a mouse, her pale face expressionless at the tale just unfolded. She had forgotten the girl. "Leonie, you should go."

Leonie shook her head. A silent no. Cecile couldn't stop to argue. It was too late anyway.

"Not much to work with here," Cecile said. "Everyone is dead. Now where is the man I'm supposed to clear? Juan Caldo."

"Juan Caldo escaped from prison almost twenty years ago. He must have left the country." John Cruz shrugged. "He could be dead."

"Maybe. Maybe not."

"It doesn't matter about him. It's his family I wish to protect from a bad name." John sounded angry, finally showing some emotion.

"Could Juan be alive?" Sister Cecile's eyebrows rose, her head tilted forward. This was an interesting aspect. Juan Caldo was out there somewhere.

"Who knows? I have names and stories of the living too."

25

John Cruz settled back in his chair. The anger was gone as fast as it had come. Now he looked amused at the nun's sudden, revived interest. "I think the murderer is still alive. As I said before. Juan? He is gone."

Cecile narrowed her eyes at him. "What people are left behind?" she asked, and settled back in her chair. Maybe there was a case after all. A case risen from the dead. A biblical case.

John told her how Juan Caldo had been tried and convicted at the Dade County Courthouse. He gave names of witnesses, addresses of several people who had been there then and were still alive and living in Miami. The list started with Nubia's widower, a man whom Nubia married several years after the incident. "He gave her AIDS and she dies. He still lives," John Cruz spat.

Cecile let it pass.

John continued with more. "Nestor's gun collection, the one from which the original gun came? It is back in Miami now. They found it in a pawnshop in Tampa, brought it back to Nestor's widow, she sold it to a local man named Ron Dubaker. Ron was around at the time of the murder, he knew Juan, knew them all. He always wanted the collection. Now he has it."

"You say there is no connection between the killing of Victor Torres and the murder of this man, Nestor Lezo?"

John shook his head. "None."

"You say." Cecile wrote something down. Then she looked up from the pages of notes. "You're sure?"

"I believe that is true. I am giving you everything connected with the case."

"Fine. Tell me about the person who has the gun collection now."

"An Anglo, Ronald Dubaker. He was a young notary public who helped immigrants."

"Helped them out of their money?"

John smiled faintly. "Yes."

They talked for another hour. Cecile wrote pages of notes. Leonie remained motionless. Cecile would occasionally look back and gesture to the door with her eyes, visual signs for Leonie to get lost. It didn't work until Cecile heard the chapel

26

bell ring, urging the old nuns to go to the small chapel for the short prayer they were accustomed to saying before meals.

Momentarily Sister Cecile was distracted from the case as she pictured the old nuns rising from the cane chairs in the recreation area to go to the chapel pews. Ten short minutes of prayer and then dinner. Cecile had reinstituted three of the seven canonical hours for prayer in the retirement community. This time was called sext.

Like Pavlov's dogs, the bell was an invitation for the community to turn from material concerns and to pray, and secondly to salivate. Soon after the short prayer time, Sister Germaine's delicious meals were served. Leonie was conditioned too. The girl rose and slipped out the door.

John was not so conditioned, and his words kept coming. Carefully, Sister Cecile wrote down everything. Finally John finished. "I think that information will help you," he said.

"I think you've done half my work here," Cecile replied. She heard her stomach growling.

"No. I've talked to no one. All this came from the telephone book, a few calls. One other thing is that I don't want my wife bothered with this. She would think I'm foolish, looking into a cousin's past." John passed a hand across his mouth, covering his expression. "It is my concern, my family, not hers, not anyone else's. So I'll pay you cash, and I'll be in touch with you. I would like this absolutely confidential, please. My name is not to be mentioned in the investigation."

"Cash?" Cecile mused, staring at John's green flecked eyes. "That's acceptable. I agree."

"I will take your card, call you weekly. When you run through the retainer, I will come by. Clearing Juan Caldo will take time. I understand that. I have money."

John pulled out a wallet overflowing with cash and peeled off a huge pile of bills. "Ten thousand dollars," he said. "Enough?"

"Uh, yes. Actually this should cover a month of investigating time. I may have results before then. Usually I take a week or two in advance. You should keep some of this."

"No. I live some distance. I don't want to make another trip. You hold it, take it as you need it." He smiled. "You are a nun. I believe you will not cheat me. That's why I chose you

27

from the telephone book. This is a delicate case. It demands trust."

Sister Cecile nodded silently.

"I will be in touch every Friday at noon. Is that good?"

Sister Cecile stared at the pile of bills. "Really . . ." She looked up. His face was shockingly serious. She couldn't refuse him. "Yes. I will expect your call, Mr. Cruz. Let me give you a receipt."

"Not necessary."

"Please. I follow business procedures. I pay taxes. This must be in my records. You've given me a lot of money." She pulled out her receipt pad, a new one with her name and address and profession in neat Letter Gothic, fresh from the new computer printer at the front desk.

Sister Cecile wrote in the amount and John Cruz's name. "Your address?" she asked.

"Not necessary." He reached for the half-filled-in receipt and took it, stuffing it in his pocket.

Moments later they rose and shook hands again. Cecile escorted her client to the door and made it back into the refectory just in time for dinner. She had missed sext. Cecile thought on that for a moment as she watched the nuns file into the refectory. They didn't often miss sext here, just sex. That was Sister Louise's joke. Nuns, Cecile thought with a sigh, will be nuns.

This week it was Cecile's turn to do a short spiritual reading before the meal. She was reading from the *Complete Works of St. Teresa*. Teresa of Avila exemplified the ideal nun to Sister Cecile: serious, but with a sense of humor and a wonderful reliance on the Lord. Cecile sat with the waiting community at the long trestle table and read from where she had left off. ". . . if I wanted a cross, there was a good one all ready for me and I was not to reject it but to go on bravely, for He would help me: so I was to go at once . . ."

Cecile finished the reading with a sense of peace. Impossible case? No such thing. She passed the dishes of food.

Tonight was Cuban night. It had been all week because Sister Germaine was on a Cuban food kick. A coincidence, Cecile thought, that John Cruz hired her to discover the truth about a Cuban.

28

Everyone was at home tonight. Currently they housed eight retired sisters, three women residents, and the two elderly couples. The secular people paid for their room and board and helped keep the community financially solvent. Of course there was Leonie too, the one face that kept everyone young.

They all said a communal grace, then dug into a pile of cider and mango roasted ham and bowls of *gallo pinto*, beans and rice.

Sister Cecile knew very well there was no such thing as a coincidence. But could a week of black beans and rice be an omen from God?

5

JOHN Cruz drove directly back to his large ranch in central Florida, a six hour drive from Miami Beach. He had left early that morning, and he wanted to be home. He didn't feel at ease anywhere but in the countryside.

He pulled up to the rambling white house and climbed out of his Mercedes. He stood for a moment in the darkness and breathed in the air that was particularly his. The thick, ripe scent of cows, sunshine, and growing crops drifted past his nostrils. The soft Florida breeze rustled the shiny leaves of a live oak that spread above his head. He looked at the long barn where the animals slept, and fought off the urge to go there first before he went in to see his wife, Pearla, the woman he had met and married twelve years ago. They had a twelve-year-old son, which said something about their early relationship. They also had two beautiful young daughters.

John felt his heart swell as he walked into the house. He was richer than a Colombian cattle baron. His new breed of milk cow had stormed the world. Little animals who produced milk, lots of milk, under adverse circumstances. The cows could live on minimal food. Farmers in Africa had introduced his new breed there, South Americans came regularly to inspect his herd and buy his animals. His family was proud, the Cruz name well-known.

His son was still up. "Dad, I want new skates. I've got to have them. I need them."

"Sure, sure, Carlito, where's your mother?" He ruffled his son's hair.

"Carl, Dad. My name is Carl."

"Carl," his father said firmly. His son was becoming a man. Pearla appeared from the kitchen as he spoke.

30

"I've prepared dinner. How was the meeting? Will they buy from our stock?"

"Yes, a good meeting, Pearla." John embraced his wife. He loved her so much it hurt. Plump after bearing him three children, she was still the most beautiful woman in the world.

"I prepared the pork, just the way you like it. And wait! A call from the Cattle Breeders Association. They want you to speak at the annual meeting. Is only two weeks away. In Orlando."

"Can we go to Disney World?" little Beatriz asked. She had come out from her bedroom, rubbing her eyes. "Mama said maybe we could all go. Can I see Mickey?"

Juan stooped to hug his daughter. "Yes, yes." He stood up straight. "I am a very lucky man. You will see Mickey."

Sister Cecile didn't speak to Leonie about the case. Instead, when she went into Leonie's room after dinner for their evening chat, she asked about homework and classes and Zoe Cabrall, Leonie's best friend from school.

"Did you finish the writing project?" Cecile asked.

"Almost. Can I use the office computer tonight?"

"Sure. Tell Sister Raphael you need it. Sometimes she just sits there playing games."

"She's really good."

"I know," Cecile agreed. "How's Zoe?"

Leonie grinned. "We speak Spanish now. I mean, she always did, but since I've been taking it at school, she makes me speak it with her. I mean, you don't learn Spanish at school; it's really a dumb class. Zoe's making me learn with her."

"You're lucky to have a friend like that," Cecile said. "Help wipe out monolingualism."

"Is that a disease?"

"It is."

"So, we should speak Spanish too," Leonie said. "You and me."

"I'm too old. Besides, I speak French and Italian."

"So, Spanish is a breeze."

Sister Cecile went to vespers with that thought in mind. Maybe she could learn the Our Father in Spanish. Then her

31

thoughts roamed again and she thought of foreign words; even the word vespers was a word from the Latin. Everyone should speak Latin. In fact, she thought, it would be nice if everyone observed the canonical hours that composed the divine office. Her community only observed matins, sext, and vespers. Perhaps they should reinstate lauds, prime, terce, none, and compline. Such beautiful words. So out of date, like Latin. The rule of the Order of Our Lady of Good Counsel said they must pray always. Sister Cecile carried that thought with her when she left the chapel, aware that, in truth, her thoughts had roamed from praying again. "Sorry, Lord," she whispered. "I'm so distracted."

When Cecile was on a case and unable to say the community prayers, she prayed alone. Nuns with outside jobs did that. Consequently, the next morning when Sister Cecile drove off Miami Beach and headed for an office on Coral Way in Miami to meet with Ronald Dubaker, the only Anglo in her new case, she prayed at every stoplight. For once she didn't see the beautiful palms, the ocean, the fast, relentless traffic.

Dubaker's office was in a mall on the second floor over a paint store and diagonally above a Cuban cafeteria. Real marble panels decorated the entry, and gold letters informed her that Ronald Dubaker was an IMMIGRATION EXPERT as well as a notary public and seller of insurance. NO PERSON REFUSED, a small sign said. HEALTH INSURANCE ONLY $75.00 A MONTH. Twenty years hadn't changed Mr. Dubaker's trade, simply expanded it. A thief of the highest order, Cecile thought grimly, a man called a *notario*.

Cecile had called first, so when she walked in, she was greeted with an outstretched hand and a Cheshire cat smile. "I'm Ron. You must be Sister Cecile. Please, come right back to my private office." The *notario* turned to a receptionist. "Olga, please take care of my other customers." Ron's smile faded just long enough for the words to come out.

The receptionist's name was on a gold plate on her desk. OLGA BORROS, engraved with thin, elegant lines.

Sister Cecile followed Ron Dubaker into his office and sat in a velveteen chair. Briefly, she studied Ron Dubaker. He was close to fifty, with a face that had spent too much time in the Florida sun. Red with broken capillaries on his cheeks, a hefty smile that showed even, but dull, teeth, brown hair that was probably dyed. He wore a Rolex.

"I called about ancient history. I told you on the telephone that I was looking into an old murder. I've been hired to clear Juan Caldo of the crime he is said to have committed twenty years ago." Cecile paused.

"This is absolutely fascinating," Dubaker said. "Victor Torres. That's the man Juan killed. Yes, I remember, but vaguely. And they caught Juan immediately. One of those gritty little love spats that happen so often. Juan Caldo, big, skinny kid from Cuba. A killer."

"Not exactly." Cecile stopped him. "There is a question about his being the killer. I've been asked to look into the case, as I told you on the telephone."

"Fascinating," Dubaker said again. "Who on earth would be interested in that? Twenty years ago? Everyone involved is probably dead or gone."

"You're still here," Cecile pointed out.

"True." Dubaker looked thoughtful. His eyes skimmed his watch. "Who was it, you say? Who hired you?"

"That's confidential, I'm afraid. A friend, is all. A friend hired me. What I'm interested in is your opinions of the people back then, a discussion of possible motives for each one. Perhaps you could go over a list I have of people who lived then. Maybe you could add to it, remember motives, things like that."

This time he really did look at his watch.

"I'll pay you for your time," Cecile said. "I know you're a busy man."

"No, no, I'd be glad to go over your list, stretch my mind to the past. It's a hard thing, thinking back then. Who was the woman involved with Caldo? Her name?"

"Nubia." Cecile looked at her list of names. "Nubia Quinjano. She died of AIDS."

"Yes, of course. Her bastard of a husband. He ran around, still runs around. He should be shot." He looked at her veil and cross. "Sorry, I forget my words. I promise to be more careful."

33

"I hear words every day," Cecile said impatiently. "What can you tell me about Nubia back then?"

"Nubia." He chewed on his lip thoughtfully. "Quite beautiful when she was young. Certainly not later. But she was eighteen and slim, I remember her then, and at the trial. She probably loved Juan Caldo. After he went to jail, she moped around, I recall. Of course, Victor was dead then. Maybe she was moping for him. And, yes! Juan escaped, didn't he? Now I remember. Yes." He slapped his knee.

"What did Nubia do then?"

Dubaker shook his head. "So long ago. Nubia? I don't know. I remember people wondering about Juan coming back and killing them all. Others said he would come for Nubia. Everyone believed he did it. I mean, why not? Torres was raping his woman. Juan never came back. Nubia married. I knew her later. I sold her husband car insurance."

"I'm curious, Mr. Dubaker," Cecile said. "How did you become involved in the Hispanic community. Are you Hispanic?"

"Call me Ron, please." He showed his teeth in a metallic half smile. "I learned Spanish early, discovered there was money to be made because these people came over and needed someone to translate their lives into American lives. I started out on Calle Ocho. Still have an office there, but now I work from here. This is my base. The Spanish-speaking community trusts me, I love them. I speak their language."

"That's wonderful," Cecile said. He looked so much like a crook, Cecile thought, so eager, so oily. He was probably lying though his teeth. She kept smiling.

"I do them a service. Some notaries take their money, claim they can get them quick citizenship, hassle-free. No such thing, you understand, except possibly for the Cubans. They have a separate status as far as immigration is concerned, as long as Fidel's communism is with us. Everyone else has problems. Nicaraguans, Haitians, people from San Salvador . . . Cubans have problems too, actually, but of another category."

"What can you tell me about Victor Torres?" Cecile asked, anxious to get on with it, perhaps to hear another lie. "Did you know him?"

"Torres? Didn't know the man. Stranger to me."

"Nestor Lezo? Did you know him?"

"The gun collector. Yes, Nestor was an interesting character. He came over here from Cuba in the late fifties and set up shop early on. He brought his money with him. Thought of himself as a very cultured, upper class Spanish type and lived in an old-style home down on the Miami River. Nice place with a big yard, fruit trees, palms. He had something of a social club for Cuban exiles when they came pouring over here, when things under Batista started falling apart. He helped a lot of Cubans get out."

"And he had a gun collection."

"Yes, Nestor's guns were antiques. The gun in question was one of a pair of real Deringer-made dueling pistols. Henry Deringer Jr. crafted beautiful pistols. Those two were something. Deringer striped the barrels to make them look like twisted, forged iron. Beautiful. The one Caldo had was not as beautiful, rather a plain gun. I have the twin."

"How did you get the gun collection?"

"They came on the market. His wife didn't want them. I ended up paying through the nose for those guns. Nestor's wife got my money. Interesting thing how they came back."

"Is Nestor's widow still alive?"

"Oh, yes, same house. I haven't seen her since I bought the guns. Long time. She's probably a different person now. We change."

Cecile looked at Ron. Who was he twenty years ago? "Could you tell me where the house is? Maybe she could help."

"The gun collector's wife?" Dubaker did something different with his lips, a sideways twist that passed for a smile. "Crazy old woman now, really."

"Her name?"

"Mirtha Lezo. I don't know the address offhand." He pushed a button. "Olga, look up Mirtha Lezo's address for my client, please. Give it to her on the way out."

"That will be a help," Cecile said.

"Probably not. Truth is, there's not much I can do to help you. Unfortunately I have an appointment in just a few minutes. We'll have to cut this short."

Cecile looked down at her list of names. "Could I take you

35

to lunch later? We could go over the list when you aren't so busy."

Ron pursed his lips. He had a very mobile face, every thought punctuated by some kind of facial tic. "Lunch. Today." He thought a moment. "Yes, I could handle that."

"My treat," Cecile said. "Where would you suggest?"

"I'll come up with something. Stop by around two. Is that late for you?"

"No. Fine. I'll be here."

6

SISTER Cecile left Ronald Dubaker's private office with a sense of leaving a minor symphony composed by a government grant recipient. Something was out of tune. The general public wouldn't subscribe. Ron had found his place with a group of needy souls who apparently paid big for the man's services. Dubaker, an aging crocodile with straight teeth; a man with a certain amount of charm and a pleasant face with years of whatever it was he did etched in every line. Not that fifty-something was old, she thought, but the man gave an impression of being around and knowing everything, of being unwilling to say exactly what he knew unless there was something in it for him. Perhaps she could come up with a profit for him in trade for some decent information. But what did she have that this man could possibly want? Or was he the killer?

Cecile paused at Olga's desk. "Mr. Dubaker asked you to find an address for me?"

"Yes, I have it here." The young woman handed Cecile a piece of paper with a name and address on it.

"Thank you so much." Cecile left quickly. There were other people in the office now. Everyone was busy or preoccupied. There was money to be made, or spent.

Outside, the day had turned from warm to steaming. Hot sun blistered the tops of passing cars, and the pavement cooked whatever touched it. Sister Cecile stood in the mall parking lot, her face already damp with sweat. Eleven o'clock now, she had three hours before lunch.

Cecile pulled out her notebook of names and addresses and looked at the list John Cruz had given her. Maybe there would be someone else in the neighborhood; an area called

Westchester on the map, it petered out into grasslands and the edge of the Everglades not many blocks west.

The Reverend Rubin Gonzalez, 130th Avenue. That would be west about three blocks, she mused. The notes beside the name said that back in the seventies, the Reverend Gonzalez ran a small mission near where the murder was committed, that he befriended many people in the area and helped the new arrivals learn English. Like Dubaker, this man had moved away from Calle Ocho, Miami's Eighth Street, where so many Cubans remained. Apparently this Westchester area was the New Jerusalem for old immigrants.

Cecile's Ford Explorer had become an oven, soaking up the rays. Even after her time spent in Miami, the nun still wasn't used to the car heat that blasted out when she opened a car door here in South Florida. In Boston, cars were refrigerators most of the time. Cecile patted the car's hood. "Ouch." Hot enough to fry an egg. Maybe she should go buy some eggs, offer to cook for lunch. Right. Dubaker had a sense of humor. Sure he did.

Cecile slid into the car. "Reverend Rubin, or the Reverend Gonzalez. I'm a Catholic nun, and I'm looking for information." She began talking as she drove, practicing her words. Maybe he belonged to a group who hated Catholics. No, he would be a good person who spent his life helping Hispanic immigrants. Noble, committed, hardworking. Hispanics belonged to all denominations. Catholicism was the original faith, but missionaries of other denominations were at work. Maybe she could reconvert this preacher. "Reverend Gonzalez, have you considered returning to the fold?"

Maybe she should just concentrate on her case.

Coral Way rolled past homes with palm trees. Palms from Malaysia, from Borneo, from the Middle East, not just native trees, because the native palms were less ornamental than foreign palms, imports like the huge date palms from California, and from Egypt before that, or the stately royal palms that first arrived from Cuba and were now such a symbol of Florida. Everywhere, hibiscus slurped at the water table and startlingly green lawns reflected chemical applications of magic green pellets. Bedding plants, rows of periwinkles, sweet williams, and begonias all cried out for attention. Cecile drove past a

38

school, a huge, windowless behemoth. "W. R. Thomas Middle School," she read.

She turned down the next street and found a small church complex. Not so small, Cecile realized. A house, a church, a school setup with children marching along the lawn to a playing field in the back. She pulled up in the parking lot in the front of the complex and climbed out.

The group of children, neatly dressed in plaid uniforms, walked past her. Eight-year-old children, she guessed. One adult acted as shepherd, a woman of indeterminate age with a huge voice urging the children to walk in a straight line. There was nothing at all dangerous about this place, but Cecile couldn't help a shudder. She remembered being eight.

Cecile ran a few steps to catch up with the woman. "Excuse me, do you know where I could find Reverend Gonzalez?"

"Reverend Ruby is in the school office." The woman gestured to the school building, a green-painted, long structure. "Go right in the front. He'll be the man in the room on the right."

The Reverend Ruby sat in an office chair behind a desk, sorting mountains of papers in a room surrounded by other desks. A secretary on the telephone talked about José Perez's attendance problems. A paper fell on the floor. There were no guns anywhere, no deadly objects, except the small pile of rubber bands on the desk. Lethal weapons.

Cecile walked in and approached a large stack of reading readiness books that rose up on the desk in front of the reverend. Over the books, his gray hair formed soft curls framing a mocha face. His eyes landed on Sister Cecile's gold cross, then moved up to her eyes, then to the veil on top of her head. "What can I do for you, Sister?"

She was struck by those eyes, pale blue in a field of wrinkled dun, questioning, innocent eyes. He was an attractive man with a warm voice. A killer? Maybe?

"Good morning, Reverend Gonzalez. I'm sorry to bother you. I can see you're busy. But do you have just a moment?" Cecile asked. She handed him her card.

He glanced at the white rectangle, then rose, genially and with soft dignity. This man was terribly, majestically, nice. "Please, sit down. I always have time." He indicated a chair

39

near his desk, a chair with a semipadded seat of very distressed plastic.

Cecile sat and met his eyes. Up close she saw red lines on the whites. He looked tired.

"My name is Sister Cecile and I'm a private investigator. I'm looking into the past of a man you may have known. Twenty years ago, quite a distance back."

The reverend's eyebrows lifted. "Twenty years ago? Do I look that old?"

Had she offended the man?

Then he laughed. "Don't be scared," he said. "I have a mind like a steel trap. Ask any of the kids here. I can go back to half their grandparents coming in for spiritual help. Of course, it doesn't hurt that a lot of the grandparents aren't much beyond their late forties. I remember everyone. So who, and why? You're a private investigator? How strange. A nun?"

"Yes." Cecile wondered if she needed to explain. Yes, she would. "You know how it is. We, who work for God, don't get paid much, so we have to do other things as well."

"Praise the Lord, it's true. Some might say the Lord is downright stingy with his money."

Cecile nodded. "You may have a point. I'm looking into the life of a man named Juan Caldo. A friend of his is trying to clear Juan of his murder conviction. Your name was given to me with the suggestion that you might be of some help."

"Juan Caldo." The preacher tented his fingers and leaned forward over his stack of papers. He appeared to be praying, with his pale eyes half closed. Then they shut almost entirely, until Cecile thought he had fallen asleep. The eyes snapped open. "Caldo. Means hot soup in Spanish. I recall thinking that man was in the soup. Yes, hot soup. Get it?"

Cecile laughed politely. "You do remember him, then?"

"Absolutely. Juan had a girlfriend, the girl was attacked by that man, a rapist they said. That man got more than one girl pregnant. Even in the seventies there were people like that. Always have been. Still are. And then we must forgive them. The Lord's work never ends, does it, Sister?"

"No, Reverend, it never does."

"Call me Ruby."

He waited, so she said, "Ruby." He appeared satisfied at that, so she continued. "The so-called rapist was killed. Juan Caldo always said he was innocent. Can you think of anything that might help me prove this? Can you remember anyone who could have had a motive for the victim's murder besides Juan?"

"Everybody in the neighborhood. Two fathers whose daughters were pregnant, several other people who had suffered from the man. Beautiful women everywhere might have had a problem with that man." Ruby appeared exhausted, suddenly. Depressed. He kept talking. "Jealousy, envy, anger, that's three of the seven deadly sins. If I believed in murder, I'd say I'd be on that list too."

"You're making this difficult."

"Yes.. But not all of us are inclined to kill. Of all those who knew him, Victor, right? That was his name?"

"Right, Victor Torres."

"See? Good memory. Okay, as I was saying, of all those who knew him, not all of us are murderers. Caldo? He was a wild sort, young, only a kid; had some brains, ambition. I was surprised he lost it and killed Victor."

"I'm trying to prove he didn't. The gun was never found. An old dueling pistol. I talked with Ron Dubaker today. He has the rest of the gun collection. Have you heard of anyone having such a gun?"

"Dubaker?"

"You knew him too?"

"Oh, yes. That man collects a lot of money for giving advice that should be free. He's out here now, in the same business."

"You're saying he's not honest?"

"God forbid I speak ill of any man, but watch your back."

"Thanks." Cecile refrained from looking around behind her at that. "You know he bought a gun collection that the murder weapon came from?"

"I don't recall that."

"Did Mr. Dubaker have anything against Torres?"

Reverend Ruby closed his eyes again. Time traveling, Cecile thought. It took a minute for him to come back. "Most people had something against Torres."

41

"You're saying Dubaker might have had a motive."

"Might have."

"Anyone else?"

"So many have moved away," Ruby mused. "There were others, of course, but they're all gone as far as I know."

Bells started ringing. Reverend Ruby glanced up at the wall clock. "I'm due to supervise some games on the P.E. court. You're welcome to wait and we can talk later. I might come up with some more names."

"Can I call you?" Sister Cecile asked.

"Yes, after three I'll be done with the school day, God be praised."

"Thanks so much, Reverend Ruby. You've been wonderful."

"I hope so. God helps those who help themselves. Just remember that."

"Yes. Thanks."

Cecile slipped away, forging through wavering lines of children marching to the P.E. court. P.E. was modern lingo for physical education. Thanks to Leonie, Sister Cecile knew all the buzz words of grammar school. Thanks to Leonie, who, she remembered, knew almost as much about this case as she did.

7

"WHAT are you doing home at this hour?" Sister Raphael asked. The older nun was knitting a pink-and-blue-checked blanket, and there were dozens of strands of fluffy acrylic fiber dangling from each square.

"This is some holy day," Leonie said. "So we only had school for half a day. We all had to go to church this morning. I don't think it's fair that I had to go too. I'm not Catholic." Leonie was still wearing her school uniform, a plaid, pleated skirt that spread awkwardly around her as she plopped down on a chair beside Sister Raphael.

"You think only Catholics go to church?" Raphael didn't even look up from her knitting.

"No, I suppose not. But I bet my father didn't go to church today."

"Not likely. This is the Feast of the Ascension of Our Lord into Heaven. We're having Mass here tonight in the chapel. I guess we can excuse you because you already went." Raphael's eyes twinkled. She always teased Leonie about God. It was the only way the old nun could deal with the girl's lack of religiosity.

"What are you knitting?" Leonie wouldn't be trapped.

"Maria's having a baby. It's a blanket."

"Maria cleans this place, right?"

Sister Raphael nodded.

"Where's Cecile?"

"On a case."

"Oh, the old murder?"

"What old murder?"

"Some guy killed someone a million years ago. Cecile's supposed to prove he didn't."

"Really? Tell me."

Leonie explained Cecile's new case in detail. She remembered every name, every event.

"Sounds difficult," Raphael said.

"We'll have to help her," Leonie said. "I mean, there's nothing dangerous about this case because it's twenty years old. So Sister Cecile won't mind."

"She might," the old nun said.

Leonie nodded. "So? Where should we start?"

"The library. We can look up the old newspapers on microfilm."

"The library?" Leonie visibly shuddered. "Ugh. I have this report on Singapore I'm supposed to do. I'm supposed to get three books for reference."

"We can kill two birds with one stone," Sister Raphael said, and she bundled up her knitting and stuffed it in a bag beside her.

"Who are you killing? Birds?" Sister Germaine, the cook, came up, smelling of ginger and garlic. Obviously she had heard the last sentence.

"Nobody," Leonie said. "We're going to the library to look up Singapore. I have a project."

"I'll call and make sure the library has what we're after," Raphael said, bobbing her head so the small white veil she wore flounced above her white hair. She scooted out, heading toward Sister Cecile's office and a private telephone.

" 'Bye, Germaine. Tell Cecile we went to the library if you see her."

Ten minutes later they were on the road, Sister Raphael driving the old nun-van, a ten-year-old blue Ford Econoline that had no air-conditioning.

"Coral Gables branch has *Miami Herald*s that go back to the fifties on microfilm. The library is on Segovia Street. It's a long drive from Miami Beach," the nun said.

Leonie straightened her seat belt and looked sideways at Sister Raphael, whose driving tended to be fast rather than slow. "I'll hang on." Then she grinned. "Maybe we should pray we get there."

Sister Cecile and Ron Dubaker drove in separate cars to Prinny's, a restaurant not far from Ron's Coral Way office.

She followed his three-year-old Dodge Caravan easily in her Explorer. She often felt that she didn't give her car enough exercise, because she reserved it for driving only while she worked on her cases. She bought it with money from her trust fund, money forever banned from being spent on religion or her convent by her father's will. The money was there to finance her detective business or to be spread among the secular poor. Cecile did both. Paul had set it up so she had a credit card with the expenditures checked by an impartial banker. Dear Paul, a good lawyer, an even better man. She wondered what he was up to now. He had been threatening to come see her again, something he did regularly.

She pulled into the restaurant parking lot next to the Dodge and jumped out. Moments later she and Ron Dubaker were in the smoking section of the restaurant. Ron lit a long cigar.

"Very aromatic," Cecile remarked as a cloud billowed her way.

"Cuban," he said. "Hope it doesn't bother you."

Cecile wondered what he would do if she said it did. Probably nothing.

Together they discussed the Old English menu. "Beef and kidney pie. Hard to imagine people actually eat this stuff." Dubaker chewed reflectively on the cigar. "Of course, Latins are quite international," he mused. "You'd be surprised."

He decided on roast beef and Yorkshire pudding with salad, Cecile chose the baked finnan haddie.

"Tell me about your wife. Is she old Miami?"

"No, she came here in her teens. Loves the city, but fell in love with my acres up in North Carolina. She'll be glad to move when I retire. We go up every summer."

"Wonderful. You're lucky." Cecile watched Ron. "Where's she from? Your wife." She stirred her iced tea, listening to the ice tinkle against the side of the glass.

"She came over in the early seventies when everyone realized Fidel wasn't any better than Batista. Huge immigration then. So many felt the revolution was going to improve things."

"Like the *New York Times* did."

"Exactly. It was a terrible time."

"Lucky thing you were there to help them get oriented. That's what you did, wasn't it?"

"More or less."

"I can just picture it. Must have been romantic for you, meeting your wife back then. You must have been like a savior to her."

"It was a long time ago."

"And I'll bet she knew Juan Caldo. Did she?"

"I don't believe so." Ron reached for a chunk of freshly delivered hot bread and stuffed it into his mouth. It was not as though he were being deliberately evasive. When his mouth was empty, he spoke: "Tell me about the person who hired you. What was the point? Caldo's dead."

"We don't know that," Cecile said.

"No? Ex-con? He's got to be dead. Who hired you?"

"That's confidential."

"Nestor's widow? Old Mirtha?"

Sister Cecile shrugged. "I'd be interested in seeing the gun collection."

"What on earth for?"

"Morbid curiosity. I'd like to see the murder weapon."

"It doesn't exist. I have its twin."

"Well, see the twin. That's what I meant. How does the gun work?"

"It's a small derringer with a percussion cap firing system. An innovation at the time. Deringer was manufacturing a lot of the old-fashioned firing style for the government, but he really got into the new model in a big way. He produced over eight thousand guns in one year alone. Still, with all the ones he manufactured, all the copies that followed, his is still worth big money, even though the copies are better."

"How does it shoot?" Cecile repeated her question.

"You simply measure in the gunpowder, pack it, put in a lead ball, and bang bang. Deadly little weapon. Beautiful gun, though. I wish I had the set. The single gun is basically worthless to a collector. I've kept it as a curiosity."

"If you had the murder weapon, then your gun would be worth something?"

"Set of dueling pistols from the mid-1800s? Any collector would pay top dollar. But I don't have the pair."

The food arrived: fluffy pudding, rare beef, bubbling fish in a creamy sauce. They ate. Finally Cecile stopped chewing long enough to ask another question. "What do you know about a man named Reverend Rubin Gonzalez?"

Ron looked up from his plate. "Ruby? He's located not far from here. He's a preacher, comes from Colombia. He came up and started tending to the local flocks. He's everyone's kindly old uncle, preaches hellfire and damnation, runs a tight ship with that school. He helps kids. Beat his wife back then. I heard."

"Beat his wife?" She thought of Ruby's kindly face. "That's hard to believe."

"I've known the man for twenty years. Wife came to me once, years ago, to find out her immigration status. She'd been working for cash, wanted a green card. That was years ago. She was covered with bruises."

"Was it really Ruby?"

"She said it was the guy she worked for. Cleaning work in a cigar factory. Pretty easy to get paid cash for that, even now. Need someone to clean the convent? Ask me. I'm telling you, it's a lot cheaper to hire under the table. The government robs us with taxes, sends the money to Costa Rica. You have any idea what the Costa Ricans do with all our money?"

"No."

"Take a drive up to Clearwater sometime. Walk along the beach to Mandelay Point, almost at the end, private place you can't drive to, you'll see a huge house the president of Costa Rica just built with rooms enough for all the kids, the in-laws, and a passel of servants. That's where the taxes our little housecleaners pay all end up. That and worse. Then tell me I don't care about these people!"

Ron poured down the last of his beer and signaled for another.

"So you think Ruby still beats her? That it really was him?"

"I don't know about now. That was years ago. She let something slip. Meanwhile I think she's turned things around, learned how to deal with men. From what I hear, she keeps Ruby going now. Maybe she beats him."

Cecile met Dubaker's eyes. He was quite serious.

"Does she have anything to do with the case? Did she know Juan Caldo?" Cecile asked.

47

"Don't know."

"Where does she work now? Is there anywhere I can find her?"

Ron picked a front tooth with his baby fingernail. "I'm thinking."

Cecile waited. Ron Dubaker knew, she was sure. He was simply deciding if he should tell her.

"No, can't say I do."

Cecile nodded. Apparently he had decided not to tell her. Besides, it might be in her notes. "What's her name?"

"Daisy Gonzalez. Big woman. Good-looking."

"Now what else can you tell me about back then? Can you think of anything else that might help?"

"Not offhand." He looked down at his plate, almost empty, and sopped the last drops of gravy with a piece of bread. "The man who was killed wouldn't have lasted much longer. It just happened to be Juan Caldo who blew him away."

"If it was Juan Caldo."

"Doesn't much matter now. Does it?"

"It does to someone." Cecile thought of John Cruz. "It matters a lot." Cecile drew out her list of names. "See if any of these sound familiar. Sanches, Paola. Ever hear of her?"

"No."

"Orta, Raul?"

"No."

"Robert Jeffries? He was a landlord."

"Never heard of him."

And so it went. Ronald Dubaker claimed not to recognize anyone, except people he vaguely remembered in passing. "Sorry, nobody on your list strikes a bell. I should know more of those names, but I don't."

"Well, I appreciate your time. Let me pay for lunch," Cecile said. She pulled her credit card out before he could object.

"Glad to help."

"I'll leave you my card. If you can think of anything . . ." She smiled politely. This was impossible. John Cruz was wasting his money. "One more thing. Could I possibly see the gun? The twin of the gun, that is?"

"Sure. Give my office a call, I'll set up a time."

"I'll do that."

48

Ten minutes later Sister Cecile was on the road heading for home. Her first reaction of discouragement was gone. The two men she had spoken with did know things. Things they weren't telling her. Ruby Gonzalez beat his wife. That meant he wasn't what he seemed, although maybe that had happened years ago and he was a reformed man. Maybe he was a good man now. And Dubaker? He was a liar about the past. He twitched at half the names she brought up. Maybe he just didn't want to know these people. Maybe he had hurt them. Maybe he just twitched.

No one said this case would be easy.

8

" 'COLONEL Magruder was challenged to a duel. His choice of weapons was "derringer pistols across the dining room table." The guns were produced and carefully loaded by the seconds. The two men took their positions at the table. The first man fired without waiting for the call. *Bang!* The foolish man found himself staring directly into the muzzle of Magruder's still-loaded pistol; his chance to shoot was gone. The adversary dropped to his knees and pleaded for mercy. Not that it would have mattered. The guns had been loaded with bottle corks.' "

Leonie put the book down. "Wow, is that cool or what! A real duel, real guns, just like the murder weapon. But they were shooting corks and this one guy didn't even know. That's a hoot."

"Very interesting. Too bad Juan Caldo wasn't shooting corks. He'd be walking around Miami today," Sister Raphael said.

They were seated at a table in the Coral Gables library comparing notes. By now Leonie and Sister Raphael knew as much about the Juan Caldo case and subsequent trial as could be learned from the newspaper. Leonie had gone one further and looked up the murder weapon in a book about classic American guns.

"We'd better grab some books on Singapore and leave," Raphael advised. "It's going to be rush-hour traffic. Besides, I've used up all my money copying this newspaper stuff."

"I'll pay you back, Raphael. My dad keeps sending me money for CDs and clothes. He forgets I wear a uniform. I mean, a unibag. I've got tons of money. Cash is in my underwear drawer if you ever need any. Besides, this is my case."

"Not exactly," Raphael said. "It's mine too."

50

Sister Cecile thought it was her case. Instead of heading back to Miami Beach and the retirement community's peace and quiet, she headed for the home of Mirtha Lezo, widow of the gun collector whose gun had been used in the murder.

It was close to five o'clock when Cecile pulled up a short driveway that ran into a densely treed lawn. Old Miami. A mango tree hung with mangoes, red and green fruits dangling down like Christmas ornaments. An avocado tree flowered, filling up a corner of the lot with shiny green leaves, a group of queen palms huddled together along the property edge. Bahamian shutters covered the front windows of the house, a single-story home painted a surprising raw orange with blue trim. The lawn was rough, not Day-Glo green like so many of Miami's prime lawns, but real stuff, a fine mixture of grass and weeds that someone cut irregularly.

Sister Cecile knocked on the door and waited. She saw the tiny peephole, too small to let her know if someone was looking out or not. She heard the noise of a door handle turning. The door opened abruptly. A woman stood there, aiming a sawed-off shotgun at her chest. The woman said something in Spanish.

"I'm sorry, I don't speak Spanish," Cecile said, staring at the gun.

"I said I don't give to religious charities."

"I'm not asking for money. My name is Sister Cecile and I'm looking into the murder attributed to Juan Caldo. Are you Mirtha Lezo?" Her voice squeaked. Cecile held out her ID, the one that said she was a private detective.

"I am Mirtha. Juan Caldo? You know Juan Caldo?" The gun remained pointed at the nun. The woman's eyes looked at the ID, then turned back to Cecile.

Cecile stood motionless, staring at the hole at the end of the barrel. "I don't know him. I'm looking for information." A hard spot of fear grew in her chest.

The gun wavered in the late afternoon light. "Why?"

"Someone asked me to prove him innocent."

"You like Juan?"

"I don't know." Cecile knew what she didn't like. This

insane conversation held at gunpoint. "Could you aim somewhere else? Please?"

"Oh, sure." The woman shifted the muzzle to point at the floor. "This thing blows a hole the size of a dinner plate. Good thing to keep around. Come in."

Cecile let out a long-held breath as she stepped into the house. She moved slowly inside a cool, silent room. A tiny breeze blew through the open windows. Patterns of light on the floor dappled the rug. A whispering ceiling fan murmured *thunka-thunka* as it spun slowly overhead. The old Florida house without air-conditioning breathed through wide-screened windows; the air was good, not dry and deadly, harboring ice age viruses at the bottom of a noisy air-conditioning unit. A huge green couch, red cushions, wall hangings of South American scenes. Unlit candles in winding cast-iron holders rested on a mammoth credenza.

Mirtha Lezo reflected the decor, a big, handsome woman, strong-looking, with gray hair cut short and pushed back. She wore hoop earrings and a baggy shirt over black pants.

"What are you wanting?" she finally said. Her accent was still heavy, some words ossified into almost indecipherable sounds. "What about Juan Caldo?"

"May I sit?" Cecile asked.

"Sure." Mirtha pointed the shotgun at the couch.

Cecile sat and stared at the dense features of the woman. She must have been very attractive when she was young. Mirtha Lezo wasn't really that old, perhaps her early fifties, which meant she had been in her early thirties when the murder happened. Still, she had a worn face, as though life hadn't played out the way she wanted. Of course, her husband had died back then as well. Perhaps she had mourned him all these years.

"I've been hired to prove Juan Caldo's innocence. What I'm looking for is some indication that he did *not* kill Victor Torres. I know he bought the gun from your husband sometime before the murder. And that your husband was robbed and killed shortly after." Cecile stopped and waited while Mirtha stared at her. The woman's coal-black eyes made Cecile uneasy. Her features held pain.

"You think I remember?" Mirtha turned and placed the

52

shotgun on a heavy-legged table, then sat down, facing Cecile.

"I hope you do. I've talked to several people. Twenty years is a long time, I know. If you could give me an idea of what it was like back then. If you could try."

Mirtha sat for a full minute while Cecile listened to the sound of the fan. She seemed to be considering the nun. Finally she spoke. "Twenty years? It was like yesterday. Victor Torres was a very handsome man. Very intelligent, big man. I will show you a picture." Mirtha rose from the red chair and went to the credenza. She pulled open the drawer and leafed through a pile of old papers until she found a photograph. She brought it to Cecile. "This is Victor."

Cecile stared at the old photograph. Victor Torres. The heart of the crime rested within him. He certainly looked like a man to bring out strong emotions. He was hardy-faced, smiling, had beautiful teeth, laughing eyes—a very good-looking man. A man he would have killed himself, had he been violent, the Reverend Ruby said. Victor's eyes stared out at the nun from beyond the grave. Cecile fingered the photograph, a large eight by ten, yellowed, wrinkled blowup of the tall man; Victor stood by a large fish hanging from a lift of some sort. No wonder the men all hated him and the girls fell in droves. Hair pushed back straight from a broad brow showed a widow's peak. He had a heart-shaped face, unusual, compelling.

Cecile looked up at Mirtha, who waited, staring at Cecile's face for an indication of something. "Yes, he's handsome. No wonder . . ." Cecile said. "Do you suppose it wasn't really a rape? Could it have been consensual? I mean, didn't he father some children?"

Mirtha sat back down, leaving the picture in Cecile's hands. "Nubia was in love with him." Her voice held the softness of reminiscence. "Juan was in love with Nubia. Juan walked in on Nubia and Victor making love. Nubia pretended it was rape. I guess this, because I knew her. She was sneaky, even then. Of course, Juan became angry and hit Victor with the gun. Juan told the police that. He said he didn't kill Victor. Nubia ran, Juan had my Nestor's gun. Juan was stupid to leave that gun on the couch."

"On the couch?"

"Here's the scene. Juan pistol-whipped Victor, knocked him down, tossed the gun behind him on a couch. Someone knocked Juan unconscious, took the gun and shot Victor. That's Juan's story. Juan was drunk too. If Juan Caldo shot Victor after hitting him on the head with that gun butt, then he deserved to be in jail." She shrugged. "Who knows?"

"Could it have been a woman?" Cecile asked. "I mean, this Victor had so many women. He was a beautiful man. What about jealousy?"

"That too is possible. Women are jealous." Mirtha frowned.

"Is there any way we can clear Juan? Can you think of anyone?"

Mirtha stared at the nun silently. Something in the black eyes softened. "Nubia. Perhaps it was Nubia. I always thought it should be her."

"Nubia? I thought you just said Nubia wanted to be with Victor Torres, that it wasn't rape at all."

"I guess now. I think Nubia Quinjano wanted him so much she wanted nobody else to have him. Everyone says Nubia left, ran away. If Juan did not kill the man, sure, maybe Nubia did it. If it was not Juan Caldo, then who knows?" Mirtha said. "But it could have been a man. There were angry men then."

Cecile thought quietly, running a finger around the photograph. Mirtha was not being very helpful in pointing at suspects. Anyone, someone, everybody did it. Cecile stared at the photograph. Victor Torres could have been an old movie star smiling out from the rumpled picture. This man caused trouble.

"Nubia," Cecile said. "What else? Can you remember about the gun collection your husband had?"

"Nestor had guns from Europe, but most from America. Guns used in the War between the States. He had a percussion cane pistol, he had hinged bayonets, a French pistol with a detachable stiletto, many more."

"Worth a lot of money?"

"Enough."

"And the collection was later found?"

54

"A dealer in Tampa who handled such things."

"And the dealer couldn't pinpoint anyone? How did he get the collection?"

Mirtha shrugged, her heavy shoulders rising and falling like a minor earthquake.

It must be hard for her, Cecile thought, forced to recall such a sore past. "I'm sorry. This must be painful for you. Your husband . . . so sorry."

"Long ago," Mirtha said, running her hands over the chair arms as though looking for strength in the formidable structure of the furniture. "Long time ago."

"The gun dealer in Tampa?"

"I have his name. I will get it. I sold the collection to Mr. Dubaker after it was recovered. You should speak with him. A *notario*."

"I've met him."

Not long after, Sister Cecile left with a promise to call back if she had any more questions. Mirtha stood by the door and said a polite good-bye. The shotgun was still on the table, the fan still turned, as Cecile walked out the door.

As the nun emerged into the evening light, a late model red Camry pulled in the drive beside Cecile's car, and a young woman stepped out, a very beautiful woman with shoulder-length black hair and a wide expressive mouth that opened in surprise.

"Hello. You're visiting my mom? Is everything all right? Did she shoot you?" The woman suppressed a smile.

"Fine, everything's fine. I was asking her some questions about the past. You're her daughter?"

"Yes." The young woman looked very serious. "Mom gets scared when she's alone. Did she go at you with the shotgun?"

"Yes."

"Mom's really a sweetie. She can take care of herself. I keep telling her to put in a security system, but she keeps the windows open. Likes the air. You know."

"I know. My name's Sister Cecile."

"I'm Rita Lezo. Next time call first. The number's listed under my name."

"Thanks, Rita."

Rita was an attractive young woman of about twenty.

Nestor Torres's last gift to his wife before he died, Cecile thought. How sad to have never seen his baby grow up into such a stunning woman.

Sister Cecile left, vaguely depressed. Murder was such a dreary subject; all these beautiful people hurt by one evil act done twenty years ago.

The long day was almost over, and rush-hour traffic would be at its worst going back to the beach. She would miss dinner, but be on time for the evening Mass celebrating the Feast of the Ascension. It would be good to pray. This case required some serious divine guidance.

9

"WHAT next?"

"Finish that report on Singapore." Sister Raphael was playing Tetris again, doing well too, from the looks of it. Raphael's fingers moved fast. Leonie's fingers were itching to get at the computer. She loved to send e-mail to Zoe, even though they saw each other every day at school.

"I've been going through all the stuff we got from the newspapers, you know?" Leonie pulled a chair up to the computer and pushed a key. "Do it this way," she said.

Raphael completed a line and it disappeared. "Yes."

"Everyone wanted this man dead, Raphael. He was a creep. I mean, it came out in court that he'd fathered two kids in the neighborhood. He was one of those."

"That's no excuse to kill him. We should pray for him. God loves everyone."

"I know, but then there's Nubia. That's the woman he was supposed to love? Juan did love, I mean. Bad taste. Now, Nubia was seen going out with the murdered man several times during the week preceding his death. I don't think she was very nice at all. You understand, Raphael? Isn't that a perfect setup for murder?"

The old nun finally looked up from the computer. "What I understand is that this case is X-rated, Leonie, and I don't like it. I think we should leave it for Sister Cecile. Why don't you bring me all the things we copied at the library and I'll take care of them."

"X-rated? I watch stuff on TV worse than this."

"Nevertheless."

"That's definitely not your word, Raphael. Nevertheless was said by a crow in a poem by Poe."

"Nevermore. Not a crow, a raven said it."

"Poe's crow. Can I spend the night at Zoe's? We have tomorrow off."

"You're rhyming. Ask Cecile. She's around."

"Okay."

Leonie left Sister Raphael at the front desk, where the elderly nun continued with her game. Leonie admired the older woman tremendously but would never let on how strongly she felt. But she did stop, turn back and give the old nun a hug before going on her way. Sister Raphael was Leonie's surrogate grandmother. Leonie missed the smile of pure joy that lit up Sister Raphael's face as the nun watched her run out.

And there was Cecile. Cecile was her mother substitute. Leonie knew it, knew it in her own way and even in adult words. She would do anything for Sister Cecile. Even solve her case.

She found Sister Cecile in the chapel, as expected, praying. The nuns wasted way too much time praying, although there were some occasions, Leonie had to admit, when she actually prayed herself. She would never tell the nuns that. Leonie moved into the pew beside Cecile. "Can I spend the night at Zoe's?" she whispered.

"It's too late," Cecile whispered back.

"It's only eight-thirty."

"You have school."

"No." Leonie shook her head.

There was one other nun in the chapel, kneeling before the small statue of Our Lady, praying the rosary. The chapel still smelled of burnt beeswax and a faint drift of incense, because Father Herra had brought everything with him to celebrate the Feast of the Ascension an hour before. The odor of holiness still lingered.

Sister Cecile blessed herself, genuflected, and turned to leave, gesturing Leonie to precede her out. When the door closed behind them, they spoke in normal tones.

"You can't. You have school tomorrow."

"No school," Leonie said. "Teacher conferences all day. I have a note about it. So can I go?"

"I never saw this note. Is it all right with Zoe's mom?"

"Sure. You know she always wants me over."

"True. I guess you can go. Be home for supper tomorrow, and give me a call around noon so I won't worry."

"Thanks." Leonie stood on tiptoe and kissed Cecile on the cheek. "How's the case going?" she asked.

"Well, slow. I questioned a lot of people today. Everyone wanted to kill that poor man."

"Yeah. So who really did it?"

"Someone suggested Nubia."

"Her?" Leonie was astounded. "She's dead, isn't she?" Cecile nodded.

"That would be a good solution. Prove she did it and nobody gets hurt."

"I may try that."

"Well, I gotta go pack. 'Bye, Cecile." Leonie paused before running off and gave the nun a hug. "Thanks." It was a good night for hugs.

Later that night Leonie and Zoe talked until midnight. "Tomorrow," Leonie said as she closed her eyes for the last time before sleeping, "tomorrow we're going to Calle Ocho and investigate. Right, *amiga*?"

"Sí, mañana," Zoe murmured, and fell asleep.

On Friday, Sister Cecile almost went to Calle Ocho herself. Miami's Eighth Street was where it all began, where Victor Torres had died, where Juan Caldo had lived. It was still the heart of the Cuban immigrant community. But it was Maria's day off, and Cecile had forgotten to ask her to come along and translate for her, so the nun decided to stay home and work on the yard. Maria's husband worked one day a month keeping the greenery in shape, but in the spring things started to grow too fast, and a trimming once a month was not enough. Many of the nuns took a hand at the lighter yard work.

Dressed in shorts and a huge white T-shirt, armed with clippers and trimmers and a shovel, Sister Cecile set to work in what she referred to as "the secret garden," a small, lush spot where a stone bench beside a winding walkway beckoned the old nuns to come and meditate.

The morning was hot and steamy. In May the weather could verge on torrid, and it was a real penance to chop and pull weeds. Today it was close to ninety degrees, and the

59

humidity made the outdoors feel like a sauna. The other nuns were all inside breathing cool, recycled air.

Sister Cecile didn't care. She loved physical work, especially when she had a problem to work out. Besides, in spite of the heat, it was a lovely morning. The sun streamed down through the trees, bugs hummed and chirped, and a sweet-tongued cardinal perched on a treetop calling for his mate. The nun's short dark hair curled wildly in the humidity, her gold cross flashed in the sunshine.

Chop. Down came the old dried fronds from a huge traveler's palm. *Chunk.* A strangler vine was uprooted and sent into a pile. *Thud.* A dead branch fell to the ground. Cecile raised the shovel to hit another dead limb. It cracked, creaked, and paused, waiting for Cecile to give it another whack. She raised the shovel and hit it hard.

A stream of zebra butterflies erupted from a nearby butterfly bush, but the dead branch remained suspended in midair. Cecile shook her head in disgust at the dead wood, felt a quick flush of jubilation at the butterflies, then forged ahead to admire a trumpet tree, something Leonie had informed her contained a powerful hallucinogen in its leaves. How did Leonie know such things?

A man walked into the garden, startling Cecile. She rested her shovel on the earth and wiped a drip of sweat from her chin. "Can I help you?"

"They told me inside there was a nun out here, Sister Cecile. You see her?"

The man was almost polite in a slightly disrespectful way. Something about the way his lips turned when he mouthed the word "nun." His speech was unaccented, American, his face belonged to a man of about thirty, and he had a long brown ponytail. He was dressed in a sport coat and shorts.

That's what made Cecile suspicious. Ninety degrees and this man had on a sport jacket? With shorts? What did he want with her?

"She's somewhere around." Cecile smiled. "What did you want with her?"

"Business."

"Oh, well." Cecile didn't know why she was being contrary. She should just graciously assure the man that she

60

really was the nun in question despite her costume, and in fact she was about to do that when the dead branch from the royal poinciana finally let loose. Maybe it was the butterfly that lit on the bough that set it off, or a tug of gravity, or God's breath, but whatever it was, the branch began a ponderous descent right behind where the visitor stood. His bland, pale eyes concentrated on Sister Cecile.

Neither of them saw the branch until it tapped the man on the shoulder. He spun around so fast Cecile's mouth dropped open. The man's gun came out fast, ready to kill.

He didn't shoot. It was only a dead limb after all.

If the branch had been alive, it would have been dead.

He put the gun back under the sport jacket. Some kind of arm holster. Sister Cecile felt a rush of adrenaline. "Do you always take aim at trees?"

He shifted his shoulders. "Miami," he said. "So where's this nun?"

"Well now, I think I remember the nun saying she had to go out. Maybe you could leave your name?" Sister Cecile asked, gripping the shovel handle hard. Her heart pounded uncomfortably.

"Too bad. I just have a message for the nun. You tell her I'll be back."

"Your name?" Cecile's voice was urgent, but the man was quick and he was gone from the garden, leaving her words hanging in the air among the butterflies and a faint stink of fear.

Sister Cecile sat down on the stone bench and stared at the empty space where the man had stood. Somehow she didn't think she wanted to hear the message this man wanted to deliver. Who was he? What did he want? Nothing good, that was clear. She could not allow gun-toting men to linger about the home for retired nuns. He couldn't come back.

Five minutes later she was at work hacking furiously at recalcitrant pampas grass that was trying to gain a foothold in a back section of the garden. Another problem to work out, more weeds to fell. The retirement community was a reformed motel. That was how Sister Raphael put it. But the motel had been neglected, and the small weedy area grew wild for several years before the nuns bought the property. It was looking good these days, but Maria's husband thought

61

pampas grass was pretty. Cecile had taken the ecological viewpoint that it was an invasive growth trying to take over Dade County, just like that hit man.

A hit man. Was that really what she thought?

While her heart gradually slowed down, while she saw the man's face in front of her eyes, superimposed on evil weeds, she chopped, pulled, and perspired.

Finally Cecile lugged the tools to the garden shed and went back into the building. Her face was bright red and her shirt clung to her body. She headed straight to the shower, and then dressed in nun clothes again. She approached Sister Linda, who had been reading in the front room where the nuns often congregated.

"Was there a man looking for me earlier?"

"A very nice gentleman," Sister Linda said.

"Nice?"

"Very polite. A little strange. The man was very hot, like he'd been walking in the heat, so I gave him some lemonade. Very hot, but cold eyes. You know we're supposed to give drink to the thirsty. One of the corporal works of mercy. Then I told him you were around in the back. Was that all right?" The elderly nun looked worried. Sister Linda had worked as a third grade teacher for thirty-seven years in a convent school in Daytona and considered herself a good judge of character.

Sister Cecile nodded. "I think the man might be trouble, Linda. If he comes back, tell him I'm not available and it might be better if he used the telephone and called me. And ask his name. That way I could find out what he wants from a distance."

"Some of that detective stuff," the old nun said. "I was thinking that. He had such old eyes for a young man."

"Yes. He did. Thanks, Linda."

Cecile went back to her office and called a familiar number.

"Miami Beach police headquarters."

"Is Detective Cypress in, please?"

"Who's calling?"

"Sister Cecile."

Moments later Jim Cypress's deep voice blasted across the line. "Cecile! How you been? I was thinking about you guys.

Stephanie was saying you and Leonie should come over for dinner sometime."

"I'd love that, Jim. How's Stephanie?"

"Five months along, feeling great."

"Raphael's promised to knit something as soon as she finishes the blanket she's working on for Marie."

"Great. What's up?"

"There was a man here today. He made me a little nervous. He carried a gun."

"This is Miami," Jim said. "Did he aim it at you and demand all your money?"

"No. He almost blew away a tree. I think he's a hit man coming to get me."

"Seriously?"

"Well, maybe I'm just paranoid, but there was something about him. Maybe if I describe him and tell you what I'm doing?"

"Go ahead."

"I only have one case right now," Sister Cecile began, and related the entire story except for the identity of the man who had hired her. Because that, she realized, was something she wasn't really sure of. She didn't even know John Cruz's address. All she knew for certain about John Cruz was that he had handed her ten thousand dollars in cash.

"You must have stirred something up," Jim said. "Maybe your client was right. Maybe Juan Caldo is innocent."

"I guess. Whatever, it happened very quickly. I started asking questions yesterday, this man walked in at eleven the next morning. If it's connected to my case, someone really moved fast. I don't like a man with a gun wandering around the convent garden. Can I come down and look at mug shots of known assassins? I mean, I'm suspicious. He looked like a pro. You must have something on him."

"High class killer?"

"Well, he looked serious."

"I can loan you a gun. I don't know how you could pick out his face. Do you have any idea how many criminals we have pictures of?"

"Don't you have specific criminals for specific crimes? I mean, sorted."

"Any thug offered enough money might qualify for hit man. You're welcome to come down and go through the books. You have no fingerprints? That could make it easy."

"Fingerprints?" Cecile's mind moved back. The man hadn't touched anything in the garden. Lemonade? Yes! "Jim, I'll call you back. There may be prints."

Cecile ran to the front room. Sister Linda had given him lemonade. "Linda! What did you do with his glass?"

"What glass?" Linda was hitting keys very slowly on the front desk computer.

"The glass that man drank from. I'm looking for fingerprints."

"I'll send this. Just a moment, please." Linda clicked some keys, waited a second, then switched off the machine. Then she rose, moving very slowly. After all, she was eighty-seven years old. "I put the glasses directly in the dishwasher."

"Could you show me his glass?"

Sister Linda walked to the kitchen and pulled open the dishwasher. There were rows of dirty dishes waiting for just a few more before the load was ready to wash. Thank goodness it was still morning and people were still getting things dirty. "Can you remember which glass?"

"Absolutely. The Minnie Mouse glass." Linda reached for it. "This one."

"Wait! Don't touch it. You might smudge the man's fingerprints."

Sister Linda stood in shock. "But my fingerprints are on that glass, Cecile! Won't they think I'm the criminal?"

"No. Just give me a sample of your prints and I'll bring them along to eliminate them. The man's will be left."

"Oh." Sister Linda still looked worried. Her old voice shook. "Are you sure?"

"Absolutely." Cecile took a towel and gingerly picked up the glass. "I'll take this down to Jim, my policeman friend."

The old nun still appeared concerned. Her upper eyelids almost obscured her deep brown eyes, eyelids that drooped with age, giving her old face the look of an aged mandarin. "I don't know about this," she said.

"Don't worry, Linda. Here's a clean glass." Cecile set the Minnie Mouse glass down, still wrapped, and took a clean glass from the cabinet, wiping it carefully with a towel. She set it on the countertop. "Just grasp this hard with your hand and there will be fingerprints."

The old nun shook her head. "It makes me feel like a criminal."

Cecile watched the old woman. Some fears made no sense, and Cecile could see her words warring with an irrational fear in the old nun's mind. Of course, when one grew old, Cecile thought, unreal fears could become real. "I would never let anyone hurt you, Linda. And this will help me."

The old nun finally grasped the glass, her face scrunching up in pain as though the world might end. Suddenly she dropped it with a smash. Glass went everywhere. Sister Linda was shaking all over.

"I'm so sorry. So sorry." Tears came to Sister Linda's eyes. Sister Cecile leaned over and gave Linda a hug and patted her back, conscious of the old woman's terrible frailty, her thin bones under the loose white habit, and her fruity smelling breath. Lemonade.

"Shall we try again?" Cecile offered. "We'll get it right."

It was well after noon before Sister Cecile pulled into the police headquarters parking lot in the visitor's slot. It had taken time to clean up the broken glass, check with Sister Raphael about answering her calls, and catch Leonie's quick call from Zoe's house that everything was fine and they were going to spend the afternoon together. "I'll be home for supper," Leonie promised.

Everything was under control.

10

"OKAY, that's taken care of," Leonie chirped. "Let's go."

"Recuerdate, de ahora en adelante solamente hablamos en espanol," Zoe said.

"From now on we speak only Spanish," Leonie translated. *"Sí. Solamente,"* she said carefully.

"We have to take the bus," Zoe Cabrall said. "And then another bus. Then we walk. It's not hard. I've come here with my dad when they have the carnival."

"Okay. Just don't talk so fast. I can't understand you."

The two twelve-year-old girls set out, one thin and blue-eyed with long, stringy blond hair, her father a CIA agent, the other a short, young version of the murdered singer, Selena, with a sharp mind grounded in the realities of her parents' import-export business.

Two buses and a considerable walk later the girls arrived at Calle Ocho, Miami's Eighth Street, the heart of the Cuban community. Both girls were aware that the Cuban population grows and spreads, constantly shifting, that it extends to every crack and crevice of Miami, West Dade, Hialeah, and New Jersey. People come and go and come again. Maybe the people they were looking for were all dead. Or lived in Hoboken.

Calle Ocho bustled in the sunshine. Small cigar factories existed beside small Cuban cafeterias, and in the park, old men played dominoes. Zoe was grinning happily. Leonie was frowning in concentration, trying to understand anything at all. "They talk too fast," she muttered.

"Cuban Spanish," Zoe said triumphantly. "It's the fastest."

"It's the worst," Leonie said.

"Everyone says that. Where shall we start?"

"Those guys playing dominoes? Why do they play dominoes?"

"Cubans play dominoes. I play dominoes."

"Okay. Zoe, you have to talk, and remember everything they say because I might miss something."

"Sí," Zoe said.

Zoe went first, approaching a cement table where four men with sun-drenched skin and gray hair sat, puffing on fat cigars and staring at dominoes. Leonie followed Zoe, staying close. She was nervous because the Spanish was impossible to understand. Mrs. LaCasa always spoke slowly and clearly. So did Zoe. These people couldn't speak Spanish right.

"Excuse me, my name is Zoe, and I wonder if I could ask you some questions about something twenty years ago. Please? If you could just spare a moment?"

Zoe was being dreadfully polite. Leonie winced. She had heard of the Maria complex, where the Hispanic woman was always subject to the male, or to the mother. Zoe was exhibiting it in her tone and demeanor. It was purely un-American.

The old men appeared to like it.

"Twenty years ago?" The oldest raised a heavy head and stared at Zoe. He must have liked her innocence. Probably too much. He spoke in choppy, gravel-voiced Spanish that had Leonie frowning. "Come here, darling, you ask me. My friends here have not been so long in Miami." He reached for Zoe's arm and patted it. Zoe didn't flinch.

Leonie looked around for the police. Coming here really stunk. She stood firm, but kept her distance, unlike Zoe, who actually submitted to having her arm patted. "Juan Caldo," Leonie said in careful Spanish, holding her arms tightly against her sides. "He was accused of murder here twenty years ago. We want to know someone who was there, who can tell us if someone else did it?"

The old man's watery eyes turned from Leonie to Zoe, baffled. "What does she say?"

Zoe repeated it in fast Spanish.

He nodded. "Not so long ago. Like yesterday. You children go away. Not your business. Go home." His voice came out like sand.

Zoe shook her head. Leonie made a mental note that the man knew of the case.

"Where are these people?" Zoe asked.

"Dead. They killed him next."

Did he say "they"? Leonie would have to ask Zoe about that. It could mean something.

"Who killed them? Who was the real killer?" Zoe asked bravely. Her voice was shaking a little. Leonie could tell. They were getting close.

The old man shrugged, patted Zoe's arm again. "Back then, maybe the women. Go home. There is no justice for us." He spat brown tobacco juice on the pavement. "Like today, justice costs money sometimes. Sometimes we get truth. You want truth?"

Verdad, Leonie thought. Truth.

"Yes." The girls said it together.

"Daisy Gonzalez. Maybe she tell you. Daisy." The old man grinned and showed a straight, perfect row of brown-stained teeth. Maybe the tobacco killed the cavities, Leonie thought. Maybe she should smoke cigars. Maybe she should drag Zoe away before something happened. The other men at the table were staring a bit too hard at Leonie's blond hair, at Zoe, whose twelve-year-old body was beginning to look like a woman's.

"Daisy Gonzalez? Is she here?" Zoe asked.

"Over there. She runs the shop. You go ask. Maybe Daisy tells you. Maybe you should go home. Where do you live?"

"Where's Daisy?"

He pointed to a small building with almost illegible brown letters over brown-shaded, wide windows. Leonie made out the name, ZARUDA'S CIGAR SHOP.

One of the other men interrupted. "Why are you asking? You little girls, go home. Get out of here." This man wasn't so old, only in his early forties, and wearing a HERMANOS AL RESCATE T-shirt. "Brothers to the Rescue," a group of men who flew close to Cuba to pick up rafters trying to escape the island.

"For justice," Leonie said primly. *"Justicia,"* she repeated. One of the Hermanos should understand that concept.

"No justice," the younger man said firmly, as though he ex-

pected to be heard. "This is not safe for children. Stay away."
He flapped his hands. Leonie took a step back.

"I will just talk to Daisy." Leonie spoke bravely.

Zoe began shuffling from one foot to another. She moved
carefully away from the older man, whose rough hands still
touched her arm, patting it, smoothing the fresh girl skin. A
slow move back, one more inch and she was free. "Thank you
so much, sir. Thank you." Zoe smiled halfway, a polite Cuban
child smile.

Time to go. Leonie echoed Zoe's *"Gracias,"* and they
walked out of the park, not looking back.

"Hairy," Leonie whispered in English.

"Scary," Zoe agreed. "Do we have to see this Daisy
person?"

"Sí," Leonie said, and they reverted to Spanish again.

The building the old man had gestured to was across the
street, half a block away. Leonie and Zoe jogged toward it, not
too fast, not too slow. Behind them laughter of old men tinted
the air, making the girls feel slightly ridiculous. Leonie whispered, "They hate us."

"No. They're like my grandfather and uncles," Zoe said.
"Not so bad if they're relatives. Still, maybe we should go
home," Zoe suggested.

"Daisy is a woman. She won't hurt us." Leonie forged
ahead. Up close the nature of the large brown building
took shape. The partially opened shades revealed women at
tables rolling brown leaves, forming tobacco leaves into long
shapes, women cutting, fitting, making dozens and dozens of
cigars. The two girls stood for a moment and stared through
the dingy windows.

"Look at that!" Zoe breathed.

"Let's go in," Leonie said.

The feeling they shouldn't be here rose like the warm,
sweet scent of prime tobacco.

Nobody looked up when they entered, two hesitant children,
standing at the door and breathing aromatic air. The women
worked fast, rolling, fitting, wetting the cigar ends, stacking the
cigars like Lincoln Logs. Leonie nudged her friend. "Ask," she
whispered.

Zoe asked.

"Daisy is in the office," the first woman answered, a very old woman with a face as wrinkled as a cured tobacco leaf.

The girls moved to the back and Leonie rapped gently on a half-closed door labeled OFFICINA. Below it was a second sign, PRIVADA. NO ENTRAR.

Leonie tapped lightly and peeked in. A woman sat at a desk drinking dark coffee out of a thimble-sized cup, a *cafecito*. Beside her a smoking cigar sat in an ashtray sending up smoke signals, and behind her a heavily barred but open window let in a stream of fresh air. The woman looked up at Leonie and deliberately picked up the cigar and pulled in a mouthful of smoke, releasing it a moment later in a dense cloud. "What are you doing here?" the woman asked in Spanish.

"Daisy Gonzalez?" Leonie asked. "Is that you?"

"Sí."

"Could I talk to you?" Leonie gestured behind her for Zoe to push into the doorway. "I'm trying to find out something."

Daisy put down the cigar. "Come in."

Leonie grinned nervously, barely focusing on the woman's face. "I'm doing research," she began. "I am studying the case of Juan Caldo. I need to know if it is really true that he committed murder."

"Investigation. You do this for your school? Caldo? That man?" Daisy looked thoughtful more than surprised. Intrigued, maybe, at a name out of the past.

Leonie plopped down on a wooden chair. Zoe remained standing respectfully.

"We're studying the legal system and I was looking through old cases," Leonie said, stumbling over the words, making them up as she went. They were studying Singapore, actually, in Social Studies class. She could make this a project next year. She would, then all this would not be a lie. "Zoe, you ask her, please?"

Zoe began to speak, talking slowly so her friend could understand. While she spoke, Leonie looked around the room. It was filled with finished boxes of cigars, beautiful boxes with elaborate pictures on cherrywood. Leonie looked down beside her and saw an open box of cigar bands waiting to be slipped onto cigars. Leonie picked up a cigar band. It was beautiful, gold with elaborate designs. It read, *Monte-cristo*. She picked up a different cigar band. It read, *Partegas*. She slipped a band on her finger like a ring, fascinated by the tiny picture and colors. She slipped the other one over her thumb.

"You like them?" the wife of Ruby Gonzalez asked. "Keep them. My gift to you. But this Juan Caldo case. Here, I have no gift. I believed he killed Victor at the time. Long ago. I was very unhappy, you understand? I was young, beautiful. Victor was handsome. You girls know how to love a man yet? You have boyfriends?"

Zoe nodded madly. She had a crush on James Henry Seibert this week. "I know all about love," she said very seriously.

"We all loved the man Juan Caldo killed. It was very ugly, very tragic."

Leonie understood the Spanish. Daisy spoke slowly, deliberately, as she recalled the past. "You're sure Juan really killed him?" Leonie asked.

Daisy stared at the blond girl for a long time. "No," she said finally. "Juan had a big temper. He was just a kid. I don't know. I remember Juan." She smiled. "I was in love with Juan too, you know."

Leonie nodded, Zoe said, *"Sí, sí."*

Leonie had a sudden attack of honesty. Her heart dropped and her face paled as she realized the consequences of what she was doing. She had better cover herself. "I have a friend who is investigating this case for real," she said, her face tense in the agony of revealed truth. "Her name is Sister Cecile and she may ask you. I thought I could help her. She'll probably come see you, and I would die if she knew I was here."

Zoe shot her friend a dirty look, but Leonie kept talking. "See, she's a private investigator, and I'm a very good help. I find out things sometimes. I've helped her before."

Daisy pursed her lips and stared at Leonie. "Really. Now what is she looking for, this private investigator?"

Leonie glanced at Zoe, helplessly. "She's been hired to find the real murderer."

Daisy nodded. Leonie stared at her, a woman who was at

71

least fifteen years older than Cecile, or perhaps just aged by her tobacco habit. Black hair held back in a shiny knot at the nape of her neck, sharp brown eyes, plump lips on a lean face; men would call her beautiful. By her own admission she had been in love with Juan Caldo, and apparently with the man he murdered as well. Leonie thought she looked tough and smart. Daisy Gonzalez was that, and she was also, suddenly, hesitant. Leonie saw it right away and knew something was not as it should be. "Who else could have killed the man?" Leonie asked.

Daisy tapped her cigar. "I could give you too many names." She laughed. "My noble husband. All the other women Victor loved. So much jealousy. The man who owed him money, the Anglo. Again there was a woman. So much love. So much hate. I would suggest to you that this is not a case for a child. Go home to your beds. Go away. There is nothing for children here." She stood up. "I will speak to your private investigator if she comes. I'm glad you told me this. I'm grateful. What is her name again?"

"Sister Cecile."

"My husband, he mentioned her," Daisy said thoughtfully.

"Please don't tell her we came." Leonie stood up, held out her hand to shake like she saw adults do. Daisy's lips turned up a fraction at the gesture. She took Leonie's hand.

"I agree to that. You are a good girl, then?"

"I am a good girl," Leonie repeated. She had some doubt about that, but maybe saying it would make it true. "Thank you so much."

"You're very welcome."

Moments later the girls were on the street, breathing sighs of relief.

"Whatever made you tell her all that?" Zoe asked. "You're totally nuts."

"It was that or be killed at a later date," Leonie said. "If that woman ever told Cecile I came here, I'd be dead meat."

"I suppose. Let's get out of here. It's creepy."

Leonie stood still for a moment, thoughtful, twisting the cigar bands, one on the thumb, one on her index finger. "There was something funny there," she said. "Daisy wasn't straight with us."

"I know," Zoe agreed. "But she didn't kill that guy. I'm sure she was telling the truth about that."

"You think? So, what is it?"

"Who cares? Let's go home."

11

JOHN Cruz prepared his talk to be given at the Cattle Breeders Association meeting in Orlando. He had read so much about his subject that he found the writing was easy, and he wrote in English surprisingly well. It was his own ideas that he questioned. He knew about cattle breeding and he knew about risk-taking in the field. He knew about genetic manipulation by tinkering with DNA from various animals. For years he had communicated with scientists, talked to local breeders, read everything. There was very little he didn't know about animal husbandry.

"Should I talk about cloning?" he asked Pearla one night. "I think for the long term development of healthy breeding stock, it's bad. So many downsides. What should I say?"

"It's unnatural, John." Pearla pronounced his name carefully, but no matter how hard she tried, it came out sounding like "Huan." "But I don't know what to say about it."

John stood up and paced the Mexican rug on his study floor. "Unnatural, maybe, but the future asks much of us that is not correct."

He paused and stared at his wife with the look she had come to recognize. She would never fully understand this man whom she had met when called in to help with a catered event in his small, primitive house. She had helped him fix the house to look good for the event. How many years ago? Before Carlito. Thirteen years? She had helped John grow with her love; she was sure of that. He had become wealthy as a result of the meeting she catered. Breeders were introduced to his new, small, milk cow. They had seen the potential, and John had sold cattle for a great deal of money. They were rich now.

Pearla loved her husband totally, and she knew he loved her. Only at moments like this when he got on some strange philosophical bent, she became confused, lost in the dark recesses of his eyes. Such a good man, John.

"I will mention cloning," he said finally. "Because it happens already. I will recall how breeds are dying out, though, because they are not what we want at the moment, that we are losing valuable genetic possibilities, immunities, characteristics that have resulted from centuries of natural development. Should we clone, should it become the new wave, think of the consequences!"

Pearla smiled, nodded, and thought how much she loved him, consequences or not. Then she answered with a question. "One disease could wipe them all out, couldn't it?"

"Perhaps. I don't know of ethics with animals, only people. But I have a feeling, purely in my heart, that cloning is not right. That isn't scientific, but I know it inside."

Pearla nodded.

"I stole my first cow. Did you know that, Pearla?"

"No." She felt shock. Why had he never told her this?

"I saved her life, she would have been eaten for barbecue. Ten years later I found the man who owned that calf and sent him some cash. I sent breeding fees to the man whose bull she mated with. I have felt my conscience should be clear." John turned and looked out the window and was silent. Pearla knew there was more to come. She knew his thoughtful mode, and she waited.

He turned abruptly. "I will make my life free," he said firmly, almost angrily.

Pearla waited for an explanation. This made no sense. Finally she asked, "Free of what?"

"Free. That's all." He sat down at his desk, a large oak affair with an elaborate computer setup. He stared at the screen saver, a herd of black and white cows wandering around. "I will finish my talk. Saturday I will give it."

"Can we come? All of us?" Pearla asked hopefully. "The children will be good. They will be honored to see their father on stage."

A shadow passed across John Cruz's face. "I hope," he said.

* * *

Sister Cecile drove down to the Miami Beach Police station and parked in Detective Cypress's parking space. She knew Stephanie, his wife, had Jim's car today, because Jim had told her that earlier. Having a parking space made life much easier. The visitor's slot was usually occupied.

Cecile gathered up her canvas bag containing fingerprint samples and went into the station, surprised, as usual, by the feeling of an almost, but not quite, male establishment. The smell of tobacco was close to nonexistent these days, but if you sniffed hard enough it could be found, perhaps the lingering smoke of a recalcitrant thug who just might talk more with a cigarette in hand, or perhaps it was smoke history, years of tobacco soaked up by the surroundings and given back to the air one smell-decibel at a time.

Within police headquarters the air of semidesperation lingered even among the calm, doughnut-eating crew. Jim Cypress waited there for her in a designated room. Cecile stopped at the front desk and said her piece.

"He's expecting you. Go ahead."

Jim was in a cubicle typing slowly at a computer. "Cecile, pull up a chair."

"I have the fingerprints. And Sister Linda's as well, so you can eliminate hers." Cecile pulled out the tissue-wrapped glass and the cup with Sister Linda's prints and set them on Jim's desk. The cup had Sister Linda's name on it, on masking tape. "Sister Linda Mascapone," Cecile read. "That's the nun."

"I'll take care of this for you."

"How soon until you find out who this man is?"

Jim lifted a solid shoulder. "Who knows?" His big face broke into a grin. "Maybe never. Maybe this guy was just stopping to ask you to subscribe to the *Herald*."

"Since when does our newspaper employ men with guns to solicit subscriptions?"

"Don't ask." Jim's big face was serious, his dark eyes cast down at his desk in the characteristic way of his tribe. Not shyness, but a rare form of Miccosukee manners. He listened without looking. Then he saw clearly. It had taken Sister Cecile a long time to figure out why he didn't meet her eyes at first. He took the time to listen, then look.

Jim Cypress looked exactly like a true Florida native. No multicolor quilted jacket could have made him resemble a Miccosukee more than what his broad shoulders did to a plain white shirt, and the dark slanted eyes did to that placid face.

Cecile studied him slowly. "You don't look pregnant," she remarked. "Most men gain weight with their wives."

"Morning sickness. I couldn't eat for three months."

"How's she feeling now?"

"Great. How's Leonie?"

"Fine. She's going to Japan soon. Her father's there."

"Come for dinner, then. Sunday night. I might have your fingerprint results and we can discuss things. I need to have Jack, our technician, reconfigure the prints numerically and put them in the NCIC computer. Jack can eliminate the nun's prints right off and won't send them in, or even reduce them to digits. Can you guys make it for dinner?"

"Absolutely. Don't you think you should ask your wife first? That's short notice."

"Why?"

"Couldn't she have other plans?"

"No. I called her before you came. We discussed it. She's dying to see you both. Besides, my brother brought in some alligator. The freezer's full. I'll throw some on the grill."

"Great."

"Sure. Just come about six, you and Leonie. If there's any problem with Stephanie, I'll give you a call."

"Sounds great."

"And bring Raphael."

"I will. And a salad. Can I bring a salad?"

"Sure. Bring a salad and Sister Raphael." Jim rested at his desk and smiled at the nun. Cecile just sat and watched him, knowing the big man was often totally silent, letting everything he felt show through his peaceful repose, a peace shown only to his friends. For a man who normally presented a blank face to the world, he had an extraordinary smile. The nun felt as though she were basking in the glow of a magnificent sun.

"You must be happy," she said.

He nodded. "Stephanie," he said. "I never lived before."

His phone buzzed.

"I'll run along. You're busy." Cecile rose.

"Sunday night," Jim said. "Don't forget."

"We'll be there."

Sister Cecile drove home. She decided to take the rest of the day off, because, in fact, there wasn't much of it left. Maybe Leonie would be back from Zoe's. After supper they could go out for an ice cream, or go swimming in the ocean. Being a temporary mother was fun. Living on Miami Beach presented so many possibilities for enjoyment. A public golf course that only charged a few dollars, the Atlantic Ocean, endless stretches of sunstruck beaches supplemented by sand brought in from various islands. Poor Miami Beach had been subject to outrageous erosion. Every time a storm came along, it wiped out tons and tons of sand. The businesses complained and the city government was once again prevailed upon to rebuild. The endless tourists never suspected that all the glorious white sand wasn't the same pristine powder walked upon by the Tequesta Indians. Or was it the Calusas? Sister Cecile ruminated on beach history as she drove back to the community.

"Is Leonie back yet?" she asked Sister Linda. The old nun sat behind the main desk, again tapping slowly on the computer.

"I saw her, just a minute ago." Sister Linda looked up and smiled at Cecile. "Is everything all right? With that criminal, I mean?"

"I've been at the police station," Cecile said. "They actually send the prints in digitally."

"Wonderful, wonderful. Technology is truly amazing. God gives us a peek at heaven through the wonders we uncover."

"True," Cecile said. She had never thought of it that way, but Linda had a point. "You're sending e-mail?" she asked.

"Oh, yes, it's wonderful. It's free. All these years, I never felt I should spend money calling my family, and now we're getting old, it's wonderful. I feel like my life's come in a circle."

"I'm glad," Cecile said simply.

"My little brother. He's a good man now. So troubled for so long, Sister. He's made peace. I thank God for that."

"We all should make peace," Cecile said. She excused herself and left to find Leonie.

Sister Cecile saw Leonie out by the pool drinking lemonade with Sister Raphael. Leonie looked so young and fresh. Her animated face was busy imitating Cecile's Connecticut prep school drawl as Cecile approached, unseen. "I thunk I'll rully have to go," Leonie mimicked. Sister Raphael was chuckling, then looked up with a guilty expression as Sister Cecile appeared.

"What's so funny?" Cecile asked.

"Regional dialects," Raphael explained, winking at Leonie.

"Thank goodness I don't have an accent," Cecile remarked, and sat down on a lawn chair. Raphael and Leonie chuckled. "Well, I don't."

"Rully?" Leonie asked.

"Rully," Cecile said. "I just saw Jim Cypress and he wants us to come over for dinner Sunday night. He's grilling alligator."

"Great," Leonie said. "Think he'll have some hot dogs?"

"Maybe. Let's go to the ocean tonight and swim. We can go right after supper while it's light."

"You'll be late for prayers," Leonie pointed out.

"The nature of my work allows me to pray later," Cecile said. "Besides, the real nature of prayer is that it's possible to 'pray always.' "

"Even at the beach?" Leonie asked.

"Especially at the beach. Want to come, Raphael?"

"I'll pray here," Sister Raphael said.

Cecile nodded. "Jim particularly invited you too to the barbecue. You can decide if Stephanie is going to have a girl or a boy."

"Boy," Raphael said firmly. "I'm already sure, and I already bought the yarn. Green and blue yarn. He really invited me?" She looked pleased.

"Yes. Doesn't green and blue mean you aren't sure?"

"They just happen to be my favorite colors. The trees and the sky. What could be more beautiful than to wrap a baby in trees and sky? I can't wait to see Jim and Stephanie."

"Me too," Leonie agreed.

* * *

Sister Cecile and Leonie drove to Third Street and parked. "Not too many people swim here, but enough so it's safe," Cecile said. She was wearing a modest black bathing suit covered by shorts and a long T-shirt. Once again she didn't look much like a nun, although it was possible that the suit was a giveaway. Not many attractive women in their mid-thirties appeared on Miami Beach with so much skin covered up. Leonie was more conventional in a one piece maillot covered by an X-large T-shirt that read, BEAST FROM THE EAST.

"Last one in's a rotten egg," Cecile yelled, and raced to the water's edge.

Half an hour later Leonie came out and plopped down on a towel on the sand. She stared at the water, a pale, robin's-egg blue, dimming in the evening light. The water felt like a huge bath. To the northern born, the water was always warm off Miami Beach. Leonie watched Cecile floating out beyond the surf and felt a flood of happiness. Zoe was her best friend, Leonie thought, but Sister Cecile had filled her life with so much that only now, almost a year after they'd first met, Leonie understood the difference between who she had been and what she was becoming. But the trouble with relationships was that they caused obligations. Like how was she going to tell the nun what she had learned in the cigar factory?

"Hi."

Leonie looked up. A man, probably about Sister Cecile's age, with eyes the color of the ocean she had been looking at, stared at her. Leonie sat up, ready to run. She didn't say a word.

"You're from the convent?" he asked.

"Why?" Leonie saw Sister Cecile out of the corner of her eye, swimming steadily in. *Hurry, Cecile, I don't like this man.* Her heart pounded. She had one bad experience on the beach with a man. No more, please.

"I saw you leave with your mom."

Mom? Right. Cecile would love that. Leonie didn't answer. She clenched her fists around some sand. She could throw it in his eyes.

"I'm looking for a particular nun from there, named Sister Cecile. You know her?"

Leonie frowned. "No." Go away, she thought. She had learned early on not to tell strangers anything. Her father had taught her that years ago.

"Your mom know her?"

"Don't know."

"You live at that place?"

Leonie shrugged. Cecile was out of the water now, coming on fast. *Hurry.*

Cecile finally arrived, gasping and dripping, and with one swoop pulled her towel up off the beach and wrapped it around herself, sand and all. But the man had looked first. Leonie already observed the pale blue eyes run up and down the nun, not the way Sister Cecile liked to be looked at.

Leonie suppressed a grin coupled with a feeling of relief that Sister Cecile was there. Cecile could handle this man.

"Hello," Cecile said. "You're the man from the garden."

"What do you do, live at the place with your kid?" he asked.

Leonie didn't like his tone of voice. Nobody should talk to Sister Cecile like that, even if she was wearing a bathing suit and looked like a real person. Leonie stared at the man, his ponytail, his untanned face. He wore a huge guayabera, the embroidered shirt with four pockets. The guayabera was worn hanging out, not tucked in, and was worn by many in the Miami Hispanic community. Except this man didn't look Hispanic. She saw the large lump under the shirt, at his waist, like he was carrying something solid beneath the baggy shirt. All Leonie could think was, gun.

Leonie began to slip on her shorts. "Let's go home, Mom," she said firmly.

Sister Cecile finally replied to the man's question about where she lived after a long pause. "Sometimes we visit the sisters."

"I need to find that nun. You're the only person I've seen there. I need to see her privately."

"She's away this week," Cecile said. "If you call a week from Monday, she should be available. Call the Maria Concilia Retirement Community and ask for her. It's listed. And I'm sure she'll speak to you on the telephone."

"What's she look like?" the man persisted.

81

"Very short, wears polyester whites and a big white veil. Short brown hair."

"Looks like a nun?" The man grinned. An evil grin, Leonie thought.

"Definitely. She looks exactly like a nun."

"Mom, I feel sick. Can we leave?" Leonie whined. A wind had come up, whipping his shirt against him, outlining the gun.

"Yes, darling. You'll have to excuse us."

Cecile turned to Leonie, who was slipping on her sandals. "We'll go right home, sweetheart." Cecile scooped up her pile of clothes and shoes and urged Leonie along. It was becoming darker and the beach was quickly changing from a lovely place to have an evening swim to a lonely spot with three fishermen and a creep. The warm night breeze that had felt so cooling and soft, suddenly felt cloying and satanic.

The stranger stared after them as they left. Leonie could feel his eyes boring into her back. "Cecile, I think he has a gun."

"I think so too. I think he followed us from the convent."

"What's he going to do when he finds you?" Leonie asked.

"I don't know. I just won't wear polyester for a while."

"Not ever. Please."

12

"WHO was he?"

Cecile drove fast. Tonight she pushed the limit, racing as fast as she could with just enough caution to avoid the skaters, the glamorous folks, and the not so glamorous strolling all over the streets of Miami Beach. She set a record.

"I think he's a hit man, Leonie. I think my investigations for John Cruz must have uncovered something."

"Hit man? Have you been watching television, Cecile? He was just a creep."

"This man is beyond the normal gun-carrying citizen. The first time I saw him he said he had a 'message' to deliver, and then he pulled the gun on a tree."

"He pulled the gun on a tree?"

"It bothered him."

Leonie winced. "Okay, maybe you have a point."

"Jim's checking his fingerprints. I'll find out if he has a record soon."

"Um," Leonie said. "Well, I guess Sister Raphael was right."

"About what?"

"This is an X-rated case."

Cecile didn't even smile. "Reason enough for you to stay away from it."

Leonie shifted in her seat.

Cecile pulled the car into the parking lot beside the converted motel. It had been one of the perks in buying the old building for a retirement community: a big parking lot. The nuns rented out spaces to local people, and usually by evening the lot was almost full, except for the spaces reserved for the community cars. Tonight Cecile noticed that the old Ford nun-van wasn't in its accustomed space. It was used by Sister Germaine to grocery shop as well as for taking nuns to various places. "I wonder who took the van out?" Cecile questioned.

"Don't know," Leonie said in a subdued voice.

"Did that man scare you?" Cecile asked as she turned off the ignition.

"That man? Oh, him. No. He was a creep, but you were there. I saw you charging up the beach. You should have seen your face."

That made Sister Cecile feel good. Leonie had been through some rough times. Too many bad times for a preteen. The nun put her arm around Leonie as they walked inside. Leonie had called her "Mom" out there on the beach.

They walked into the lobby, still dripping sand from their towels. "Right out back, Leonie. We can leave our towels to dry outside."

A group of nuns was watching the television on one side of the room, another group was sitting at the round table, playing Old Maid. Cecile stopped by the card table. "Who's out in the van?"

Sister Germaine looked up. "Raphael. She took a call that was for you and went tearing out."

"Really? What did she say?"

"I heard her," Sister Emma said. "I think it was someone named Jim. Raphael said she could take the message."

"Oh, great," Cecile murmured. Sister Raphael was taking charge again.

"Raphael's doing it again," she said to Leonie as they hung their sandy towels over a lawn chair out back. The nuns had a good-sized swimming pool, part of the old motel structure that everyone enjoyed. Tonight the pool gleamed dully in the light cast by a series of electric lanterns someone had recently donated. The water looked clear and inviting even after the ocean dip, or maybe because of it.

"Can I jump in and rinse off the salt?" Leonie asked.

"Good idea." Sister Cecile watched as Leonie took off her shorts and shirt and slipped into the pool, the blue-bathing-suited girl looking like a wood nymph playing in a dark forest pond. Cecile stood and worried for a moment, thinking of how that man had approached Leonie so boldly. Then she worried about what Jim could have said that would make Sister Raphael go driving off into the night. "Please help them, Lord," she prayed. "Everything is in your hands." She really shouldn't worry, she told herself.

A minute later she jumped into the pool beside Leonie. The water was great.

Sister Raphael met Jim at the Cuban cafeteria a few blocks away from the police station, on Washington Street. They sat in a small, green plastic booth. The old nun had a guava jelly and cream cheese pastry in one hand, a cup of decaffeinated coffee in the other. Jim was poking a fork into a salad.

"Stephanie has to eat a lot of vegetables," Jim said. He devoured a huge chunk of tomato.

"Good." Sister Raphael took a bite of the pastry and chewed for a moment. "Now, I can understand your not wanting to talk on the telephone if this were a federal case, Jim, but you said it wasn't that." The old nun's eyes were bright with curiosity. "If it isn't dangerous, then what?"

Jim picked at the salad for a moment. "I'm not sure how to handle this, Raphael. You're older. You're kind. Wisdom with age, right? That's why I'm just as glad to talk to you before I speak with Sister Cecile."

"Just how old do you think I am?"

"Not as old as Linda Mascapone."

"Sister Linda?"

"Sister Linda." Jim stabbed another slice of tomato and ate it. "Here's the deal. Cecile brought me a glass with two sets of fingerprints on it. Sister Linda's prints and an unknown male's. Also, Cecile brought me a cup with Sister Linda's prints alone, for elimination. Well, I dropped the cup and it broke."

"Was it one of the good cups?" Raphael asked worriedly. "Did you get cut?"

"No, no. What it meant was that we had to run both sets of prints from the glass."

"Oh." Suddenly Raphael saw the picture. "So?"

"Linda Mascapone drove a car for a hit man in 1944. A mob leader named Caruso Vincinti was taken out. Her prints

85

were obtained from the steering wheel of the car, a car that was later abandoned, found half submerged in an old quarry in Rhode Island. But they were able to lift the prints. They connected the prints with Linda Mascapone because she had a prior, grand theft auto when she was nineteen. Because the drive-by shooting was part of a major felony, the prints were never taken out of the system."

Jim paused and took a breath. Sister Raphael was staring at him, her old blue eyes wide in astonishment. Jim continued. "Luckily everything's automated so nobody knows the results of the fingerprint testing except for myself. The technician handed me the material, and I ran it."

"Sister Linda? She was a driver for a hit man?" Sister Raphael's voice was so quiet it barely came out at all. "She's been a nun for years, but she joined the order late. She was in her thirties, and she did her novitiate at the mother house in Paris, France."

"They caught the shooter in 1956 and he plea bargained, confessed to the crime, served some time. He died in 1978 in a car accident. His name was Ralph Mascapone. As far as I can figure, he was Linda's older brother."

"Poor Linda, my poor, dear Linda. There's a warrant out for her?"

"There's no statute of limitations on murder. But she's a nun, eighty-seven years old. What's she like?"

"Linda taught third grade in Daytona at a parochial school. She received the Teacher of the Year award seven times. She was a wonderful teacher. She retired at the age of seventy and ran a hospice for recovering drug addicts; later she got into AIDS assistance programs. Now she just helps at the front desk and prays a lot. She has trouble walking but she gets around."

"That's why I wouldn't talk on the telephone. You have extensions, right?"

Sister Raphael nodded. "You were wise. Linda? How incredible. How terrible for her. How dreadful."

"She helped commit murder."

Raphael sighed. "So long ago. It's sad, isn't it. Maybe the guilt was the impetus for her becoming a nun. I'm sure she confessed the sin years ago."

"Maybe. I'm sure your Sister Linda hardly remembers. I'm not going to tell Cecile. Cecile's young, it would weigh on her mind, even though she wouldn't pursue it. Do you think that's wise? And I should report it. I should." Jim frowned. "It's part of a crime. It's accessory to murder."

"Don't."

Jim looked stolidly at his plate. "I'm a good cop," he said. "Always have been. I should."

"You still are a good cop. The very best. And a better man if you let this go," Raphael said slowly.

"Why is it I never had an ethical dilemma until I started hanging around with nuns?"

"Interesting question, Jim. Maybe we made you more aware of what's right and wrong."

Jim continued to look at his salad plate. "Could be."

"Please don't ruin the end of what became a good life." Raphael's blue eyes were sad, as though in her own past there was something worth forgetting.

"Then that's settled." Jim took a large forkful of finely chopped lettuce and stuffed it in his mouth.

Sister Raphael took her fork and dug out a sticky glob of guava jelly. "You'll let it be?"

Jim sighed deeply, eyes on the salad again. "I guess."

"Well, what a thing," Raphael said. "But it's done with. Thank God."

Finally Jim looked up from the decimated salad. "The really bad news is the other set of prints."

Raphael's blue eyes popped open behind the wire-framed glasses she had put on to see the pastry better.

"His name is Jeffrey Cloud, he's thirty-nine years old, and he's from Providence, Rhode Island. The only reason he's in the computer is from an arrest when he was twenty, for aggravated assault. Since then there's been nothing."

"A small-time crook," Raphael said.

"No. I called Providence. They tell me he's associated with a group of high-paid assassins. Not the mob. A group of independents. High-priced, low profile. Instant death. You make a call, the party you want eliminated is dead by the next day. Someone flies in overnight. They charge a lot for their service."

Sister Raphael's pale cheeks grew whiter. "Dear Lord." She closed her eyes after addressing her maker, then opened them. "I don't like this at all. We must tell Sister Cecile about Mr. Cloud immediately. I guess she was right to have you check into this. And it explains why he appeared so quickly."

Jim nodded. "Where did you say she was?"

"She took Leonie for a swim in the ocean. They should be back."

"I'll come over. Will that be okay? I won't scare anyone?" He grinned.

"No one but Sister Linda," Raphael said softly. "That poor dear. She's been learning how to do things on the computer while she's at the desk. In fact she's been sending e-mail to old friends, she says. Do you suppose she's still in touch with those people?"

"They're probably all dead."

Sister Raphael gave Jim a strong look. "Don't underestimate the dead," she said.

Jim Cypress sat and stared at Sister Raphael, bemused or thoughtful, one or the other, and basked in the wisdom of age. "Let's go see Sister Cecile."

He picked up the check.

13

Sister Linda was not in the lobby when Jim and Sister Raphael arrived. Raphael was glad for that. No sense scaring the old nun to death, although there must have been moments in her life when fear came too easily. Maybe Linda Mascapone had learned to rest in God's grace a long time ago.

"Where's Sister Cecile?" Raphael asked the group of card players.

Sister Germaine answered. She was holding the Old Maid card and was about to pass it off to Sister Louise. "She and Leonie dripped by ten minutes ago. I think they went out back."

"Probably swimming in the pool," Raphael muttered. "Come on, Jim."

"Am I supposed to see her swimming? I mean, she's a nun."

"We have big towels. I'll go first."

They walked through the lobby, around and past the chapel and out the big sliding door to the pool area. Sure enough, giggles could be heard, and the sound of water splashing wildly.

"Yoo hoo," Raphael announced.

"Hey, who's there?" Leonie's voice.

"Me and Jim Cypress," Raphael's voice came out.

The giggles stopped. "Just a minute, please," Sister Cecile said. Her voice sounded very dignified, and Jim turned his back on the pool, momentarily.

"I'm out," Cecile's voice said. "You can turn around, Jim. What's going on?"

The young nun was liberally wrapped in a huge purple towel. The nuns had bought a massive collection of towels from an elite downtown hotel which had prided itself on its strange colors. "Have a seat."

Cecile was already in one of the plastic chairs. All that was visible of the nun was her head and feet and a few inches of arms and hands. Even so, she maintained a sense of dignity. She sat up straight, her hair slicked back, her demeanor businesslike.

Jim and Raphael pulled up more chairs. Leonie lingered in the pool, hanging on to the edge closest to the group.

"News about the prints," Jim said.

"Bad news. That's why you came by?"

"Not good," Jim agreed and went on to tell her what he had already told Sister Raphael about Jeffrey Cloud. He didn't mention Linda Mascapone. "So, you'd better be careful," he said.

"But don't you see what this means?" Cecile said, sitting up straight. "It means I'm on to something. It means my man is innocent."

"Stirring the water brings up scum," Jim said. "This particular scum is lethal. I think you should drop the case."

"That's an old cliché. Besides, I've been paid. I like the man who hired me. I have a chance of proving a man charged with murder is innocent. I can't stop now."

"Your ego is showing, Cecile," Raphael pointed out. "All those I's. Bottom line is that we don't want to lose you. He's a hit man."

Leonie let go of the edge of the pool and began to float, breaking away, then swimming back. "You think you can stop her?" she asked softly, rhetorically, mouthing a question not meant to be heard.

"What would you do, Jim?" Cecile asked.

"As a policeman? I'd find out who hired Cloud. The group is based in Providence. There must be a weak link. I'd go at it that way."

"That's just what I was thinking," Cecile said. "He's from Providence? That's a mob town, right? Paul's mentioned the fact. I think he knows people there. I may give him a call. Yes. That's exactly what I'll do."

"Paul?" Jim asked.

"That's Cecile's lawyer," Raphael put in. "He takes care of her money and proposes once a year or so."

Jim nodded. "He knows the score?"

"I would say so," Cecile said. "I told Mr. Cloud I was away for a week, so he probably won't be around for a while. I'll use the time to follow up some leads, be in touch with my client, and then I'll take off for Providence."

"You told Mr. Cloud?" Jim's placid features opened up.

"Well, we did run into him at the beach tonight," Cecile said.

"What a creep," Leonie remarked from the water. "Slime bucket."

"What are you talking about?" Raphael asked. She gripped the arms of the plastic chair tightly.

"Okay, I guess he followed us from here, and he approached us," Cecile said, omitting the fact that the "us" had really been Leonie alone on the sand. "He was still looking for me, but he doesn't realize I'm me. I gave him a description of a short nun in polyester."

"And she's never, ever going to wear polyester again," Leonie said from the water.

"I never have," Cecile confirmed.

Jim stared at her. "I give up," he said.

"I'm just telling you, Jim, I'm okay. I'll keep checking on things quietly, then I'll go to Providence and work from that end. Paul is very good. I'll give him a call tonight."

"I hope he's good." Jim stood up and paced the long deck of the pool. He stood at a distance and stared into the heavy bushes where the nuns' garden began. The three females watched him ponder from a distance.

Sister Cecile whispered to Raphael, "Jim's a wonderful man, but he doesn't have a great deal of imagination."

"He's alive," Raphael pointed out.

"Well, that's true," Cecile agreed.

Shortly after, Jim Cypress left. "Be careful," he said. He sounded like Sister Cecile admonishing Leonie about life. And probably with no more impact.

Leonie grabbed her towel and dried superficially, tossed the towel back on a chair and excused herself. Sister Cecile and Sister Raphael didn't think anything of it. They had other things on their minds. Jim was gone, leaving them with

91

warnings and a reminder to tell all the nuns in residence that Cecile was out of town.

Five minutes later Leonie returned, dressed in shorts and a T-shirt. Sister Raphael was nowhere in sight. Sister Cecile was sitting alone, still wrapped in the huge purple towel, reading the prayers for vespers.

"You should go in," Leonie said.

"It's a warm night. I'm praying."

Cecile put the book down in her lap and turned to Leonie. She pushed the chair back into a half-reclining position and closed her eyes. "It's so peaceful. Sometimes Florida is wonderful. A good state to pray in."

Leonie tried to make her chair shift back and it wouldn't go. She punched it. "Ouch."

"There's a little button underneath."

"Oh." The chair slid back. "You're going north?" Leonie asked.

"I'll give Paul a call and talk to him about it."

"I went somewhere today," Leonie said.

"Where?"

"Zoe and I, we figured we could speak Spanish."

"How'd you do?"

"Not bad. Zoe had to explain my words a little. The guy didn't understand me at first."

"What guy?"

"The old guy playing dominoes on Calle Ocho. Did you know all the Cubans play dominoes? It's a cool game. I'm going to have Zoe teach me."

"In Spanish."

"Sí."

"So there you were on Miami's notorious Eighth Street speaking Spanish to an old man playing dominoes. And you asked something about my case, didn't you?" Cecile's hand moved to her prayer book.

"Actually, it sort of came up."

"And the old man said?"

"He said to go home."

"Smart man."

"So, we just kind of kept on asking."

"Kind of?"

"Basically he said, 'Get lost, kids,' in so many words. So we were just about to do that when he mentioned Daisy Gonzalez. She runs a cigar factory right near there. Really neat place, all these old women sitting and rolling cigars. Anyway, Daisy has an office in the back, so we went there and talked with her."

"Daisy Gonzalez? For heaven's sake, Leonie, you've messed everything up! How could you?"

"I'm helpful," Leonie said stubbornly. "Besides, we spoke in Spanish."

"Is your Spanish this good?"

"You'd be surprised," Leonie said, squirming a little. Sister Cecile hadn't gotten really mad yet. That was a bad sign.

"What did Daisy Gonzales say?"

"Basically she said 'Get lost,' just like the old guy. But the point is, there was something funny about her."

"Like, really funny. Two twelve-year-old kids in a cigar factory looking at an old murder is really funny. Did she offer you a cigar?"

"She was smoking one," Leonie said. Sister Cecile was being sarcastic now.

"What else?"

"Well, I got these cool cigar bands." Leonie held them out for Cecile to look at. "She let me have them. And she also said she didn't kill him herself, and I really believed her, because then she said she was a little bit in love with Juan Caldo. He must have been a nice guy. I get that feeling."

Cecile looked at the cigar bands and listened to Leonie talk. "What else?"

"Everyone hated Victor Torres. Anyone would have killed him. Her husband, she even said. Who's her husband?"

"Never mind." Cecile stared at the cigar bands. "Pretty," she said, and handed them back to Leonie. "My father smoked Montecristos," she recalled. She still didn't sound angry but her voice sounded funny.

"No kidding."

"Leonie, why are you telling me? I mean, I know you. You know I want to beat you for a week. I won't, I'll just yell inside, try to keep from screaming too loudly on the outside. You *know* better! I'm very upset about this. I really am."

93

Cecile stood up and walked away. Leonie knew about Cecile's anger. She was in for it. Grounded forever.

"I was afraid you'd go to Daisy and she'd say something," Leonie admitted just loudly enough for Cecile to hear her across the distance. "So I figured I'd better tell you first."

"That's a likely scenario." The nun walked back to her chair.

"Not to mention the fact that you might never have found Daisy. I did. And I think she's very important in this case. You needed this information," Leonie said stoutly. "And I found it out."

"I already knew about Daisy Gonzalez. Now what?" Cecile paused. "Thank God you told me. Are you scared enough now? There's a hit man out there following us? You messed with my investigation. Don't do this to me."

"I'm sorry. Mr. Cloud is scary."

"Sorry." Cecile fumed quietly. "How can I make you stay safe, Leonie? What can I ever say?" Now Cecile sounded scared. She wasn't mad, she was scared. Leonie hated that, because the nun was scared for her.

"I won't do another thing, Cecile. I promise."

Cecile's gray eyes opened wide. "Do I believe you?"

"Really. I'll just hang out with Zoe. When you go to Providence, I'll hang around Sister Raphael. Besides, I'm going to Japan in a couple of weeks. Maybe Raphael can help me get ready."

"Yes. You'll be safe in Japan."

"What am I ever going to do in Japan all summer?" Leonie asked.

Sister Cecile shook her head. "Only God knows."

14

CECILE used the lobby telephone to call Paul. Most of the nuns had drifted off to bed. Only a few were still there, watching television at the other end of the big room.

The phone rang twice and Paul answered. Sister Cecile didn't respond for a few seconds. She listened to his voice.

"It's Cecile. How are you?"

"I was just thinking about you."

She laughed. "I'm sure."

"Really. I was thinking I needed to come down."

"How about I come up?"

"Really?" Paul sounded suspicious. "Why?"

"Well, I have this case involving a hit man from Providence. You know some people there, don't you?"

"Sure. Who's the hit man going after?"

"Me."

"Great. What'd you do to deserve that?"

"Not much. I opened up a twenty-year-old case and started a stone rolling, apparently. I want to trace the connection, and figured going to Providence would allow me to find the horse's mouth."

"Are you mixing your metaphors? And placing yourself in jeopardy? Cecile, this is crazy. You said a hit man?"

"Don't worry, I'm safe and sound and totally invisible. Woman of a thousand disguises."

"You look like a nun no matter what," Paul said.

"Believe me, this is all but wrapped up. I have to come to Providence, that's all. Can you help me out? Do you know anyone in Providence?"

"Actually, I know this judge. He'll be glad to marry us on short notice."

Cecile laughed. "Someday you'll stop proposing."

"Someday you'll say yes. When are you coming?"

"How about Saturday? Can you book me a flight to Providence? Can you meet me? Can you ask your mob squad friend there to give me a hand?"

"All of the above. And, I'll be there. With a sidearm. I'll make the arrangements. On your credit card, of course. Want a car?"

"A nice little American machine," Cecile said.

"Bulletproof, if I can find one."

"Nothing will come of this hit man, believe me, Paul, forget I said that. I'm fine. This trip is just for research."

"Right."

"So make reservations to Providence. Please."

"It will be good to see you, Cecile."

"You too."

A few moments later Cecile hung up and lingered by the phone a minute. Paul was forbidden fruit, a classic vanilla sorbet, to mix another metaphor. God had chosen her years ago, and she had said yes.

She started to hum as she wandered away from the phone and bent over to straighten things out around the card table. Just as she put the last chair in perfect alignment, Sister Linda approached.

"I was watching television," Linda said carefully.

Cecile nodded.

"I heard you on the telephone."

Cecile nodded again. "I hope it didn't disturb you. I'm sorry."

"No. I heard you say you were going to Providence. That's Rhode Island?"

"Yes."

"Can I come too?"

"Providence? Why?"

"Well, I have some relatives there." The old nun stood up very straight. "I haven't seen them in a great many years, and I know I'm old. I never hoped to go back. We've kept in touch, of course, and recently Sister Raphael showed me how to use the e-mail, and it's been so wonderful." A tear formed in the cloudy brown eyes. Sister Cecile wondered just how much this old nun could see.

"I could bring you," Cecile mused. "I mean, I'm going on a case, not nun-business, and I plan to use my credit card. You aren't visiting any religious, are you?"

The elderly nun raised a hand to her mouth and giggled. "No," she said. "My baby brother. I come from a large family. Only Vinny is left, and his wife, and a great many nieces and nephews. I would love to see Vinny. Vinny could pay for me. But I don't dare travel alone these days."

"Oh. I can pay. You know about my credit card. Anything that isn't connected to God."

"Vinny isn't connected to God," Linda affirmed. "But he's a good boy."

"Fine. We leave next Saturday."

The old sister threw her arms around Sister Cecile and gave her a big but gentle hug. "God bless you, Sister," she said.

Before she went to bed that night Sister Cecile left a message on Paul's machine, because he was apparently out, or had gone to bed. "Make flight reservations for two, Paul. Please. Me and Sister Linda Mascapone. I'm bringing a guest. Thanks. I'll call."

The days rolled by to Sunday, and the Lord's Day progressed in a flurry of prayers and food. Mass in the morning, then Sister Germaine's Sunday dinner, served at two o'clock in the afternoon. Today she served seafood Newburg served on fluffy baked potatoes. Scallops had been on sale at Publix this week, so the creamy sauce was chock full of them. An occasional quarter of a shrimp appeared along with some other undecipherable chunks of marine creature. The retirement community loved Sundays. At four o'clock the nuns would often go out to a movie in the rickety nun-van, driven, usually, by Sister Germaine. Today was no exception. Because the community housed several secular couples, and two widows, these folks were always invited along, but generally they refused, going about their own business. The seculars, as they were called by the nuns, occupied the spare rooms and contributed needed cash to the running of the home.

"We're going to a barbecue," Leonie announced to Jean

Bestard, one of the widows who occupied the best of the spare rooms and paid royally for it. "Alligator barbecue. Isn't that cool?"

Jean nodded politely. "Sounds delightful."

"Yeah, we have some friends," Leonie said. "They always have hot dogs for me."

"My son's coming by later. We'll be going out too."

Sister Cecile overheard. "Give my best to Gustavo, please. I'm glad he's looking out for you."

Jean smiled. "Once in a while he amazes me. He's a good boy."

"He can be," Cecile agreed, and recalled Sister Linda's use of those same words in describing her brother. Gustavo walked the edges of criminality. Of course Linda's brother wouldn't be like that. "Leonie, are you ready? Jim asked that we come early."

"Almost ready," Leonie said.

Twenty minutes later Sister Raphael, Leonie, and Sister Cecile headed out to the Cypress's small house in North Miami Beach. They arrived and received a huge embrace from Stephanie, Jim's blond wife, who looked, Cecile thought, a lot like Leonie. Initially jealous of her, Leonie had become something like Stephanie's little sister, and the two blondes immediately disappeared together into the kitchen.

Sister Raphael wandered over to inspect the grill where slabs of meat cooked slowly over chunks of aromatic wood coals. "It's not green," she said. "Want me to keep an eye on it, Jim?"

"Please."

"Jim, I'm going to Providence next Saturday," Cecile said. "Anything I should know?"

"Wear a Kevlar vest," the Miccosukee said.

"Why?"

"You know why. Other than that, I don't know anybody in Providence."

"That's okay. I guarantee Paul has connections."

"Be careful."

"I will. Jim, do you have a Kevlar vest? I mean, seriously."

Jim's big forehead creased in a dozen frown lines. "Yes. I'll get it for you before you leave. Take it home. Wear it everywhere. Even in town. That man is hard core, Cecile. He won't hesitate to shoot. It's his business."

After that they avoided shop talk. Four hours later they left the Cypresses' house and drove home. Sister Cecile carried a grocery bag containing the bulletproof vest fresh from Jim's closet. Sister Raphael carried a bag containing a helping of barbecued alligator for Sister Germaine to try. The evening had been a perfect interlude, and Sister Cecile was content that Leonie had such good friends. She needed the example of young marrieds, and the Cypresses were a wonderful couple. For a girl without relatives, Leonie was managing to assemble a vast number of role models.

While Sister Raphael headed to the kitchen with her bag of food, Sister Cecile checked the front desk to see if anyone had called. There were messages for various nuns, and one written down for her, from Jean Bestard. "Sister Cecile, a man called for you. I told him you weren't available and to please call tomorrow morning. He wouldn't leave his name."

Sister Cecile stared at the note. The caller had to be Jeffrey Cloud. Paul always left his name. Cloud, as she called him in her mind, now knew that she was available, that she hadn't gone away for a week. "I should have told everyone," she murmured as she slipped the note into her purse. "This is very bad news."

"What?" Leonie asked.

"Cloud. He knows I'll be around tomorrow. He may call. But I'm more concerned that he'll just stop by. I don't want to tell everyone who lives here to lie for me and say I've left. It just doesn't work. You know how some of us are."

"I know. Nuns don't lie well."

"Some don't," Cecile agreed. "I'll just be careful."

15

Sister Cecile spent an uneasy night with visions of herself in the Kevlar vest. She had gone so far as to try it on. It was heavy and slightly bulky, but she would wear it if she left the community.

Except she didn't put it on first thing in the morning. She woke early enough to drive the van to morning Mass at St. Patrick's and drop Leonie off at school. Daily, weekday Mass was an option, and today six of the oldest members of the community came along, including Sister Raphael and Sister Linda. She left the vest on her dresser, certain that Jeffrey Cloud was not an early riser.

The church was cool and dark. There were the usual regulars and the priest who said the Mass for the feast of St. Bernardine, whose feast day it was. The nuns were all in their white habits, and it felt good to be a part of the community, praying together for the souls of mankind, for peace, for so many things. Sister Cecile worried that with the shrinking of religious orders going on, the world was going to run out of prayers. She thought of Sodom and Gomorrah, how the Lord had been looking for even a few good people. A poverty of praying people certainly wasn't new. There would always be holy people, she realized, men and women of faith, folks who took care of each other, exhibiting the spiritual and corporal works of mercy. Briefly, she stopped worrying.

But when Sister Cecile went out later, she dressed carefully, preparing for the worst of humankind, and left a message with Sister Louise at the desk that she would be away for an indefinite time.

In fact, she headed for Calle Ocho, driving the Ford off Miami Beach, passing the gorgeous plantings on the cause-

100

way, zipping along I-95 and down into the heart of Miami's Cuban community. Towering clouds had piled up in the west. Today there was lightning in the distance, a spectacle that didn't usually occur until later in the afternoon.

Cecile felt the heat. She was foolish to overdress in Miami. But she had. Wearing an oversized habit, Sister Cecile felt awkward and faintly foolish, because Cloud couldn't possibly be out there where she was going. Perhaps the habit wasn't a good idea. But did Cloud know who she was? Would he shoot at anything in a habit, or would he shoot at that woman he had seen two times already? By now he would have a description of her. According to Jim, the assassin wasn't a man to be underestimated.

Leonie had told her where the cigar factory was located, and the name, Zaruda's Cigars. Cecile parked nearby, stepping out onto the busy street. She looked up and down for a pale-eyed man in a long ponytail, but saw only the dark brown eyes of a multitude of people from that island ninety miles off shore. Too late, she realized she was stuck if Daisy Gonzalez didn't speak English. She should have brought Marie to translate.

The cigar factory was as Leonie described, the name barely discernible on the faded, peeling sign above the building. Cecile stood outside and looked in. Semidisguised, she looked like a fat nun with a big gold cross. Finally she entered, smiling, nodding, progressing to the rear of the room, conscious of the slowly revolving ceiling fans pushing the sweet scent of tobacco in pungent swirls. Air-conditioning either didn't exist or perhaps the day wasn't considered quite hot enough to turn it on. The breeze coming down from the ticking fans made the room bearable. The soft murmuring of spoken Spanish wafted among stacks of tobacco.

The door to the back room was open and Cecile saw the woman, slightly older than herself but ravishingly attractive. The Reverend Ruby Gonzalez's wife.

Sister Cecile knocked lightly on the door.

"*Sí?*"

"I'm sorry, I don't speak Spanish," Sister Cecile said very slowly with hopes of being understood. "May I come in?"

"Sure. The little girl told me. You're the nun?" Daisy stepped

101

forward, hand out. She spoke impeccable, unaccented English. A huge cigar smoldered on the ashtray on her desk. An open bottle of wine decorated the desk, and a small glass, half full of wine, glowed like a deep maroon jewel through the smoky room. The large, barred window in the back opened to a gentle breeze from an alley, not quite enough breeze to clear the air. "Sit down. Please."

Cecile sat. "I'm really sorry about her, about Leonie coming here," Cecile said, starting right off with an apology. "She shouldn't have come, shouldn't have been here."

"She was great. So was her friend. I'm glad to see an Anglo speaking Spanish. Have some wine. If you could wait just one moment, I have to make an important call. Then we talk." Daisy produced a clean glass from a bottom drawer and poured Sister Cecile a glassful. "Don't tell me sisters don't drink." She picked up the glass. *"Salud,"* she said. "Repeat that. Your first Spanish lesson."

"Salud," Cecile said and took the glass.

"You speak no Spanish?" the woman said thoughtfully. "None?"

"Sorry."

Daisy made her call, speaking in hurried Spanish. Cecile didn't understand a word, except *ahora*, which Daisy said several times. It meant "now."

Sister Cecile sipped politely from the wineglass. It was bad, pure plonk. She contemplated the busy businesswoman across from her. She pictured Leonie and Zoe in this same room. Cecile felt redundant, somehow. She probably couldn't learn any more than Leonie had.

Daisy hung up. "Sorry," she said.

"I should learn Spanish," Cecile murmured apologetically.

"Of course." Daisy's eyes gleamed. She picked up the cigar and puffed. "We make a good cigar here. My workers all come from Cuba." She showed perfect but slightly brown teeth, then rinsed them with a drink of wine. "Best of both worlds. McDonald's and *gallo pinto*. We put it all together, enjoy everything."

Cecile stared, not talking, letting Daisy speak. She hadn't expected this kind of welcome. "Yes," she agreed. "You've been here a long time?"

"I worked here. Learned the trade in my country. I supported my husband in the beginning when he was a preacher. One of the church members ran this place, Carlos Zaruda. I gradually took over the management from Zaruda. A good man," Daisy said. "He was getting old and I asked him if I could buy it. Not a chance, he told me, but when he died a year later, he'd left it all to me."

"A mixed blessing, that he had to die," Cecile said.

"Yes, unfortunate." Daisy tapped the cigar. "I'm very careful with these things. One a day. Only good quality."

For the best quality cancer, Cecile thought. "How old was Zaruda?"

"Fifty-five. We were very close." She turned around a photograph on the desk. "See?" The former owner was a short, dark-haired man with a beatific smile. His arm was around a younger, even more beautiful Daisy.

"He looks kind," Cecile said.

Daisy swirled the glass and touched it to her lips. Then she became serious. "Zaruda was everything. But you are not here for that. Your child said you were searching the past for Juan Caldo. Why?" She tossed her hair back and leaned forward. "Tell me."

"I was hired by someone, confidentially, to prove Juan's innocence. I've been asking around and seem to have stirred something up. So perhaps my client is right; there is something to be learned."

"Interesting. Since the girls came, I am thinking about this. You spoke to my husband, of course. He told me. He was annoyed because even the memory of that man annoys him." Cigar smoke twined around her hand, a hand decked out with fingernails painted a deep red, almost the same color as the wine. The look in her face was stony, and Cecile wondered about Ruby, and if he had really beaten this woman.

"You mean Ruby didn't like Juan? I didn't get that impression."

"No. He despised Victor Torres. Still does."

"Everyone seems to have hated Victor. A murder waiting to happen. Did you ever suspect your husband?"

"Not a chance. We were together that night. We were at Mirtha's, a small party."

103

"Do you recall who was there? Or more important, who wasn't there?"

"Nestor was not there, but it was a woman party, so he would not be. Ruby brought me over and we ended up in the kitchen talking to some friends from Cuba. See, this was brought out at the trial. Everyone talked of this. We all left early, but I stayed with Ruby. We went home together. Very possessive man, my husband. I thought at one time, maybe Ruby sneaked out late at night and killed Victor, but not Ruby. Ruby is righteous, walking in the path, you know? Your kind of path."

Cecile wondered about that. "Do you know a man named Dubaker? Ron Dubaker? Was he there at the party?"

"Ron?" Daisy laughed scornfully. "No. His wife, she was not there either. She was a friend of mine before she married that man. One of us, then one of them."

"What's her name?"

"Graciella. She is not important in this. She is run by her husband. Those kind of people." Her lips twisted in scorn.

"You certainly don't appear to be run by anyone," Sister Cecile said. "You seem a very competent businesswoman."

"Yes. I am."

"Too many people had the motive. Who had the opportunity?"

"The trial ruled out nobody. In fact, we all separated early, like I said. I went to the trial. I was pregnant then, very young. We went together, Mirtha and I. We were both pregnant, so we could talk together about those things, you know? Go to the bathroom from the courtroom every five minutes it seemed. We watched the trial, we testified."

"I met Mirtha's daughter. She's very beautiful."

"And so is mine," Daisy said.

"If she looks like you, she is exceptionally beautiful," Cecile said honestly.

"You flatter. I become old too quickly. But all that aside, you should speak to Nubia's sister." As she spoke she turned a photograph around and showed it to Cecile. "My daughter," she added.

Sister Cecile stared at the photograph. The stunning young

woman looked back, showing direct brown eyes and a challenging look. Her hair was swept up in a dark crown.

"Beautiful," Cecile agreed. She wiped a drip of sweat from her chin. The room seemed very hot. Maybe it was the wine. "Nubia's sister is named Lourdes Sanches," Cecile said, mentally going over her notes, getting back to business. "Where is she?"

"She sells in Burdines. They live out in Kendall somewhere. I don't see her these days."

"Maybe I could go to the store. Do you know which Burdines?"

Daisy took a sip of wine and closed her eyes. She looked old as her face relaxed. When she opened her eyes again she became young. "Dadeland. Ask at Personnel."

"Yes, I will," Cecile said. "Is there anyone else who might have an idea?"

Daisy shook her head. "Not that I remember. It was a difficult time for so many of us. Murder, death, you know how many lives have been lost since then? Our people coming to this country? You people don't understand."

Cecile didn't speak. Her gray eyes saw the pain, the triumph, and, as Leonie had said, something else. This woman was just slightly nervous about something. "Perhaps we will never understand. And perhaps your grandchildren, or even your children, will never understand either," Cecile finally said.

Daisy tapped her desk, like an applause. "You do understand something. I see."

They continued to talk. Daisy rambled about old times, about the people then and now. Cecile finally stood and held out a hand. "Thank you so much. You've been helpful."

Daisy shook her hand. "No. I haven't been helpful at all. It was good to meet you, Sister."

"Oh . . ." Cecile paused before rising. "If I could buy one of your best cigars. I'm seeing a dear friend next week. I'll pay, of course."

Daisy turned behind her and removed a small cherrywood box from a pile of similar boxes. "Please. Take this. There are none better made in this country."

"How much?" Cecile asked.

105

"No. You take them. Don't embarrass me with your money."

"Thank you," Cecile said simply. "My friend will be so happy."

"Good fresh cigars. He will enjoy."

They shook hands. Sister Cecile placed the box in her large black purse and pulled up from the chair, moving awkwardly in the habit's layers of cotton. She should have worn secular clothes. It was allowed. She did it often on a case. Now she was drenched with sweat and her face was red. She tossed the long strap to her bag over her shoulder and walked toward the door.

"Good luck," Daisy said in a clear voice that followed the nun out through the cigar factory like a promise.

Sister Cecile made her way past the cigar workers. Their fast-moving fingers rolled, shaped, rolled again. She stepped outside into the Florida sun, blinking. It took her a moment to orient herself and make a left from the door. She had parked only a short walk away. She looked around at the bustling street, hearing only Spanish, until she looked up, straight ahead about half a block distance. She saw a familiar figure, and heard a familiar voice calling her name. "Sister Cecile!"

She responded automatically, her eyes opening wide, her mouth ready to speak, when she saw the gun. "Cloud," she whispered.

What was later identified as a slug from a .357 Magnum Ruger GP-100 ripped through the hot air and slammed into her chest. Sister Cecile toppled to the cement sidewalk.

16

EVENING found the majority of the community at vespers. Only a small group wasn't praying, they had prayed earlier, and, if possible, even more fervently. Leonie had joined in. The small group gathered around the big kitchen table and nibbled on leftovers and talked seriously. Leonie's face was tearstained.

"We have to plan a funeral," Sister Raphael said.

All Leonie could think of was that her mother had died when she was four, and she could still remember the funeral. "No," she said.

"It brings a sense of closure."

"I hate that word," Leonie growled. "My English teacher uses it. There should be no funerals, no closure. Things should be left open. Forever." Her still, pale face wore a stubborn look. There was no arguing with Leonie in that state.

"I phoned in the obituary, but I didn't give any details," Jim Cypress said. "Maybe we could leave it at that. Nothing else will appear in the newspaper. I've hushed it up."

"The body was shipped directly from the funeral parlor to Connecticut for burial in the family plot," Sister Cecile said. "That's what we can inform anyone who calls. I just have to remember not to answer the telephone. Everyone here knows I'm dead now."

Leonie looked over a pile of cold chicken at Sister Cecile. Leonie was a part of this, had been from the beginning. Besides, she had answered the telephone when Cecile's call had come in from the hospital emergency room. The bulletproof vest had worked, but Sister Cecile's bruised rib hurt, and she had been given a tranquilizer. Her conversation with Leonie from the hospital had verged on the peculiar, but Leonie was quick and had called Jim Cypress immediately, over Sister Cecile's protests.

Leonie cried later when all the implications hit home. So did Sister Cecile.

Jim immediately contacted the hospital after Leonie's call, then swung by the community to pick up Sister Raphael, who had another set of keys for Cecile's Ford. Only after that was taken care of did Jim pick up the young nun at the hospital.

"Okay," Leonie said. "The body's gone north. What else do we have to do?"

"Catch that—" Jim stopped on the verge of using an inappropriate word. "Catch Jeffrey Cloud. I've put out the APB. That's virtually useless. He's probably on his way back to Providence by way of New Orleans. Job's done as far as he's concerned. He's a pro. He'll have proof he was somewhere else at the time of the shooting. It's hardly worth pulling him in. Waste of time."

"I'm going to be in Providence myself," Cecile mused. "I suppose I should wear that vest again, and maybe some kind of disguise. I'm not going to go looking like a nun."

"Heaven forbid," Raphael said. "I don't think you should go at all. You've done enough."

"No," Leonie put in. "Don't go. It's too dangerous."

"It's much safer now. They think I'm dead."

"But you don't know who they are," Jim pointed out. "Stay here. There's no reason for the trip."

"Don't go," Leonie said again.

"The fact that I'm not dead is going to come out eventually. We have to catch the man. We have to find out who's behind this. Nothing has changed." Sister Cecile wore a stubborn look. "I'm going as planned. I spoke with Paul last night. His friend is willing to meet with us and discuss the situation. Paul already made reservations. It pays to do this stuff in person. I need to talk with these people."

Sister Raphael reached for a chicken drumstick and started eating it. She had skipped the evening meal. They all had. It had been a worrisome time. Leonie followed suit, removing half a breast, picking off the skin. Jim watched them eat, then helped himself to a wing. Nobody wanted to talk about promising leads. They all wanted Sister Cecile out of this case. But they all knew there was no point in arguing about it.

"Southern fried chicken," Cecile said unnecessarily. "I could warm up the cream gravy and mashed potatoes. Anybody?"

"I'm too upset to eat," Raphael said. She reached for a piece of celery from the vegetable tray.

Jim wiped his fingers on a paper napkin, then grabbed a chicken thigh. "I can't stop you from going, Cecile, but I can arrange for you to pick up a gun there. I know you can shoot."

"I don't shoot people," Cecile said.

"Even when they shoot at you?" he asked.

"Don't know. Right now I'd be inclined to pray."

"I suppose you're praying like mad for that Cloud person," Leonie said with a touch of scorn in her voice.

"Not yet. But I will tonight."

"A gun," Sister Raphael said, "sounds good, but it might just be a cumbersome thing. Besides, who's going to shoot Cecile now that she's dead? Nobody. But, Cecile, you have to lay low all week. No investigation, you understand. You can get back to that later. Or maybe you'll find out who hired Cloud and end the case."

Cecile nodded and said nothing.

"I have a report of the shooting," Jim said. "Careful notes about how it's connected with the job you're on. When you pull out the name of the man who hired Cloud, we can take over. Then it becomes a gun-for-hire case."

Cecile still said nothing.

"Zoe and I can do anything you want," Leonie said.

"No you can't," Cecile said, finally responding. "All right, I'll be quiet all week. Except John Cruz is calling on Friday for a report. He doesn't know I'm dead, and I need to talk to him. Everyone else in this place knows I'm dead. I made the announcement at dinner. They were surprised, but they can handle it. I'm sure some of them are praying for the repose of my soul right now."

"Good idea," Jim muttered, and Cecile threw him a dirty look.

"On Friday," Cecile said, "I want you, Raphael, to take all incoming calls until John calls in. I don't want any slip-ups."

"Okay," Sister Raphael said.

"Leonie, you go to school as usual. Don't say anything about anything. Zoe is a dear girl, but because of that very fact, she might let something slip to one of her parents, and then one might say something, and so on. Just act normal. Don't talk about me. Do you understand that, Leonie?"

"Of course."

Sister Cecile removed a large chicken breast from the platter and took a bite. She chewed for a moment. "I was hoping to visit some of those people again. People on my list. I really wanted to see the gun collection that Ron Dubaker has. The matching gun to the murder weapon. I really wanted to see that."

"Why?" Raphael asked.

"Maybe take it to Providence with me?" Cecile smiled at her feeble attempt at a joke. "I mean, you all think I should carry." She took a huge bite of chicken, almost unladylike.

"An antique dueling pistol," Jim remarked, "would be very inappropriate, if not downright silly. I really think the trip to Providence is silly too."

Cecile finished the bite. "Anyway, I have some ideas. I want to speak to Dubaker, to Mirtha, to everyone, in fact. Ruby, for example, I see in quite a different light now that I've met his wife."

"We don't know any of these people," Jim pointed out. "But one of them is the murderer. Right?"

Cecile rubbed her nose. "Probably. That gives us a field of three, plus or minus a few of their friends with whom they may have spoken. I'm very pleased to be able to tell John Cruz that he's right. His old friend Juan Caldo is most likely an innocent man."

"If you live that long." Leonie spoke, and she looked miserable, almost ready to burst into tears again.

"Leonie, I'm going to be fine. Tomorrow after school we'll go shopping for your trip to Japan. School is over in ten days, and you'll be off to a great vacation."

Leonie pushed back a pale strand of hair. "I want some of those baggy pants," she said firmly.

"I'm not sure they allow them in Japan."

"I'll let you know."

When the meeting broke up a few minutes later, Leonie

was in better spirits, but still tossed Sister Cecile an occasional worried frown as though she didn't quite trust the nun to pull off a trip to Providence without her help.

Jim didn't look very happy either, but he plastered on a half smile as he left the community. And Sister Raphael ended up talking to herself. "Should I begin to knit a shroud?" she said. "What does a shroud look like, anyway?"

Sister Cecile hid out the next day, going over the convent accounts, cleaning her room, visiting with the old nuns, all of whom were thrilled with the concept that she was dead. One call came into the community from a strange voice, as reported by Sister Germaine, who picked up the call on the kitchen extension and said the voice sounded like it belonged to a killer. The caller asked for Sister Cecile, and Germaine reported that she had replied in a very solemn voice that the nun in question had gone to her eternal reward.

The caller hung up abruptly. Everyone was convinced the call was from either the hit man or from the person who hired him.

Sister Cecile put on a disguise, a secular costume, a full, fluffy skirt and a loose knit top, and took Leonie shopping after school. They bought one pair of wide, low-waisted jeans, some tight jean shorts that showed off Leonie's belly button, and some cotton tops.

"I can't believe you'll wear this stuff," Cecile grumbled, but she paid with her credit card. "And I insist on some dresses."

"Dresses?"

"Absolutely. You'll be glad you have them. And what about shoes?"

An hour later they were done with Leonie's wardrobe. "Now me," Sister Cecile said. "I need a wig. Long and blond, what do you think?"

"You'll look like my mom," Leonie said.

"Okay. As long as I don't look like me. Where do we buy wigs?"

"On Washington Street near Fifteenth Street," Leonie said. "All the gay people shop there. Drag stuff. They sell everything."

"Let's go."

The shop in question catered to the males of Miami Beach who like to dress like females. There were a number of patrons in the store, all resembling women, but most were over six feet tall wearing three-inch heels, wild hair, and a great deal of makeup. Sister Cecile looked at Leonie. Leonie looked at Sister Cecile. They both shrugged and went inside. Nobody paid them the least bit of attention until Cecile began trying on wigs in front of a large oval mirror.

"That's beautiful, darling," a person said to Cecile. "But I think you'd do better just one shade lighter. Let me help you." The voice belonged to a man, the face to someone else, quite beautiful with flawlessly applied makeup.

"I like straight hair," Cecile said. "Shoulder length."

"Bangs?"

"What do you think, Leonie?"

"Maybe bangs. Let's see."

"Have you ever considered going auburn? We have some lovely shades of red here, darling."

A half hour later Sister Cecile and Leonie left the shop carrying two wig boxes, not one. One box contained a blond wig, shoulder length, straight hair with wispy bangs. The other box held a red wig. "Very daring," the salesperson had chortled when Cecile tried it on. "You'll knock 'em dead in this one."

"Just so they don't knock *me* dead," Cecile had replied. Then she smiled so as not to give anything away.

17

On Friday at noon John Cruz called for Sister Cecile. Sister Raphael answered the phone. "Who's calling please?"

"John Cruz."

Raphael nodded. She recognized the voice. "Just a moment, please."

Sister Cecile was nearby. In fact she hadn't gone farther than the garden since wig-buying day. "John, how are you?"

"Fine, Sister. Do you have any news?"

"Yes. I've definitely stirred things up. Someone's apparently hired a hit man to come after me."

There was a long silence. "Well, you should get off the case."

"Oh, no. It proves Juan Caldo is innocent. Don't you see? This is good news."

"I already knew he was innocent. But you can't lose your life pursuing this. Has there been any problem?"

"Well, he thinks I'm dead."

"Drop the case. It's not necessary to continue." The voice sounded distant, sad.

"Oh, no. I'm getting close. I have something planned for this weekend. Things will be resolved."

"Sister, this is no good. It's not worth another life. Drop it."

"I haven't earned my fee."

"Lose it, I said. Keep the money."

Sister Cecile stared at the telephone. This was her boss speaking, in so many words. She should drop the case. "I've planned a trip for this weekend. Reservations have been made."

"Cancel them. I'll pay the added cost."

Sister Cecile didn't know what to say. The trip to Providence was more than a chance to solve the case. She was escorting

113

an eighty-seven-year-old nun to see her family for the last time. She was going to see Paul. "Well, I'll consider myself off the case. But if something turns up, John, I'll certainly see it through. I've stirred things up. Things may not settle down. Can I call you? In a week or two?"

"I'll call you. I really want to thank you for undertaking this, Sister. I'm sorry for the way it turned out. Really I am. All I want in this life is peace and justice. Perhaps I'll have to settle for peace."

"Peace is more than most of us dare hope for," Cecile said.

"This is true. I've been blessed," John Cruz said. "Thank you, Sister."

Cecile hung up a moment later. Raphael hadn't been far away.

"Well?" the old nun asked.

"Peace. He'll settle for peace. No justice."

"A wise man."

"Perhaps," Cecile said. "But I'm still going to Providence. Paul's already made the reservations. Everything is set."

"Speaking of wise," Sister Raphael said. "The trip is not."

Sister Cecile didn't exactly shrug, or stick out her tongue, but Sister Raphael got that impression nevertheless.

Nobody realized that Sister Linda was going to Providence because nobody had mentioned it. Sister Cecile had a lot on her mind, with her own sudden death, and Sister Linda never caused any commotion. The very old nun, in fact, was downright secretive. She packed quietly, readying only a small bag with a few changes of underwear and a spare habit, a sweater, and a huge string of brown rosary beads. Sister Linda did spend some time on the computer, sending e-mail to points north, but nobody knew what was said, because she had her own password with America Online on the community computer.

Sister Cecile played the trip down, because everyone would just tell her it was a mistake. However, she did spend some time packing, gathering several outfits to match the wigs, clothing that was unquestionably not nunlike. Wearing her blond wig, dungarees, and a T-shirt, she made a quick trip Friday afternoon to the Lincoln Road Mall. She used her credit card in some of the more unique boutiques. For the blond persona, she chose matching outfits in beige and blue. Wearing them, with the wig in place, she noticed she looked like a modern-day Grace Kelly.

The redhead was another person entirely. Wearing a roguish red lipstick, Cecile bought a bright green outfit and another of searing pink. She looked sensational, but not at all discreet. She should have bought a short, black-haired wig and some sedate clothes to melt into the crowd, she thought as she headed for home. It was too late now.

That night after vespers Sister Cecile paid a visit to Sister Linda in her room. The old nun was inspecting her toothbrush as Cecile entered.

"I have all my teeth," Linda said in awe, contemplating the frazzled yellow brush. "I gave up sugar for Lent when I was twenty-nine. I haven't used any since. No cavities."

"That's wonderful. Are you all set?"

"I could use a new toothbrush."

"I've called a taxi service. It will pick us up at seven o'clock tomorrow morning."

"I'll be all ready."

"I guess I already told you, we're taking Southwest. It flies directly to the Providence airport. We're flying out of Fort Lauderdale."

Sister Linda nodded. "My brother Vinny's meeting me."

"Wonderful. My friend Paul is supposed to have a car for me, or meet me himself. I'm not sure which. He's supposed to call tonight."

"I'm so happy," Sister Linda said in a quivery voice. "You don't know how much this means to me. It's been a long time. I've missed my family, but I've prayed. God filled my life, but, you know, family." She sighed. "So many have died."

"I know," Sister Cecile said. The old nun's joy was tangible. "I think I might have a new toothbrush somewhere. I'll stop by with it."

"You're a dear girl, Cecile. A very dear child."

The following morning the two nuns slipped away, Cecile dressed as a blonde, Sister Linda as a nun. They prayed the

115

morning prayer together as the taxi drove to Fort Lauderdale. The sun was already hot by the time they walked into the airport, past clusters of people and up to the Southwest counter. "I'll check all the bags right through," Cecile said. She carried both their bags.

"Fine. Now, I'm coming right along, Cecile. I'm just slow. Do you know where the bathroom is?"

"Right this way."

Pearla Cruz was looking for the bathroom too, but not in an airport. She was in the Grand Orlando Hotel, one of a great army of hotels set in the Orlando area. The Cattle Breeders conference bustled with over three hundred souls, cattlemen and their wives gathered to discuss innovations in breeding, brag about what was being accomplished in the field, and discover how to do things better.

"Mama, I hafta go," little Pearlita said for the fifth time.

"It's just down here," Pearla said. She should have left the children with a neighbor. But they were so proud! Their father would be up there in front of that huge group of men and women talking about his cows and his ideas on the future of the industry. Carlito accompanied his father. He wore cowboy boots, just like all the men, so thrilled to be one of them.

She was a lucky woman.

Carlito walked with perfect posture, head up, face serious. He was sure to be mistaken for an adult, because he was tall like his father and wore brand new boots. Twelve years old, but still a boy, still possessor of a child's voice. Soon that would change. Soon he would be a real man.

When it came time for his father to talk, Carlito, or Carl, as he preferred to be called, took a seat in the back of the room. He was not going to say "That's my father" to anyone, although he felt like shouting it.

The moderator introduced John Cruz. John took the stand and stared at the filled conference room. Perhaps forty people sat with notepads and pens, ready to take notes. His talk was one of four given each hour and a half, and John's was titled, "A Success Story: Breeding the Old Way for the New Way."

The title was controversial, but that was good. John took a deep breath and began to speak.

He's good, Carlito thought as he settled into his chair, ignoring his mother and sisters, who were several rows ahead of him. The girls were giggling. Pearla was radiant. Carl was cool.

His father's words filled the room. John covered his breeding techniques clearly, he discussed artificial insemination and said his piece about cloning. He explained how his new small breed had brought prosperity to family farms in desolate areas and how governments in third world countries were buying his stock. The roomful of people clapped wildly when he was done. He was inundated with questions.

Carl turned to the man beside him, a dark-haired, pock-faced man of about forty-five years of age. He was going to say that it was his father up there, at least until the man spoke to a friend on the other side of Carl, talking directly over Carl's head. "That speaker dude looks like Juan Caldo. Remember that guy? I'd swear it was him. Same voice too."

"Who the hell's Juan Caldo?" the other man said.

"He's a killer. Killed a friend of mine twenty years ago. Caldo went to jail for life, but he escaped. Never got caught. Wouldn't it be a hoot if that was him?"

"Caldo, yeah, I remember the prison escape. Man vanished off the face of the earth. Cold-blooded son of a gun."

"Looks like him, don't it?"

"Take off twenty years. Yeah. Could be. Funny thing. Maybe we should ask him."

"Sure, the man's gonna say, 'That's me, killer.' No way. Maybe we oughta ask around."

Carlito ducked from in between the two men. His face was bright red, tears stung his eyes. He slunk to the door and stepped out, gasping for air. How could those men be talking about his dad like that?

He raced for the men's room and found an empty stall. He sat down for a long time until the tears were under control. Then he came out and splashed water on his face, dried it and went out to find his dad.

John was surrounded by a group of men, all talking animatedly about a new development in cattle feed. Carlito saw his

117

father, dressed in that red plaid shirt he had thought so wonderful when his father brought it home from the store. Now it was like a red flag waving, "I'm a killer." The boy wanted to race up to his father and rip it off. Or maybe warn him.

Carl waited until he could speak to his father alone. His father was on his way to meet Pearla at the bar/restaurant downstairs. It was five o'clock and time for happy hour.

"Dad," Carl said stiffly.

His father put an arm around him. "How was it, Carlito?"

"It was so great, Dad. Really. I gotta talk to you. I mean, private. Right now."

John loved his son, and Carl knew it. His father respected his ideas, believed in him. They had a great relationship. So Carl wasn't at all surprised when his father simply nodded and said, "Sure. We can take a walk outside. Your mother won't mind if we're late."

They didn't speak until they were outside the hotel, in the back where a pool and a lagoon waited for the guests' pleasure. Tables and benches and chairs were arranged in anticipation of the Texas-style barbecue planned for later that evening. They sat together on a bench, looking into the lagoon.

"What's the trouble?"

"I sat in the back and listened to your talk. It was really great."

"Thanks."

"Then, when it was over, these two guys started talking about you. They said you looked just like this guy that killed somebody twenty years ago. Named Juan Caldo. Did you ever hear of that guy?"

John Cruz didn't say a word. His expression didn't waver.

Carl looked at his father, hoping to see a perfect denial. Hoping that his father knew of the man, or knew of the resemblance. Or something. "I was going to punch them, Dad. Like they were making fun of you."

"Well, that's interesting. Twenty years ago? I guess I was in New Jersey then. I didn't come to Central Florida until later. I'll have to look up a picture of this man, see if he's some cousin from Havana, maybe." His dad's voice sounded normal.

Carlito breathed a huge sigh of relief. Not that he had been

118

scared, just angry. "Sure. You have a lot of cousins in Cuba, right?"

"Sure do. What else did they say?"

"That you had the same voice, even. They were going to ask you, then one of them laughed and said he'd ask around about you."

"No kidding. Any idea who they are? I could talk to them."

Carl's eyes roved the barbecue area. There were only a few waiters setting things up and a chef standing at a huge grill, basting a large chunk of beef. "Not here. I don't know, they just had on dungarees and cowboy boots, like everybody. I didn't have my glasses on."

"You should wear them," his father said.

"I want contacts."

John nodded. "Soon. Meanwhile, don't worry about this. I never killed a man, twenty years ago, or ever."

"I know. It just made me feel funny."

John gave his son a hug. "Let's go find your mom and the girls."

18

THE Cruz family stayed in a motel that boasted a huge cutout of Mickey Mouse in the lobby. Pearla had packed food so they wouldn't have to go out to eat. She never seemed to remember that they were rich now. Over the years she had done everything with John, helped with the books, helped with the cows, with the deals they made with distant buyers. She knew the business, but Pearla was eternally thrifty.

"We're rich, Pearla," John said that evening. On the round, motel-room table, she spread out beans and rice, soft drinks, some chicken, carefully kept cold in a cooler. "We could go out."

"This is so much nicer," she insisted, handing Beatriz a plastic spoon.

John eyed the chicken. It did look good. "Tomorrow we have breakfast out, then the entire day at Disney World. Then the next day we can do Sea World. Restaurants. No dishes for you to clear. No work. I've decided."

"But the children have school."

"We can give them a day off. Let's be together."

Pearla agreed, reluctantly at first, but then she got into the spirit of things and became as happy as the children. John seemed happy too, relaxed, loving.

Monday night they returned home. Pearla immediately began fussing with the little girls, getting them washed, ready for school the next day, ready for bed. Carl got on the telephone with his best friend. John went out to the barn to be among the animals. Milk cows, breeding animals, several prize bulls. He loved the barn with its low, animal sounds, the sounds of cows munching hay, a soft, lowing moo now and then, the rustle and kick of heavy animals at peace. His over-

120

seer took excellent care of the animals now, and like John, he regarded each animal as an individual with its own special needs. In fact, John had made arrangements for Mike Baxter to assume part ownership of the ranch; a small percent with each paycheck went into a partnership fund, something John dreamed up because he understood that to own was to have pride. Mike's percentage of ownership could never go above twenty percent. It was an unusual deal, but the farm prospered. They had some hired hands who came in, everything ran smoothly. The farm barely needed him anymore, John realized.

John's overseer lived in a small house on the edge of the property, and after visiting each one of the animals, John walked the half mile to the house where Mike lived with his wife.

Mike was watching television, drinking a beer. His wife was reading in the other room. "Hey, John, how'd the talk go? Knock 'em dead?"

"Three potential orders," John Cruz said. He took an armchair and stretched out his legs.

"Hold on a minute." Mike went to the kitchen, pulled a cold beer out of the refrigerator and brought it back for John. He flipped off the television. "Good work. Things went well, then."

"Looks excellent. Some calls should be coming in this week, gentleman farmer from Venezuela is very interested, a couple of others promised to be in touch. Think you can show them the animals?"

"You not going to be here?"

"Sure, I'll be around." John shrugged, gave his distant smile. "There were some cows up north. I might take a trip up. You have the key to my office, so use it. As a partner, you can make any deal I can."

Mike swirled his beer around in the can. "You gave me a chunk of this place. You're something else, John. Not many owners would do what you've done for me." He looked nervous. Mike was only twenty-six.

"You can handle it. Hey, Carlito could sell a bull to this guy."

"Okay. I'll spend some time in the office."

"Sure. Any deal you make is okay with me. That's always true. You understand that, Mike?"

John Cruz sat for a while. They chatted, then watched some television. John finished his beer and finally headed back to the main house. He walked slowly. The stars shone down on him from a black sky, and he remembered nights in the forest with only himself and one small calf for company. So many years ago, yet it felt like yesterday. As he walked he studied every tree, tasted the clear, soft air. He loved the peace, but knew it wasn't for him.

The next morning John kissed his children good-bye as they headed out to catch the school bus. He stared at Pearla for a long time over his coffee, a strong cup, American style, with no cream, no sugar.

"What is it, Juan?" she asked him, using the name she had once used every day.

"I love you, Pearla. You'll never know how much."

"I love you too, Juan."

Early that afternoon, John told Pearla that he had to go to the bank. He took the Mercedes and went into the small town where they kept their accounts. He withdrew $100,000 cash from their joint savings account, leaving behind something in the vicinity of half a million dollars. He put the car keys into an envelope addressed to his wife and dropped it off at the post office.

People in town said he hopped on the bus for Orlando, but nobody was able to say for sure where he got off.

Sister Cecile and Sister Linda landed in Providence at two o'clock in the afternoon. They retrieved their bags, Cecile carrying hers and Sister Linda's. They moved very slowly toward the front exit. Linda couldn't move fast. "Paul left me a message early this morning," Sister Cecile said, a wisp of her long blond wig moving gently in the still air. "He was called to Washington for a deposition. He can't meet me. Plus, he hadn't gotten the rental. I suppose I'll take a cab, or one of the shuttles that take you to the rental car agencies. I've been thinking of just using taxis, because I don't know my way around here, anyway. It might be easier."

"Where will you go?"

"I'll hop in a cab. Then find a motel. I can conduct my business, and we'll be leaving on Wednesday. You have your ticket somewhere safe? I mean, your number?"

"Yes. No tickets. It's odd these days with this ticketless travel. Times are so different. Cecile, I can give you a ride to a motel. I mean, my brother's meeting me. It won't be any trouble at all."

"I don't know what motel."

"Vinny will know a good one. Vinny's been a good boy for a long time." Sister Linda's face took on a peculiarly blissful expression.

Sister Cecile didn't quite know what to think of that statement, but the fact was, a native could be very helpful. The automatic doors swung open and they walked out into New England. "Well, I'll take you up on that ride, Linda, if you're sure your brother won't mind." She looked up and down the pickup area. The Providence airport was small and lacked the insanity of bigger, international airports. Still, there was a sense of urgency under the crisp, blue, Rhode Island sky.

"There he is," Linda said, waving her arms.

Cecile saw a huge black limousine. It pulled up and the driver's window rolled down. A pockmarked face looked out. "Linda Mascapone?"

"Jimmy! Jimmy Gigliardi. My dear boy. You look exactly like your father." Sister Linda almost danced to the window and kissed his face. The limo's side door burst open and another man appeared, an old man, stooped, dressed in black, using a cane to get out. Linda saw him and rushed to his side. Hugs and tears followed. Tears from Linda, anyway. Her brother Vinny did look happy, kissed his sister on each cheek and stared at her.

"Forty years, Linda. Blessed Mother's been looking after you? Just like you said? Everything okay, Linda?" His hand was on her arm as though he feared she would vanish in a cloud of holy incense.

"My God, Vinny, you've gone and gotten old on me."

"Seventy-nine years old, whaddaya think?"

Sister Linda sighed and hugged him again. That, apparently, was enough for the old man. He stepped back.

"Well?" he asked. "Well?"

Sister Linda looked around and breathed deeply of the familiar air. "So good to be home," she murmured.

"I never thought I'd see you," Vinny said, shaking his head. From ten feet away Sister Cecile saw the emotion in the elderly man's face. "I wish Mama was here."

Vinny looked around then, and he quickly spotted Sister Cecile close by, patiently guarding the luggage. "Who's the dish?" he asked.

"Oh my goodness, that's Sister Cecile. She's in disguise. She's had some problems, Vinny. Why, everyone thinks she's dead. Maybe you can do something for her. She needs a ride, first of all."

"Nun? This is a nun?"

"Sister Cecile," Cecile said, and stepped forward holding out her hand.

Vinny didn't take it at first. He stared, looking Cecile up and down. The sharp black eyes didn't look seventy-nine years old. "Problem? Like you're dead. I know about stuff like that." He finally shook the nun's hand. "You come out with me and Linda, we can figure something out. We got a little party going on at the house. Got the family. You wanna come?"

Cecile brushed back the blond wig hair and attempted to look dignified, and perhaps even holy. She would rather get right to work, but Sister Linda was bobbing her head and saying yes, and brother Vinny sounded as though he really wanted her to come. "That would be lovely," she said.

It never paid to look a gift horse in the mouth.

19

John Cruz rode a bus to Orlando. From the bus station he took a taxi to the airport, and from there he booked a seat on the next flight to Atlanta. He paid cash all the way. For lunch on Southwest Airlines he received a snack pack containing a small sandwich and some peanuts. He drank a gin and tonic and settled into the seat to plan his itinerary. He would spend two days in Atlanta in an airport motel, then catch a flight to Chicago, switch again, maybe travel to Dallas, and finally Mexico City. In Mexico he could buy a cheap car and set out for a place somewhere safe and go on with his life as best he could.

In his pocket John Cruz had an American passport under the name of Juan Calderon. He had kept the passport up to date over the years. Juan Calderon would live a life of safety and discretion. And sorrow. Pearla might think her husband was an escaped murderer, an innocent man, whatever, but he would not be there to trouble her anymore. His son Carl would be devastated, his young daughters would forget him, but someday, somehow, he would make things right. In his mind he wrote Pearla a long letter.

That night, John Cruz had dinner in a motel dining room. Underneath a vent that blew an icy gale down on him, he ate a perfectly cooked sirloin steak with rubber edges and plastic peas. He missed the beans and rice that Pearla cooked so well. He missed his family.

After the meal he went to the pay phone in the lobby armed with a handful of quarters and Sister Cecile's card. He dialed the number and inserted an endless stream of quarters until a metallic voice said, "Thank you."

The telephone rang in Sister Cecile's office where Sister

Raphael was sitting behind the desk reading C. S. Lewis's *Screwtape Letters*. Raphael finished a sentence, then picked up the telephone. "Sister Cecile's office," she said.

"Is Sister Cecile in?"

"I'm sorry, no. May I help you?"

"Who's this?"

"This is Sister Raphael, Sister Cecile's assistant. Is this John Cruz?"

"Yes. Will she be in later?"

"She's out of town for a few days."

"Could you tell her for me, ask her for me, to please continue the investigation? I asked her to stop."

"Yes," Raphael said. "There was some trouble."

"Danger, yes. She told me. I don't want her to take chances, but it's essential she discover the truth. Essential."

The man's voice sent a chill down Raphael's spine with its intensity. He heard it himself, must have, she thought, because he coughed to cover it up, not aware that she could read voices like a book.

"Something came up," he continued. "I've left where I live. I won't be home for a while, but I'll forward some more money this afternoon. Tell her, please keep trying, but please be careful. It's urgent."

"I'll tell her. She may be close to the truth, John. She's still investigating. Sister Cecile has a hard time letting go."

"Thank God. I'll be in touch."

"Your three minutes are up, please insert coins for additional time," the mechanical voice said.

"I've got to go. I'll call."

John hung up the telephone. His face was drenched with sweat. His fingers wouldn't unbend. That night he tossed and turned in a motel room that smelled of a thousand passing souls and a damp air conditioner. The air blew too cold, then too hot. He dreamed of Pearla. How could he leave her? He saw his children running across the field. How could he ever return?

The following morning Juan made coffee in the small pot provided in the motel room and wrote a long letter to his wife on motel stationery. He told her there was a problem in his past. He told her he had never done wrong, but people thought

126

he had. He told her how much he loved her. He didn't mention that he was a convicted murderer, and he didn't tell her where he was going. He mailed the letter the next morning.

Sister Cecile left the gathering at brother Vinny Mascapone's house, to be driven to the Biltmore Hotel by Jimmy Gigliardi. Vinny escorted her to the door. "You're coming tomorrow at one. Right?" Vinny said.

"Right. We meet on Federal Hill at that restaurant you told me about. We talk about my problem." Sister Cecile nodded agreeably. She was dumbfounded by Sister Linda's family, who were, in the popular sense of the word, Family. Who would have ever guessed that sweet Sister Linda had such relatives? Cousins, nieces, nephews, all hugging, kissing Sister Linda, talking too fast. At least five of the men carried guns in various places on their bodies. Between courses of *pasta fagioli*, crisp salads, shrimp scampi, and meatballs, Cecile saw two shoulder holsters, three at the belt, and one strapped to an ankle. This was a family that could help!

"I'll talk to some people tonight. They'll be there," Vinny croaked. His scratchy voice had not improved through the evening, although after numerous toasts honoring his sister's return, he was even more voluble than ever.

"My friend will be coming down from Boston," Cecile said. "Would it be all right if he comes too? He was supposed to meet me today, but he was delayed. I'm calling him tonight."

"Who's he?"

"Well, he's a lawyer. He's going to help me."

Vinny jammed a finger at his chest. "Here you got real help, Sister."

"I see that."

"You wanna bring a mouthpiece? You sure about that?"

"He's my best friend."

Vinny's sharp brown eyes stared at the nun. Her oval face looked surreal surrounded by the long blond hair. "Friend?"

"Yes. Friend."

"Okay. You tell him he can come. He's not some fed lawyer?"

"No. Private practice."

127

"Okay. Maybe we can use the help." Vinny turned to Jimmy Gigliardi, who was standing six feet away, fingering the keys to the limousine. "You can take the sister now, Jimmy. You see she gets a good room."

Sister Cecile arrived at the hotel at midnight. The Providence Biltmore was a grand hotel in the old tradition, but Cecile didn't really notice the nicely decorated suite, the fresh roses set on the round table, the well-stocked bar. All she saw was the bed. She pulled off the wig and stared in a mirror at the sweat dampened brown ringlets. Names of a dozen Italian women rolled through her mind. Selma Gigliardi, Patricia Rogerio, Donna Mascapone, cousins, nieces, niece-in-laws, some very nice women, some strangely hostile. All were intelligent, and able to converse on everything from the expanding universe to the philosophy of St. Thomas. And the men. Nobody bothered to introduce them to her, but she overheard one conversation on computer engineering that boggled her mind.

One of the women had thrust a recipe into her hand, Claudia Amato's *insalata di fagioli*. Cecile pulled the recipe out of her pocket and studied it before tucking it into her suitcase. She would pass it on to Sister Germaine. The last thing Sister Cecile did before she turned out the light and said her prayers was to call Paul's answering machine and leave a message: "I'm staying at the Biltmore Hotel in Providence, meeting some people for lunch at one o'clock at Capito's on Federal Hill tomorrow. I hope you can make it. I'll be a blonde."

She was asleep ten minutes later, her rosary still in her hand.

Federal Hill in Providence, Rhode Island, could be described as an authentic parcel of Rome transported magically to a city ruled like ancient Florence. Providence was a fiefdom, Cecile had heard. In fact, she discovered that it was a beautiful city with an abundance of hills, cool, flowing water, two-family houses, and hundred-year-old, redbrick buildings. The rough parts were plentiful and best avoided or driven through fast. Her taxi driver did just that on the way to Pius X Church for the eleven-thirty Sunday Mass. The cab picked Cecile up at the church when Mass was over and bounced her up and down streets, past the marble statehouse and through even more endless neighborhoods of two- and three-family wooden houses, finally depositing her under the huge arched gate to the Italian section. A large, bronze artichoke decorated the center of the arch. She had arrived at Federal Hill.

Sister Cecile stared at the big artichoke. Maybe it was a pineapple, but no, Claudia had made a point of mentioning it last night. Sister Cecile strolled under the vegetable, then walked past the small shops, selling all things Italian. She walked by groups of men speaking in Italian, she stared into store windows where various objects and food *d'Italie* were displayed, and finally walked into Capito's restaurant. The dark, red-and-gold-decorated lobby smelled of ancient garlic. A small fountain tinkled water from the mouth of a marble fish, and there, beside the fountain, grinning, stood Paul Dorys.

"Paul!"

They hugged, then stood back and looked at each other.

"I had second thoughts, Cecile, when I saw you coming at me. I know you said blond, but I still thought you'd look the same. You don't. You look really beautiful."

"Thanks a lot."

Paul chuckled. "Well, of course you always look beautiful."

"Sure." Then she laughed. "So do you. Really, I'm so glad to see you. It's been a while."

"Too long."

She nodded.

"Why blond? Is it real? Something new on my favorite nun?"

Cecile shook her head. "Not a chance. I came in disguise, and after meeting Sister Linda's relatives with it on, I figured I wouldn't confuse them by removing it." She lowered her voice. "Much less do I want them to see the real me. They're Mafia."

"Really?"

"You'll see. This hit man who's after me isn't Mafia, so this seemed like an opportune way to approach things obliquely. I mean, who could know more about assassins?" Cecile's voice was low, the words barely discernible through the music of the fountain. "It's very possible they'll find out who hired Cloud."

"I don't like it, Cecile. These people."

"Sister Linda's people, I'm afraid. Linda's told me enough times how good Vinny's become. He's her brother. I can trust him."

Paul took Cecile's arm. "Let's go in and find out."

They walked into the main dining area, where a waiter stood by the door. Small groups of people sat around tables, but Cecile didn't see Vinny or any of the family. "May I help you?" the man by the door asked.

"I'm meeting Vinny Mascapone here," Cecile said.

"This way, please."

They were taken through a red-padded door to a room beyond. Four men were already seated around a table: Vinny, Jimmy Gigliardi, and two strangers. Paul and Cecile were seated and Cecile introduced Paul as simply "my friend, Paul."

The two strangers stared at the newcomers. "I'm Sal," "I'm Joe," they said, and the waiter poured wine, then proceeded to bring food. Apparently the meal had already been ordered.

A huge antipasto was followed by bowls of minestrone soup, then fresh, broiled scrod with a side dish of spaghetti with meat sauce. Business was not discussed. Yesterday's Red Sox game was dissected. The mayor's latest incident where he had saved a citizen from a hostage situation was expanded upon endlessly. "We have a world-class mayor in this town," Sal said. "Buddy Cianci. Now there's a mayor. Boston could do with the likes of him."

"Remarkable man," Paul agreed. "I hear he's even come out with his own spaghetti sauce."

"Not every mayor does that," Joe said, nodding, sparks coming from his black eyes. He had eyebrows that extended a good inch out from his old and deeply freckled face. "Gotta try this sauce, Sister. You see to it, Vinny, she takes some of it back to wherever it is with her."

Vinny agreed, not stopping his eating to speak.

The meal ended abruptly. The table was cleared, small cups of cappuccino arrived, cigars came out and the men became silent.

130

"What's the trouble I heard about?" Sal asked.

Cecile felt four pairs of brown eyes on her, and Paul's, which were blue. She looked at Paul first and he winked. "Well, I believe someone hired someone to kill me. The hit man is from Providence. His name is Jeffrey Cloud. I was hoping that by coming here I could discover who hired him."

"You're not looking to get rid of him?" That was Vinny.

"No. I'm only concerned with staying alive and discovering who's behind this."

"Means you gotta ice him," Joe said.

"Maybe not," Sal put in. He puffed the cigar and let a huge cloud out, thoughtfully blowing it to one side as though well-trained by dining with a wife.

Paul's eyes went from one man to another, finally stopping on Jimmy Gigliardi's face. Jimmy was looking blank, the complete associate who exemplifies the best virtues of the three monkeys. Cecile saw Paul's stare and looked at Jimmy herself. She saw nothing out of the ordinary and wondered what was bothering Paul. Paul spoke, finally. "You know the man, Cloud?" he asked. He stared at each man in turn.

All four nodded. "He's not one of us," Vinny said. "But I hear Dom Baggio used him. You hear that, Sal?"

Sal nodded. "He did. Cloud's one of a group. They have an answering service, gets forwarded to one man or another. Cash in advance. Guaranteed work."

"Would it be possible to find out who hired him?" Cecile asked. "That's all I want to know."

All four men seemed to shrug simultaneously. *Omerta*, Cecile thought, the vow of silence that they all took. She had read that somewhere. No reason it should extend to Cloud.

Vinny answered finally, looking at Paul, not Cecile. "See, that's not going to be so easy. The answering service contacts one of the group, the member calls back, gives his number if he likes the feel of it. Things are worked out very privately."

Vinny pushed a finger into his mouth and picked at a back tooth for a minute. "We don't use these guys. We don't do anything like this."

Sal and Joe and Jimmy all nodded simultaneously. "See," Sal said, "we're legitimate businessmen now. I invest in the market. Joe, here, he has a little greenhouse outside of town,

131

grows flowers. Jimmy, he does a lot of work for everybody. Jimmy? Got some ideas here?"

A scar on Jimmy Gigliardi's forehead wrinkled as he looked at Cecile, the first one to actually look at her, she felt, since the questioning began. "I might've heard something. Lotta young punks out there now. I'll ask around."

"Thanks, Jimmy. Thank you all. I appreciate this," Cecile said. She looked from one man to the other, hoping for something, anything, even an acknowledgment that she was the one asking, not Paul. But it had become a male thing. Not an eye flickered, and the only thing she felt was Paul's arm, warm against her, giving her just the slightest nudge. She knew Paul very well. That nudge meant "back off."

"Well . . ." Cecile smiled brightly. "I'll be at the Biltmore Hotel for a few more days. I'm going back on Wednesday with Sister Linda."

"Oh, yeah, you came down with Linda," Sal said as though that were the most important thing Cecile had said all evening.

Maybe it was.

The waiter brought in a late dessert, oddly placed beyond the discussion of important business. Perhaps they liked things to end on a sweet note.

"Pesche con vino e crema," Vinny said. "You're gonna like this." Then he proceeded to slurp the peaches noisily. Everyone else ate more quietly, but then, Vinny was an old, powerful man and had probably never been held to good manners. Cecile looked at them all again, one at a time. Even the young were old men, slurping peaches, caught up in some kind of life she didn't want to even guess about. Ten minutes later the party broke up and Cecile and Paul said good afternoon and thank you.

"I'll be in touch," Vinny said as they parted. "Maybe Jimmy's gonna come up with something. Good meeting you, Paul."

"Just call the hotel," Cecile said. "Thanks, Vinny. I appreciate this."

She and Paul walked away from the group, an odd group that vanished in the daylight. From nowhere Cecile saw the limo arrive, Jimmy transported to behind the wheel. Then they were gone.

132

She and Paul walked away, feeling the crisp light of spring sunshine in New England. "Nice city," Cecile remarked.

"Nice friends, Cecile."

"Sister Linda's brother. Vinny Mascapone. I never knew."

"I don't like that Jimmy," Paul remarked.

"Why?"

"He blinked. And he looked at you."

"That's a sure sign of evil intentions," Cecile said.

"It is."

20

SISTER Cecile and Paul spent an hour wandering down by the water that flowed through the city, wondering if they should ride the gondola, deciding not to. "I miss New England," Cecile said. "I wish I were back here. Much as I love Florida, it isn't home."

"Come back," Paul said.

"It isn't so simple, Paul. You know about the rule of obedience, right?"

"You've mentioned it." They were standing by an iron and stone fence watching the water flow by on its way to the sea. The smell of fish, of cotton candy from a nearby vendor, the burst of laughter from a family walking by; it all felt very Northeast to Sister Cecile.

"Poverty, chastity, and obedience," Cecile said without preamble. "Those are the vows. I belong to Christ. My money is there to help anyone, so that takes care of the poverty. I don't care about that. Chastity? I'm a bride of Christ. If you belong to Christ, you stay alone. But obedience, now, that's exceptionally difficult."

"You're talking to yourself."

"I really want you to understand, Paul. Not just know, but understand." Paul could be very annoying sometimes.

"Seriously, I should think obedience would be the easiest thing," Paul said. "Can't you talk reasonably to your superior? Just say you want to come home? You're acting medieval."

"Not really. It's the simple doing of what your superior says. If Mère Sulpicia tells me to run the community in Miami, that's what I do. I don't say no. You know about obedience. Jewish people know the Ten Commandments."

"Sure. But it's easy to go along with them."

"Really? Not if it's inconvenient. How about, 'Thou shalt not kill'? How about, 'Honor thy father and thy mother'? and the old saw, 'Thou shalt not commit adultery'?"

"Oh, those Ten Commandments," Paul said.

"So, I do what I'm told, and perhaps, if there's something I need, or the community needs, then I get in touch with Mère Sulpicia and we talk. But there's no need for me to come back here."

"We moderns go after what we want," Paul said thoughtfully. "Kids. They want, they get."

"Everyone's a kid these days."

Paul didn't have an answer to that one, at least not for a minute. "Why do you have to believe so hard?" he finally asked.

"God doesn't like half-ass commitment," Cecile replied. "I do try to be whole in what I do."

"A complete ass," Paul said. "Interesting concept."

Cecile's laughter turned the heads of two ducks on the river. "Back to our problem," she said.

"We're going to the police station. My buddy there decided to cooperate. He's in today, I gave him a call this morning. His name is Pat Landow. He's from Boston, originally, moved to Providence a few years back and does well on the force here. He's a good man."

"Is he expecting us?"

Paul glanced down at his watch. "In twenty minutes."

"Jeff Cloud is known as the 'Dirty Breeze,' among certain circles," Detective Pat Landow said, handing Sister Cecile a computer printout. "See, the only thing we have on him is some priors. At age fifteen, he was arrested in high school for malicious mischief, later was caught with a gun; he was seventeen, but nothing came of it, and later one assault with a deadly weapon, a shod foot. He was a kid. Since then he got real smart. He lives right here in town in a very nice home on Elmhurst Avenue. Has a wife and kid. He steers clear of the mob. We watch, but we don't see anything. Everything is talk. But it's real. This man's a killer."

Paul nodded at that. "What does he do for a living? I mean, why do you even know about him if he leads such a fine life?"

"Informants tell us about him every so often, but we need more than talk. What facts we have came from an IRS probe. He submits his income tax forms, calls himself a consultant. Meanwhile everyone in town knows he's a hit man. A couple of feds wanted to pull him in on something so they looked at the tax forms."

"What happened?" Cecile asked. "What did they find out?"

"He flies around the country, deducts his airfare, talks to businesses about creating ads, gets paid cash. He pays his taxes, the deductions fit with the travel. The income he declares fits in with his lifestyle. We suspect he's stashing cash out of the country somewhere. Meanwhile we can't find anything. He goes out of town, we lack jurisdiction. If we ever had a decent suspicion of a crime, we could watch him, maybe even follow him. But there's nothing. The man's smart and slippery."

"How about the fact that he shot me in Miami?" Cecile said. "It's on record."

"Who shot you? Do you have proof it was him?"

"I saw him."

"Anyone else see him?"

"No. Actually my friend. Leonie saw him once, but she wasn't there when I was shot."

"Leonie's twelve," Paul put in.

"This man will have six witnesses lined up to swear he was in Iowa. He won't be registered at any hotel. There won't be any flights in his name. How close was he when he shot you?"

"Actually quite a distance."

Pat shook his head. "He's home free."

"That's exactly what my friend on the force in Miami Beach told me. No deaths are traceable to his movements?" Cecile asked.

"Sure, there's always deaths, but nothing out of the ordinary, nothing that seemed to warrant the hiring of a hit man. We know he's doing it. We can't pin anything on him. He kills carefully."

"He tried to shoot me. I mean, he actually did shoot me. If I were dead, wouldn't that strike a bell?" Cecile asked.

"Not necessarily. People get shot. Where were you?"

"Calle Ocho, Miami."

136

"That wouldn't have raised an eyebrow. Call it ordinary."

Paul's face had become tense during the last few moments. "You were shot?" he asked softly.

"Jim gave me a Kevlar vest," Cecile said. "I was wearing it at the time. Don't worry, Paul."

Paul's face was very pale and he closed his eyes. "Damn it, Cecile."

"Shhh. No big deal. See, Cloud thinks I'm dead now."

"As you come bombing into Providence, his hometown," Paul snapped. "Why didn't you tell me? You think he doesn't know you're here now?"

Cecile placed a hand on his arm. "Don't *worry*, Paul."

Paul shook her hand off. "I'm sorry, Pat. This is crazy. You don't have any idea about Cloud's connections? How about his answering service that refers calls to him for jobs?"

"How the hell'd you hear about that?" Pat asked.

"I heard."

"We tried to put a tap on it, but the judge wouldn't go along. He said there was no probable cause. I could give you his address, but that won't do any good. He's an upstanding citizen, in theory."

"And there's nothing more you can tell us?" Paul asked.

"Just to be extremely careful. And should you get anything real on this guy, give me a call."

"Absolutely. Thanks, Pat." Paul got up, pulled Sister Cecile from the chair and said, "We've got to go. I really appreciate this."

Pat Landow gave the couple a knowing look. Cecile still wore the long blond wig, still wore secular clothes, this time wearing a pale beige suit that made her look like a young executive. "Sorry I don't have any more information. Keep in touch, Paul."

Outside the police station Paul let loose. "How could you do this! Why didn't you tell me!"

An incoming policeman stopped and stared at the couple. "Everything okay, folks?"

"Fine, officer, really. Just a discussion," Cecile said, but they both noticed that the policeman stood by the door and watched them resume their conversation with lowered voices.

"People always try to kill me, Paul. It's the nature of my job."

"How about quitting that job?"

"I'll write Jeff Cloud a postcard. Dear sir, I quit. I don't care about helping John Cruz anymore. Please don't kill me."

"Exactly," Paul muttered. They turned and walked down the steps to the sidewalk. "Kevlar. Did you bring it with you?"

"Yes, it's at the hotel."

"Good place for it. Promise me you'll wear it from now on? Until this man is taken care of?"

"It's hot. It's heavy."

"It's bulletproof."

"It does work," Cecile admitted. "After I was shot, they took me to the hospital. Only a bruised rib."

"Darn all, Cecile."

"I'll wear it. Plus, there's a place in New Jersey that makes designer clothes with Kevlar. Maybe I'll give them a call."

"Stop being so fatuous."

"I'm not being silly. I'm very serious."

"You should be serious. This man is deadly."

"The problem is, it makes no difference now whether I quit the case or not. The man is in business, and he's been hired to do the job. So I need to find him before he finds me." Sister Cecile let out a deep breath. "I'm scared, Paul. All my praying, and I'm scared. I'll call home and ask all the sisters to pray tonight at vespers. A special intention."

They dined out that evening at the Florentine Grill. Sister Cecile wore the vest under the blue suit. She had called the community late in the afternoon and spoke to Sister Emma. "Could you please have everyone pray for my safety and the just disposition of Jeffrey Cloud?" Cecile asked.

"Dear Sister Cecile, I'll have them do an entire extra rosary for your intentions," Emma said. "After all, you're dead."

"Oh, I forgot." Cecile chuckled and the old nun burst into laughter.

"Seriously," Sister Emma said. "We'll pray. I know this is difficult for you."

138

"Thank you, Emma."

Sister Cecile explained what she did to Paul. "I didn't talk to Raphael or Leonie, just Sister Emma. She promised all the prayers."

Paul looked at Cecile. "Are you wearing the vest?"

She nodded. "It was easier under a habit. I wore a big habit, sort of loose. This suit is stuffed over it."

"Keep it on."

"I promise. I know all the prayers will be heard."

"I spend my entire life trying to make things work for you, Cecile. Just shut up and stay alive and appreciate it."

"I know, Paul." She almost suggested that he stop worrying, that God could take care of her, but Paul just wouldn't get it. He didn't understand that the mushy God that current humanity promoted, the God of the politically correct who could fit any religious inclination, really wasn't the way things were. God of love, yes, but there was justice out there too, and even anger. God was not soft. So Cecile took a spoonful of possibly the most delicious ice cream this side of heaven itself and kept quiet.

"You have that 'God is on my side' look, Cecile."

"That's not exactly true. It's a great mistake to say that you know everything, and then think you're humble."

"Who said I was humble?"

Cecile twinkled. "I wish. No, that's a quote from Teresa of Avila. I had to throw it in. God is on my side is a nice thought, but he seems to have left us to our own devices on this one. Still, I wish we'd get some kind of revelation about Mr. Cloud. I'm worried."

"Me too."

"I hate to count on Sister Linda's family."

"This is Providence, Rhode Island. Your friends should be able to sort it out."

Cecile took the last bite of ice cream. "I'll have better luck in Miami. I wish I could leave tomorrow."

"You can."

"I have to wait for Sister Linda. She's seeing relatives. I can't drag her away early."

"I suppose."

Cecile looked at Paul over the empty ice cream dishes. He

was as dear to her as ever. "If I had it all to do over, Paul, it would still be this way. You know that, don't you?"

Paul was silent for the space of a dozen heartbeats. A legion of emotions swept across his face, his intense blue eyes didn't waver. "I do," he said, and they both laughed in unison at the irony of his words.

"I brought you a present," Cecile said suddenly, and opened up her large purse. She drew out the box of cigars that Daisy Gonzalez had given her. "I know you'll like these."

Paul took the box of Romeo & Julietas with both hands.

"For real?" he asked.

"What do you mean?"

"I mean are these real Cuban cigars?"

"Well, Daisy gave them to me."

"Daisy?"

"Daisy Gonzalez. She runs a cigar factory in Little Havana in Miami. She gave me these before I got shot. Luckily they were in my big purse and I had the presence of mind to hang on to it."

"Cuban contraband. These are almost worth getting shot for, Cecile." Paul carefully slit the box open and pulled out a cigar. He sniffed it carefully. "Woody and spicy," he murmured, and lit up. He sat and tasted the cigar, puffing out a delicious aroma. "Have you considered there may be something more to this case than a Cuban murdered twenty years ago? How about cigar smuggling? This may be why they're after you. This is big business. You have any idea what these things go for?"

Cecile remembered the cigar band Leonie had showed her. Another Cuban cigar, she realized. "A major smuggling operation," she said. "I never thought of that. How incredible!"

"Well? Could that be it?"

"It's something to consider, but I don't think it's Daisy. Her husband's a minister. Besides, I was shot leaving her shop, plus Cloud was snooping around a long time before that."

"You'll have to wait for the mob to come up with something," Paul said.

Cecile nodded glumly. "Sister Linda, and family."

"They could cause trouble," Paul advised. "I'd avoid any

more meals with the family. Go to the zoo, or something. Providence has a nice zoo."

"Oh, no. Vinny's a good man. I'm sure. Linda said so, and if I can't trust her, who is there?"

"Hardly anyone."

21

PAUL left her off at the hotel. He headed back to Boston, only a short hour away, and Cecile was on her own. She stopped at the front desk to check for messages. The clerk handed her one.

"Thanks," she murmured, and opened the piece of paper.

"One of our contacts has come up with something. Could you come over to the house tomorrow at one." The note was from Vinny.

Cecile felt a current of electric excitement charge through her. Paul had warned her to stay away from family gatherings, but what did he know? Things were happening. One o'clock fit in with the Mass schedule. She could do the same routine as yesterday, go to the weekday noon Mass, then a meeting with the Mascapones.

She walked down the hotel corridor, her footsteps silent on the soft green carpet. She slipped the magnetic card into the door lock and watched the little green light go on. Such security, she thought. Nobody could possibly get in her room with this new system. She looked around to be absolutely sure.

Everything appeared to be exactly the same as when she left. Her bedcovers were pulled down and a small candy and a rose rested on the perfect folds. The flowers on the table had been perked up. The one drooping gladiola was trimmed back. Fine. That was as it should be. Then she looked at the dresser. Hairbrush in place, map of the city exactly as she had placed it. She opened the closet where three suits were hanging. She had left them pushed to one side. They were all evenly spaced now. Would a maid have done that? Maybe. She began to sweat, the wig was making her head way too hot.

Something was off. What was it? She went from the closet to the dresser, walking fast. The top drawer was open a fraction of an inch, just enough for her to peek inside and see the thin wire. It stretched from her field of vision to something dark beside her underwear, something that was not underwear.

"Darn," Cecile breathed. "There goes a good night's sleep."

She picked up her purse and carefully walked out of the room and returned to the lobby, where she went to the public telephone and called the Providence Police Department. "Is Detective Landow still in?"

He was. She told him what she had found.

"You actually think there's a bomb in your dresser?"

"Yes."

The silence from Pat Landow said more than a good expletive could. A bomb threat in a major downtown hotel was going to screw things up royally in the department. Headlines, maybe. Cecile felt guilty for causing so much trouble.

"Don't say anything. I'll be along with the bomb squad. Wait in the lobby."

"I'm there."

"Hang on."

It was beyond embarrassing. Such a lot of anxiety for the people in the rooms surrounding hers. The hotel guests didn't enjoy being routed from their beds at eleven-thirty at night, but the hotel security was not about to have its patrons blown to kingdom come in case the bomb squad man, Officer Sgro, made a mistake and cut the wrong wire. Bad enough a policeman should blow up without taking out some poor visiting businessman.

Cecile's mind raced between fear that everything would go up in smoke and the embarrassing thought that the bomb was in her underwear drawer. Underwear was the one area of her life where she truly skimped, preferring low cost items that had a tendency to fray and have holes. And her old bras. Policemen would see her bras. Nobody should ever see nun underwear.

She waited downstairs in the lobby and prayed for the bomb squad officer to remove the bomb without injuring himself or anyone else. She paced, she stared at the elegant hotel fixtures, marveled at the marble floor and soft rugs, and prayed quietly. An hour later Detective Landow appeared. She jumped out of her chair.

"All set," he said.

"Was it?"

"Yes. Something fairly immediate. It wouldn't have hurt anyone but you. Sgro is good. He disarmed it without too much difficulty."

"I'm glad to hear that. I'm really sorry about this. I hate to cause all this inconvenience."

"When are you going back to Miami?" he asked hopefully.

"Wednesday. I suppose I should move to another hotel. Do I need to make a statement?"

Pat Landow frowned. "I took down everything this afternoon. The bomb will be clean, no fingerprints, I can guarantee that. Unfortunately there's nothing to connect this to your man. We can't really pull him in on hearsay. What surprises me is that this isn't really Cloud's style as we've figured it."

"Times change," Cecile said quietly. "Desperate times, desperate measures. I was supposed to be dead already."

"That could do it. You've messed up his record. We'll be checking the hotel personnel. Where will you be staying?"

"I don't know. Could you suggest somewhere? It's late."

"Any preferences?"

"No. Some obscure motel. I'll have to take a cab. Just give me an address."

The policeman rubbed his chin. "I know just the place. You keep in touch with us until you leave town. Call me at eleven, tomorrow morning. I'm coming in late. Meanwhile I'll have someone drop you off at the Roger Williams Inn. It's just off the interstate. Nice place, clean, no mob connections that we know of."

"Wonderful. Can I go up to my room and get my clothes?"

"I'll come along."

Cecile checked into the Roger Williams Inn at two o'clock in the morning. It was a spotless, Colonial style motel, but beyond that she didn't really notice a thing. She went through the ritual of hanging her clothes in her room. Here, there was no closet, just a rack opposite the bathroom. She didn't open the dresser, just left everything else in her suitcase. No more

144

dressers, please. Finally Sister Cecile went to bed and lay there for at least an hour while her heartbeat slowed to normal. She said two complete rosaries. The cooling drone of the air conditioner lulled her to sleep.

Waking up the following morning in the motel was a generic experience. The air blew too cool, the curtains were too dark. Sister Cecile lay in bed, trying to catch all the events of the preceding day and put them in manageable order.

Eventually she felt good enough to wonder where the coffee was. She pulled herself out of bed and turned on a light. Then Cecile saw it, the small electric coffee pot, the creamer in small packets, even sugar and aspartame. "Thank you, God," she whispered, then realized she should thank the motel staff. "Thank you, staff," she said more loudly, and fixed some coffee. She said matins alone, placing herself in God's presence at the foot of a motel bed in Providence, Rhode Island.

An hour later Sister Cecile emerged for the day. She went to the motel office and booked the room for another night. Barring bombs, she would be back in this room tonight. She headed across the street to the Waffle House. From there the nun dialed Paul to tell him she had left the Biltmore.

"Hello, Paul?" She smiled into the telephone.

"Nice to hear from you. I called the Biltmore this morning." He sounded furious.

"Oh. Did they say anything?"

"Just that you'd checked out. What the hell is going on?"

"Well, this is going to take some explaining."

"Where are you?"

"Outside a Waffle House. Now, here's what happened."

Paul didn't interrupt except for an occasional expletive, and Paul customarily didn't use expletives in her presence, at least not since she had become a nun. It was one of his ways of showing he had a modicum of respect for it all. At least that's what Cecile told herself. His using them was a real sign of concern, something to his credit, she thought. "I'm fine. I do check my room. I saw the wire."

"Thank God."

"There you go again. I know you really do believe in God."

"Just an expression."

145

"Well, I'm going to Sister Linda's family's home right after noon Mass. I think they know who's behind Cloud. A message at the Biltmore said as much."

"Wear the vest."

"Absolutely."

"And call me. Call from Sister Linda's. Promise?"

"I promise."

Then she called Pat Landow. "I'm still alive. I'll be at the motel tonight," she said. "Any news?"

"Nothing. No one saw anything."

"How could they have gotten into my room?"

"Don't know."

"Well, I'm sorry," she apologized one more time.

"No problem."

Sister Cecile hung up. No problem. Right.

After a breakfast of waffles, sausages, and eggs, she returned to the motel and put on the bulletproof vest.

22

THE taxi driver who drove Sister Cecile from the church to the Mascapone residence had a Russian name and a thick accent. Times hadn't really changed much, Cecile thought as he dropped her off in front of the white house with the cement steps leading up a hill covered with pansies and sweet williams. New England still had an immigrant labor pool, bad and good neighborhoods, crisp white homes, heart-stopping, exhilarating air, fluffy clouds. It was a day in which only good things could happen.

Right, Cecile thought, feeling her bruised rib. It still hurt if she thought about it. Nevertheless, she felt buoyantly optimistic. She rang the doorbell, ready for the solution to her problems to fall into her lap.

Sister Linda opened the door, old brown eyes shining. "Sister Cecile, I'm so glad you came. Jimmy says he has something for you. Selma's little boy. And they want me to take back the family organ. It's going to make our chapel sound just exactly like heaven! Isn't that wonderful?"

Cecile gave the old nun a hug. An organ? Was she talking about a liver, or something musical? And what did Jimmy Gigliardi have?

"I'm so glad you're enjoying yourself."

"I had so much to make up for. I made a bad mistake a great many years ago. I finally could say I was sorry, in person," Linda whispered. "That's so important. Restitution, you know? Everything is right now."

Cecile didn't know what Linda was referring to, but she was glad if Sister Linda was glad. "Yes," she said.

"Come see the organ." Sister Linda took Cecile by the hand and drew her along through a lace-curtained parlor, past

147

an elegant dining room table laid with a white tablecloth. A vase of red roses sat in the center. They went into a room off to the right, a library, but with several computers set up on wide tables. In the back between some bookshelves stood a mahogany pipe organ. The pipes were small, perhaps six feet by four feet; the organ was the size of an upright piano.

"Why, it's beautiful," Cecile said.

"See the pallet box? Vinny just had the soundboard checked, and the trackers and stickers are in perfect shape! And Sister Emma plays. Did you know that? And of course I play. All those grammar school musicals . . ." Sister Linda beamed. Vinny wandered in, looking equally pleased with himself.

"We wanted to give this to you. It's just sitting here," he said, his voice lower and scratchier than ever.

Cecile just stood and smiled, wondering how on earth they would ever get this monster back to Miami. A moving van? Piano mover? It really would be wonderful in their chapel. "Beautiful. We really do appreciate this. Thank you, Vinny."

"And Jimmy's got the news you was after," Vinny said. "He's in the kitchen having a bite with Selma. That's his mother."

Linda almost bounded ahead of Cecile. She seemed to have lost ten years. "I'm just so happy. I feel so wonderful, so close to God."

In the kitchen, Jimmy was sitting at the big Formica table dipping some bread into a bowl of olive oil, sipping a glass of red wine. The bread smelled fresh. Cecile wondered suddenly if maybe they would offer lunch. "You found out something, Jimmy?" she asked.

He wiped his mouth on his sleeve and reached down behind the table for something in his pants pocket. "Yeah, I got something for you."

The only one who realized he was reaching for a gun was Sister Linda. "No! Jimmy!"

An instant before the gun went off, aimed directly at Sister Cecile's heart, Sister Linda threw herself in front of the younger nun.

Jimmy pulled the trigger at the same time that Linda leaped. Instead of hitting Cecile, the bullet hit Sister Linda.

148

Automatically Sister Cecile's arms flew out to catch the falling nun. Sister Linda, not a small woman for all her years, lurched against Cecile and together they crashed to the kitchen floor. Another shot rang out and Cecile felt a familiar pain, lighter this time, because the second bullet went directly through the fleshy part of Sister Linda's arm before it hit Cecile in the chest.

A third shot rang out. Vinny had arrived and he stood in the kitchen door, his gun smoking. Jimmy Gigliardi fell over. His gun clattered to the Formica tabletop.

Selma was screaming. "My baby! My baby! You killed my baby. You son of a bitch, Vinny!"

From her awkward spot on the floor underneath Linda's dead weight, Cecile shut out the screams. She had to help Sister Linda. Cecile struggled to get on her knees beside the old sister. She had to save the wounded nun. *Dear God, don't let it be too late,* Cecile prayed, and managed to turn Sister Linda over. No movement. The bullet had stopped the old nun's heart. Linda was dead.

Cecile looked around frantically. Jimmy was splayed on the table, his gun a foot away from his lifeless hand. Vinny Mascapone stood in the doorway, holding a revolver as big as a cannon.

Suddenly there were people everywhere. The kitchen began to resemble the last scene of an Italian opera. Selma ranted and raved, half in English, half in Italian. Tears, howls, and a madcap explanation of what was happening, or of what just happened, floated through garlic-scented air.

What happened was easy to understand. Jimmy had tried to kill Sister Cecile. He killed Sister Linda instead. And Vinny shot Jimmy.

Why it happened was another story entirely. Cecile worked it out from the chaotic words streaming through the air of the Mascapone kitchen. The gist of it all was that back in 1947, Linda had been along for the killing of Selma's favorite uncle. Selma had never forgiven Linda and had made a vow, as a small child, to take vengeance, but Linda had slipped away to a convent. Jimmy Gigliardi had known this, knew his mother had never forgiven Linda, and that Sister Cecile deserved no consideration, because she was on Linda's side.

And Jimmy had been in touch with Cloud. Jimmy's plan was to kill both Sister Cecile and Sister Linda Mascapone. The double murder would have meant big money to Jimmy Gigliardi and satisfaction for his mother.

"He was gonna kill you, nun," Selma spat, her arms forcibly held behind her by Vinny. "He was gonna get half the money Cloud had. And you'd be dead," she crowed, "and *holy* Sister Linda would have seen you die right here. Right in front of her traitorous eyes! And then she'd get hers." Selma gave a great lurch, trying to get away from Vinny, her hands like talons trying to claw at Sister Cecile. "Now she's dead, the bitch!"

"Shut up, Selma, you wanna be in a conspiracy to murder? You got enough trouble just being a human bean," Vinny growled, clutching the woman with all the force of his seventy-nine years. "Okay, Cecile, here's what we're gonna do."

"Let me go, Vinny, you old bastard," Selma grunted, wrestling her arms. But Vinny held on, his raspy voice dominating the room.

"Soon as Sal gets here, he's gonna take you home, get you outta here," Vinny said. "We got a regular case, what with me shooting your bozo son in self-defense. Crazy fool killing people in my own kitchen! Killing my sister!" Suddenly Vinny let out a huge sob. "My own big sister! She was like a mother to me."

Someone must have made a telephone call because people were arriving. Sal walked in, panting from running up the steep steps to the front door. He was followed by Joe and a convention of women who raced to Selma and dragged her out of the kitchen. They were swearing softly in Italian.

The kitchen was silent. Sister Cecile, who had been sitting on the kitchen floor the whole time, pried herself loose from Sister Linda. Cecile had been praying semiaudibly, crying, listening, slowly making sense of everything. She rose from the floor, her beige suit stained with a huge puddle of Sister Linda's blood. The old nun lay on the floor; Jimmy Gigliardi was flopped over on the kitchen table, his face in a pool of olive oil.

"We should call a priest," Cecile said with a catch in her throat.

150

"I'll do that. You got any cop friends might believe what went on here?" Vinny gurgled thickly.

"Detective Pat Landow," Cecile said.

Vinny Mascapone wiped the tears from his face. He was only a tired old man who had just lost his sister. In the next room Selma Gigliardi was sobbing quietly. Sister Cecile couldn't help herself from crying. Sal stood beside Vinny, patting him on the back. Joe, the fourth man from their lunch yesterday, wandered around the kitchen. "Maybe we oughta toss this gun?" he asked, eyeballing Jimmy's pistol.

"Leave it," Vinny growled. "Leave it."

After Vinny got off the phone with the parish priest and Cecile called Detective Landow, Sister Cecile called Paul. "I need you," she said.

"I'm on my way."

Three hours later the bodies were given conditional last rites of the Church by a local priest, and were well-photographed by a police photographer. The mortician was called and the corpses were removed. Cecile vouched for the fact that Jimmy had shot Linda, that Vinny had come to her aid and shot Jimmy in what could be considered self-defense. There was no crime to pursue. There was only sorrow and the end of a half-century vendetta that should never have happened.

Paul was there, had been there for some time. Cecile told him in whispered words what had happened. He stood by her, spoke for her, held her hand.

Finally it was over. The police left, lights still flashing, the group of women had departed with promises to return with casseroles, mountains of funeral food that was as much a part of a funeral as the body itself. Donna Mascapone, Vinny's daughter, took over the house and saw to it that everything was put in order. There was a funeral to consider. Two funerals. Sister Linda would be buried in the family plot.

Cecile prepared to leave, Paul at her side. Vinny came up to her, his face haggard. "Sorry," he said.

"No, I'm the one. I'm sorry."

"Not your fault. Jimmy, he was bad. I shoulda taken care of him a long time ago."

"No," Cecile said. "I guess there's no way of knowing what

151

was behind it. I mean, Jimmy was going to collect half of Cloud's fee if he killed me. Would Selma know who was behind it?"

"No. Jimmy hisself probably didn't know. I'll ask around. Meanwhile I think you gotta take that organ back with you. Like a memorial to my sister. You know what I mean? This is real important to me."

"Organ?" Paul asked.

"Pipe organ," Cecile explained. "In the back room."

"I'll have a plaque made," Vinny said. "Bronze. Like, 'In Loving Memory of Sister Linda Mascapone.' And then maybe the dates. So you gotta take it back." His face crumbled and a tear dropped from one corner of the deep brown eyes, eyes that looked like his sister's.

"I will."

Vinny wiped the tear with a fist. "I'll check into this Cloud stuff. Meanwhile, you better get outta Providence. I think that's a smart thing to do."

"I agree with that," Paul said. "Come on, Cecile."

Sister Cecile followed Paul outside and down the steps to the street, where Paul had parked his big gray Cadillac. "I never rented a car," Cecile said. "Somehow cabs seemed safer. I guess it wouldn't have mattered."

"No. It wouldn't have mattered." Paul was silent as he helped Cecile into the car. When they were on the road, he finally spoke. "Where to?"

"Can you find I-95 going south? The motel is right off that."

"So you didn't need the vest after all," Paul said, choked up. "You had Sister Linda."

"No, I did need it. There was a second shot. This is getting crazy, Paul. I don't know where to go, what to do. Linda's dead, and in a way, it's my fault."

"I think Selma would have gotten her revenge one way or another. I never saw so much hatred. All those old women dragging Selma away. She wanted to kill you too. I don't know how you get into messes like this, Cecile."

"Selma was crazy because her son was dead. Even bad guys have mothers who weep." Cecile wiped her eyes.

"Bad mothers who weep," Paul said.

"It seems as though the word 'mother' has a feeling of good in it. Only lately things have changed."

"Greek mythology is full of bad mothers." Paul tapped the steering wheel. "Being a mother is no guarantee of sainthood."

Cecile didn't reply to that, just lay her head back against the headrest. "What time is it?"

"Seven. You can change and we can grab a sandwich."

"Food," Cecile said. "It's been a long time. And I have to deal with that organ, Paul. How am I going to have it delivered?"

"Have it shipped."

"I'd like to drive it. Maybe I can rent a van."

"And drive how many miles? You're crazy."

"No. I want to do it for Sister Linda."

"You just had an old nun die in your arms. Someone tried to kill you. You aren't thinking rationally."

"I need some time to think," Cecile said thoughtfully. "Maybe I could work things out in my mind. There has to be a key to all this craziness. I could drive and think and pray. I'm sad, Paul, really sad."

"You could fly and have it shipped. Forget sad. You're alive and you have to stay that way."

"That's the easy way. Next exit, Paul. That's where the motel is."

23

On the evening of the day John disappeared, Pearla Cruz found a note from her husband. The envelope was propped up on her dresser, leaning against her hairbrush. John knew how Pearla took care of her splendid, long black hair, how Pearla always went upstairs after dinner to brush it out before they settled down for an evening of talk on the front porch, or to spread out on the big couch in the family room and watch television, or to play games with the children. He loved to see her hair down, and this was the only time of the day she let it free.

The message was written on his office notepad, the one that read, "From the desk of John Cruz." He was so proud of that, of his office, of his name. She remembered his name when they had met. Juan Calderon.

Dear darling Pearla,

This is the hardest thing for me to do because I love you more than life itself. But I do not want to hurt you, or to destroy the life you have here. The animals are doing well, Mike Baxter can sign anything because I made him a partner. He's a good man, his wife will help you. Anything that needs doing he can do. If I stay it will only cause you pain. Now when they come for me you can say you don't know anything, that I just left.

Do not believe them. I never did anything wrong, except I saved Pastele from death. Long ago I sent money to that man. You know about that. Someday maybe I can come back. Someday I will be free.

I love you, Pearla.

Juan

Pearla read the note several times. Juan was gone? No. It couldn't be true. He was only out in the barn as he so often was. He had forgotten about dinner. He did that all the time, so wrapped up in his cows, such a hard worker.

Pearla said nothing to the children, who were busy playing in the family room. Alone, she went out to the barn and looked everywhere. The stalls were filled with cows, the paddock held the small bull, Pablo. Soft animal sounds were all she heard. The hired man had gone home, and Mike had left for the day.

And of course the car was gone.

Pearla said nothing. Her mind moved into a vacuum. He couldn't do this. Not Juan. She couldn't accept it. She waited until the next morning when the two older children were in school, and she left the house with the toddler in the care of Raisa, their housekeeper. Mike was in the barn checking some breeding records.

"John said he was going somewhere?" Pearla asked.

"He said something about a meeting. He was vague." Mike looked puzzled. He should, Pearla thought, and it was going to get worse. She finally understood Juan was gone.

"He went somewhere," Pearla agreed. "But I don't know where. He said you should handle things."

Mike opened his eyes wide. "What gives? He came down to my house the other night, said I'd have to handle the paperwork. He sick?"

"No. He did say you would have to do the paperwork." Pearla nodded. "He didn't say why?"

"No."

Pearla pushed back the tears. She couldn't afford to cry. "All right. We will run things as always. I will help with the papers. I know them. We can do it together. We may have to hire another man. Can you do that?"

"Where is he?" Mike asked. His voice vibrated with emotion.

"I don't know."

Pearla returned to the house, shaken. How could this be happening to her? What was happening? What did they think Juan had done? She thought of him as Juan, never John. She trusted Juan with her life, Juan Calderon, John Cruz, whoever he was. She would tell the children he was away at

155

school, away at meetings because he knew so much. He was away somewhere and he was so important he could never come back.

But what could she ever tell herself?

Pearla cried in her room, then wiped the tears and dismissed the housekeeper for the day. She took care of the baby, three-year-old Beatriz. Then, with Beatriz at her side, she cleaned the house. She would make it spotless so that whenever something happened she would be ready. First the kitchen. Beatriz wiped the low cabinets with a soft rag. "Make them shiny," her mother had always instructed her, and Beatriz polished ferociously. Then the living room. Pearla vacuumed, dusted, lifted every book from the shelf and wiped it with a special rag that collected the dust. Beatriz stacked blocks neatly on the floor while her mother worked. Then they went into Juan's office.

The office contained breeding records for the past eighteen years. The original magazines that he had pulled from a Dumpster at the edge of a forest were carefully preserved. Pearla had longed to toss them in the trash, but she didn't, and she looked at them today with pain and a desire for the man she had met so many years ago. The bookshelf behind his messy desk was stuffed with articles, books, papers, everything relating to cattle breeding. Pearla dusted everything on the shelf carefully, then she turned to the desk.

Six pencils with broken leads, several pens, paper clips, an inkstand that he used as a paperweight. Under it was an orderly pile of bills. These would go to the main office in the barn, a well-turned-out room where Mike worked occasionally. She would have to bring everything current over there, Pearla realized.

She saw a pile of new magazines on animal breeding. Maybe Mike would like to read them too. Pearla set them aside. Bills, records, sheets of information from the conference John had spoken at just a few days ago. Everything in this pile was a jumble. Two dirty coffee cups, the telephone sitting crookedly, a pair of scissors, mileage charts to Orlando, one of Beatriz's stuffed cows, three calendars.

What happened that had made Juan flee? Was it something

at the conference? She hadn't seen anything. Maybe Carlos would know.

Pearla continued to arrange things. She looked at the magazines she was going to take to Mike. Three of them were opened to articles on pigs. Pigs? Since when did Juan have an interest in *cerdos*?

She lifted the coffee cups to take to the kitchen, then put them back on the desk as something tangible that he had touched, relics to be preserved, maybe. She left them there and opened the top desk drawer.

Pencils, erasers, Carlito's ruler, which Juan had borrowed last week. Pearla looked at the clutter in the drawer. Juan was so organized in his mind, but it didn't always show in his possessions. She began to read the newspaper clippings for a hint of where he could be.

Articles on breeding pigs. Articles on a new kind of cattle food, new animal antibiotics, cloning, and then a pile of cards from the businesses Juan frequented. Harvey's Feed Store, the Automotive Center, Sister Cecile—Private Detective, Miami Beach, Florida.

Pearla stopped. Private detective? Why would Juan have this card? Sister Cecile? A nun? This made no sense. Little Beatriz began to whine. Lunchtime; the child was hungry.

Pearla put the card in the pocket of her dungaree shorts. "We have some lunch, okay, Bea? SpaghettiOs okay?"

"I want SpaghettiOs," Beatriz squeaked. "With dinosaurs!"

Pearla fed Beatriz, but she didn't really eat herself. She drank a cup of strong coffee with milk and ate a teaspoon of Beatriz's leftovers. She took the baby outside for a walk to the barn to see if Mike had everything running smoothly; then she and Beatriz returned to the house. Nap time for the baby, and then she would call this detective in Miami. Maybe there was an answer.

Beatriz finally settled down for her afternoon nap. The two older children wouldn't be home from school for another two hours, and it was quiet time. This was the time when Pearla and Juan sometimes escaped to their bedroom and made love. Pearla thought of the last time as she stared at Sister Cecile's card and slowly began to dial 305, the Miami area code.

* * *

Miami steamed. The air-conditioning unit for the retirement community struggled bravely to keep the rooms cool. Sister Raphael had just come in from inspecting the big fan outside and she was seriously depressed. The fan squeaked loudly. The old nun went to the main thermostat and turned it to a higher setting. Everyone would just have to be hot for a few hours until the sun went down. Otherwise the old system would die, and Sister Cecile wasn't here to contend with it. But there was a solution at hand, at least it seemed that way, because Sister Raphael was sure some money had just arrived in the mail. They really needed to have a new cooling system installed.

A thick manila envelope had arrived in the noon mail, mailed from Orlando, addressed to Sister Cecile. It had to be from John Cruz, but it said "Personal" on it and Sister Raphael didn't dare open it. She walked into Cecile's office and picked up the fat envelope one more time. It felt like money. Maybe it was another ten thousand. If it were, they could call the air-conditioning people and have the system repaired, or buy a new one.

Raphael lowered herself into Cecile's chair. She sat for a full minute and contemplated the manila envelope and felt the room become hotter and hotter. Then the telephone rang. Raphael reached eagerly for the receiver. She had been expecting to hear from Sister Cecile since Friday and the anticipation showed in her voice. "Hello?"

"Is Sister Cecile there?"

"Who's calling please?"

"My name is Pearla Cruz."

"May I help you? Sister Cecile is not available."

"I found a card in my husband's desk today," the voice said. A soft voice with a trace of a Cuban accent. "My husband is Juan Cruz." She pronounced it "Huan."

"Yes?" Raphael said.

"Has he been there? My husband?"

Sister Raphael didn't know what to say. She should say that it was a confidential matter, that clients were protected, but there was something in the woman's voice. Something lost. "I saw him here," Raphael said at last.

"He was all right?"

"Fine," Raphael assured her.

"When was this?"

"A week or so ago."

"Oh." Utter disappointment.

"I'm sorry."

"Do you find missing people?" Pearla asked slowly.

"Yes we do," Sister Raphael answered unhesitatingly.

"Juan is gone. My husband. I know he came to see you, I know there is a reason, but I don't know why. I want you to find him. I can pay."

"Yes. I'm Sister Cecile's assistant," Sister Raphael said, wondering just how close to the truth that was. Of course she was, she just didn't have a title. "And I expect her to be home on Wednesday. Could you come by on Thursday?"

"Thursday? Do I have to come in?"

"Well, I suppose not. Maybe if you could call on Thursday."

"I can overnight money. How much will it cost?"

Sister Raphael thought about a new air-conditioning system. This one could be replaced for ten thousand dollars, a huge, new system that wouldn't squeal. Raphael wondered how much this woman had to spend. For the very first time she understood Sister Cecile's dilemma in charging people. She heard herself saying what Sister Cecile always said. "We charge a flat rate of six hundred dollars a day, barring unusual expenses. You could pay by the week or the day, or designate a lump sum."

"I'll send a bank check for ten thousand dollars," Pearla said, and Sister Raphael wondered if she had some kind of mental connection with her husband, who had come up with that exact figure.

"I think you should wait," Raphael heard herself say. "You must talk with Sister Cecile."

"I don't want to wait."

"Can I have your number? I could have her call you."

"Yes, of course."

"As soon as I hear from Sister Cecile I'll give her your number, Mrs. Cruz. She should be in touch soon. Will you be in tonight?"

"Oh, yes, I won't be going anywhere."

24

SISTER Cecile and Paul spent a long evening discussing how to proceed. Paul insisted they stop for a six-pack of beer at a convenience store. He pulled in at a pizza shop and ordered a pizza with anchovies and olives. Pizza topping was one of the few things they ever agreed on. They set up the meal on the table in Cecile's motel room.

"I don't want anyone knowing about this crazy plan," Paul said.

"It isn't crazy. I can drive. I love to drive. All you have to do is rent the van and go pick up the organ. Tomorrow I drive."

"All the way from Providence, Rhode Island, to Miami Beach. That's something like sixteen hundred miles, isn't it?"

"I love driving by myself. Nobody makes any of the important decisions except me. Like where to eat, when to stop, when to get gas. Do you know how aggravating it is driving when seven nuns all have different ideas? It defies the rule of obedience. Someone always has to go to the bathroom. No, this way I can set my own schedule, drive slowly, roll into South Florida in three days."

"You don't know how to drive slowly."

"Well." Cecile liked that. "So what?" She poured a quarter of a glass of beer for herself and ate one olive off the pizza.

Paul took a piece of pizza and rolled it sideways before inserting the end in his mouth. He was thinking. Cecile could tell from the look in his eyes as he chewed. He had almost come around to her plan.

"I already spoke with Vinny about it. He thought the van was a great idea. He really wants the sisters to have the organ.

He has the bronze plaque all designed in his mind," Cecile said, pushing it.

"No doubt Selma will tell Cloud exactly the color and make of the van you're driving," Paul said, picking up another slice. "And you'll be dead before Connecticut."

"No. You're going to rent the van. You're going to go pick up the organ. Private mover, Paul Dorys, esquire. It will be safer than if I take a plane. I don't care what they say about airport security, I'm dead if I go on the plane. Really, Paul."

Paul wiped his lips on a paper napkin, then took a drink from his beer. "It might work. It just seems so slow. Three days on the road."

"Slow is good sometimes. I need time to think about all this. It's been a bad week." Cecile picked up her beer, looked at it, and put it down again.

"I know," Paul agreed.

"Sister Linda and all."

"She was very old. How old?"

"Eighty-seven. And she was able to say she was sorry. It wasn't her fault Selma wouldn't accept the apology."

"Forgiveness," Paul said. "That's a tough one."

Cecile's gray eyes met his blue ones. "It's good to forgive, good to be forgiven. That's what we pray for. I guess it's one of those important things. It takes two, the forgiver and the forgivee."

"Even in the real world," Paul agreed. "You aren't eating."

Cecile stared at the pizza, looking at one particular configuration of anchovies, cheese, and olives. Very pretty, but she couldn't eat another thing. "Take it with you, Paul."

Eight o'clock Tuesday morning Paul rented a large blue Ford Econoline van with heavily tinted windows. The seats had been taken out for a previous renter, and the company was happy to send it off to parts unknown. The rental fee was outrageous, but it all came from Sister Cecile's account. The fact that the organ was coming along for the ride did not negate the fact that the entire trip to Providence was for business purposes.

Paul bought a map of the eastern United States, a map of Rhode Island, one of Connecticut, and one of New York. He

161

stocked the front area with bottles of fruit juice and water and boxes of crackers, hoping Cecile would at least eat something on the road. Then he headed to Vinny Mascapone's house, where he had arranged to pick up the organ.

"I'll be driving it myself," Paul said to Vinny and the four husky men Vinny had rounded up to help move the organ. "I've been needing a trip to Florida. This is a great excuse. I'll head down the Keys and do some bone fishing after I drop off the organ."

Vinny nodded in agreement. "Good plan. So, how's the nun getting back?"

"Oh, she still has an airplane ticket," Paul said.

"When's the plane leave?" Vinny asked.

"Wednesday, around noon," Paul replied, aware that everyone was listening, everyone from the movers to the women in the kitchen who were fussing with funeral food. Cloud would probably be at the airport, bomb in hand. Cecile was right.

Half an hour later the organ was successfully stowed in the van. It barely fit, but it worked.

Vinny appeared from the kitchen carrying a case of red glass jars. "Spaghetti sauce," he grunted, and stowed the sauce in the space before the empty front right-hand seat. "This here's the mayor's own spaghetti sauce. You take this right to the convent along with the organ. Not every town got its own tomato sauce."

"Thanks, Vinny. The nuns will appreciate this." Paul shook Vinny's hand, slipped some money into the hands of the men who moved the organ, and said good-bye. He drove away, directly to the second rent-a-truck business he had found in the yellow pages. He drove into the lot, parked the Econoline, and rented a Big Budget white Chevy utility van. He bribed three men at the company to help him move the organ from the Ford to the Chevy, unloaded and reloaded the spaghetti sauce, maps, and food by himself, and said he would be back in a half hour to pick up the Ford van.

Cecile came out of the motel room when he honked. She jumped up into the white van and they drove back to pick up the Ford. "I'll drive the Ford around Providence tonight, picking up this and that," Paul said. "Meanwhile you can get started. By the time Cloud discovers you aren't on the airplane, you'll be gone."

"I'll leave early in the morning," Cecile said. "I called the state troopers for a road check, and there's work being done on the road at night. It's actually much better during the day."

Paul shrugged. "Suit yourself. I think you'll be safe. I'll return the Ford to the rental agency lot late tomorrow."

Cecile nodded. "Cloud will be after a blonde driving a blue Ford van. I'll be a redhead tomorrow, driving a white Chevy."

"I hope it works."

"Piece of cake," Cecile said. "And if I sense someone on my tail, I'll leave the van behind, hire someone to ship the organ, and vanish. Or something."

"Or something. Just don't take any chances. Promise?"

"Promise."

They drove back to the first rental company, where Paul had left his car. He had parked the blue van downtown in a parking lot with plans to move it around, just for effect. It was time to say good-bye.

"Good-bye, Paul."

They stood on the black tarmac and smiled, then gave each other a hug.

"Don't worry, Paul. Everything will work out in the end."

Paul pulled back and looked at Cecile, holding her at arm's length. "Which end are you referring to?"

"I was thinking 'Last Judgment.' "

Paul shook his head. "I was afraid of that."

Cecile clambered up into the white van. "God bless. I'll call."

"Every night. Be careful!"

Cecile drove away, heading back to the motel. The van drove heavily because of the load, the huge organ and all its pipes jammed in by the rental company workers who had helped Paul reload it. In fact, they had been so rough that the small locator bug that Selma had placed on the underside of the organ's pedal board had been knocked loose and now lay, sticky side up, on the green rug lining the floor of the van.

Back in her room at the Roger Williams Motel, Sister Cecile settled down in her bed, totally exhausted from the emotional stress of having Sister Linda die in her arms, of the

163

thought that her own death had been twice averted by the bulletproof vest, and by Paul, whose very presence was so wonderful and terrible that it left her ragged. She lay in bed and flipped the television remote, watching everything and seeing only flashes of Sister Linda, of Paul, and of the bloody suit that she had dumped in the motel trash outside.

It was nine o'clock at night. She should call home. Sister Raphael needed to know everything.

Sister Raphael answered the telephone herself. "Cecile! How wonderful. I have some very interesting news."

"So do I."

It took fifteen minutes to catch up, Sister Raphael stopping for a good three minutes to weep and blow her nose over Sister Linda's demise, and then to finally return to the fact that not only had John Cruz vanished, but that his wife was ready to hire Sister Cecile to find him. "I said you'd be back on Thursday," Raphael said. "Is that too much to hope?"

"Probably. I'll be driving slowly. I have a heavy load."

"An organ," Raphael breathed. "That really will be lovely."

"And a case of the Mayor's Own Marinara Sauce."

"What did we do to deserve that?"

"I don't know."

"What should I tell Mrs. Cruz?" Raphael asked.

"Nothing. I'll call her right now. It's not too late, is it?"

"She's so worried. Just call her. When will I hear from you again?"

"I'll call from the road. I should be around Richmond, Virginia, by tomorrow night. Maybe further."

"I'll be expecting your call. Oh, and Cecile, this is important. There's a letter here from John Cruz, at least I think it's from him. No return address, but an Atlanta postmark. How dumb, with everything, I almost forgot."

"What does it say?" Cecile asked.

"I have no idea. It was marked 'Personal.'" Sister Raphael sounded smug.

"You didn't steam it open?"

"I wouldn't think of such a thing." Raphael paused. "I'll open it now."

Cecile heard ripping noises. Then, "Money, lots of cash. And here's the letter." Sister Raphael read, "'Dear Sister Cecile, Something urgent has come up and I am leaving town for a while. It is more important than ever that you discover the killer of Victor Torres, so I am rescinding my request that you stop the investigation. Please do not endanger yourself in any way, but if it is at all possible, find the guilty person. I will call you in several weeks for a report. Thank you very much. John Cruz.' "

"Well, well, well," Sister Cecile said. "I wasn't wasting my time here after all."

"If trying to get killed is wasting time," Raphael put in. "It looks like ten thousand dollars."

"Good. Put it in the bank."

"If the air conditioner dies, can I spend it?"

"Dies?"

"It sounds terrible sometimes. I have to turn the motor off and the building gets really hot."

"Why don't you call that repairman who advertises in the church bulletin?"

"Someone told me he's a crook."

"Then ask around. We need that money for so many things."

"If we need a new system?" Raphael asked hopefully.

"Spend it. I'll call Mrs. Cruz now."

"And I'll inform the community about Sister Linda. We'll miss her."

Cecile hung up, rose from the bed where she had been sitting and talking, and took a turn around the room. John Cruz was missing, but had rehired her. His wife wanted to hire her. It was going to be difficult to decide what charge went with which Cruz.

Sister Cecile dialed the number Sister Raphael had given her. An accented voice answered.

"I'm calling for Mrs. Pearla Cruz. This is Sister Cecile."

"Oh, Sister Cecile." The voice stopped. Cecile could hear a television, loud in the background. "I'll go to the office phone. Could you hold on a minute?"

"Of course."

Pearla Cruz told Sister Cecile all she knew about John Cruz's disappearance. "Can you find him? Why did he have your card?" Pearla asked.

"He hired me on a case," Cecile said. "Do you know a man named Juan Caldo?"

"Caldo?" There was a moment of silence. "No. When I met Juan, his name was Juan Calderon. He wanted to become more American, he said, so he became John Cruz."

"I see. And there was nothing unusual to precipitate his departure?"

"Excuse me?"

"Nothing happened out of the ordinary before John left?"

"Oh, no. He gave a wonderful talk about cattle breeding in Orlando. It was a great success. We've received several calls. People want to talk with him. I don't know what to say." Despair racked the woman's voice.

Cecile thought for a moment. "I'm up North right now. I'll actually be driving by Orlando in a few days. Could I stop at your home? Would that be acceptable? Maybe I can come up with something then. Maybe we can discover something together."

"Yes, come directly here. And you will find Juan?" Pearla asked.

"I'll do my best."

"I'm so glad. Then you will find him." Pearla sounded very positive.

"I'll try."

Later that night when Sister Cecile turned over for the fifteenth time, unable to sleep or even become comfortable in the huge motel bed, she wondered if she had been strictly telling the truth to Pearla. It was very likely there was a good reason Juan Calderon-Cruz didn't want to be found. Maybe she shouldn't find him. Maybe nobody would be happy if she found him, particularly Pearla Cruz.

25

THE Chevy van pulled out of the Roger Williams Inn at ten in the morning, because Sister Cecile had overslept. She never overslept, but this morning she didn't wake up until nine o'clock. Of course, she hadn't gone to sleep until four A.M., so it was probably a good thing.

Sister Cecile barreled down I-95, heading south. The huge organ blocked the rearview mirror, but the side mirrors gave an excellent view of what was behind her. The van moved at a steady sixty-five miles per hour, downhill all the way. The pain and confusion of the past days drifted slowly away and Sister Cecile felt the peace of the open road.

At eleven o'clock she exited the highway. Exit ninety, Mystic, Connecticut. Years ago she had seen the movie, now it was time to have a genuine Mystic pizza. Paul had wanted her to eat something. She would eat.

The pizza parlor was located directly on the main street of the town where everything suffered from quaintness. Sweet little shops, a drawbridge and a scattering of white boats, a beautiful church at the top of a hill, and the pizza shop itself with lovely glass decorations and a beautiful dog weathervane. Cecile ordered a small moussaka pizza with eggplant, extra sauce, and mozzarella. She settled into a booth at exactly twelve o'clock, the time she would have been checking in at the Providence airport.

She pictured the airport in her mind. Jeffrey Cloud was probably standing right next to the check-in booth, or perhaps out front, holding a bomb under the *Providence Journal* or clutching that huge gun he had shot her with before.

Sister Cecile said a quiet grace, blessed herself, and picked off a slice of eggplant. Thoughts of the gun had just taken away her appetite. This pizza was "a slice of Heaven," proclaimed by several prominent signs in the shop, but she just couldn't eat it right now. Heaven could wait.

Cecile packed the pizza in the carryout box and went on her way.

Cloud was furious. The nun should be dead. Everyone had screwed up. Selma Gigliardi's vendetta meant nothing to him, but when the old lady had offered to stick a tracer on the organ, he'd agreed. But then the damn lawyer had driven off with it. Shit, damn. So he waited at the airport. No nun.

He returned to his car and checked the tracer. Maybe the damn nun was driving after all. He couldn't let her make it back to Miami alive.

Cloud stared at the device that tracked the locator bug, watching the red light blinking on the screen. The organ was heading southwest. He pulled out of the airport drive, stepping on the gas. It had to be the nun driving the organ, had to be! A blue Ford with tinted windows driven by a blonde. Selma had told him about the wig.

Still in Mystic, Sister Cecile lingered. She took a walk up the hill and looked at the church, she wandered back to the river that led to the sea and inspected the boats. She stood by the water and prayed.

By the time she pulled the van back onto the main highway, Cloud was five minutes ahead of her and thoroughly confused, because suddenly the direction finder had switched. He kept going, but very slowly. Finally he pulled completely off the road, because the red finder light indicated the van was approaching slowly from the rear.

Cecile drove at only sixty miles an hour. She was feeling placid, peaceful after her prayers by the bridge. She spotted a blue van identical to the one Paul had originally rented. It would be fun to drive alongside a blue van, she thought, because, in truth, she was supposed to be driving a blue van. Maybe this blue van was going to Florida too.

The blue van had heavily tinted windows. Cecile wondered, idly, if it contained an organ. She paced herself behind it, put the Chevy on cruise control at exactly fifty-nine miles per hour, and drove across Connecticut three car lengths behind a very attractive, blue Ford van.

The blue van did not take the Whitestone Bridge, as Cecile had initially planned to do, but took the Cross Bronx Expressway. Maybe the blue van knew something she didn't, Cecile thought, and followed it, three cars behind. Cecile ate some crackers as she drove, then pulled out a juice drink, one of many that Paul had set beside the driver's seat. She drank and then located a New York City radio station that played golden oldies. She tapped her fingers on the steering wheel to the beat of "Yellow Submarine."

Traffic was moving well; it was the right side of rush hour and people were coming rather than going. The two vans rolled along, across the George Washington Bridge, down, and eventually onto the New Jersey Turnpike. Sister Cecile was ready for a rest room and a tank of gas.

So was the blue van. So was Cloud, a thousand yards behind.

The blue van's blinker went on just as it pulled into the rest stop. It had been going fast and this must have been a last minute decision. Cecile squealed a right and followed it in. She pulled up directly beside it and watched a young woman emerge, a slender woman with long blond hair. It could have been her only yesterday, Cecile thought.

Cecile visited the rest room, then returned to the van. She checked the floor. The empty fruit drink bottle had rolled away when she made a sharp turn toward the gas pumps. It could start to roll and cause trouble, Cecile knew, maybe roll under the brake pedal, or smash against the organ if she made a sudden stop. She found it, finally, where it had rolled into the back, close to the organ. She picked it up and tossed it into the trash, unaware of the small bug with the adhesive backing that had somehow become stuck on the container as it rolled around. As she filled the tank, she saw that the blue van was still parked where it had stopped.

Miss Blue Van must be having a meal, Cecile decided. Too bad, but Cecile didn't want to wait. She had miles to go.

Cloud saw the blue van turn into the rest area. He saw Cecile's van too, but didn't think much of it. He parked at the end of the lot farthest from the two vans and saw the blonde leaving the blue van. "Looks good as a blonde," he said, half aloud. Selma had told him about the hair color. He barely noticed the redhead crawling around in the back of the white Chevy van except to think that she had a cute figure when she'd trotted into the restaurant. And the organ had been covered with a quilt and could have been anything. He didn't notice the blip on his locator screen as the juice bottle hit the refuse can.

While Cecile was at the gas pumps, Cloud continued to wait. He should have used the facilities himself, he thought, but was wary of his quarry leaving, so he stayed put. More than once he had seen unpredictable things happen in similar situations. Luckily, his new black Honda was good on gas.

The woman from the blue van apparently had a regular meal, because she didn't emerge for half an hour. She wore dark glasses and her pale hair was long enough to partially obscure her face. Cloud started his car and drove slowly behind her to the gas pumps, where she stuffed the hose into the van and waited. He stayed out of sight and put gas in his own machine. Five minutes later Cloud was on the road again, two cars behind the blue van. This was easy. He would wait until they were on an empty section of the Jersey Turnpike, if such a thing could ever happen, or wait until dark. Then he would simply drive up to the van and blast the driver. Mission complete.

It was all so effortless, Cloud didn't even look at his locator screen until the blue van exited the turnpike at Moorestown, New Jersey. He followed the van off the road. Something must be wrong. Or maybe the nun was visiting relatives. Then he glanced down at the locator screen. The red light was still blinking, but north. Very north. What was going on here?

It didn't take Cloud long to realize he'd been buffaloed. The locator said loud and clear that it was back north somewhere. Way back north.

The nun must have ditched it, somehow. He continued to follow the blue van. It turned off the main road onto a very exclusive street lined with tall, redbrick homes set back, and for the most part surrounded by tall, privet hedges, or wrought-iron fences with electric gates. Traffic was minimal except for one Rolls-Royce and any number of Mercedes-

Benzes. It all felt highly irregular to Cloud, but he had heard the nun was rich. Apparently she was.

Finally the van stopped in front of a large gate, and the driver honked. Perhaps the woman had phoned ahead on a cell phone. That was likely because several people came running out of the big Tudor house. A ten-year-old boy pulled at the van door and the slender blond woman emerged.

Cloud was parked across the street in the black Honda, invisible behind the tinted window. He had his gun out and ready. He got his first good look at Sister Cecile in a blond wig.

It was not Sister Cecile.

26

WHILE Cloud wended his way back to I-95, Sister Cecile tore down the same road, intent on making it beyond Richmond by nightfall. She had studied her maps and come to the conclusion that it would be smart to avoid Baltimore and Washington, D.C., altogether, because there would be too much traffic. The route through Delaware looked like a pleasant alternative. She would leave I-95 and hop on Route 13 somewhere above Washington, D.C.

Three hours later Sister Cecile was wishing she hadn't. Route 13 had traffic lights, one after the other. It had slow drivers, and it had chicken trucks.

Nothing against chickens, Cecile thought as she rejoiced that the road had become two lanes going south instead of one. Her windows were down and she was relatively comfortable. She drove steadily south through the Delmarva Peninsula.

Suddenly she smelled an amazing smell. A terrible smell. Dead ahead was a huge truck filled with small crates of live chickens; hundreds and hundreds of chickens crammed into small spaces, yet open to the air. Half alive. It wouldn't have been so bad, but the air the chickens polluted was her air.

She stepped on the gas and roared past the thousands of chickens about to become nuggets, buffalo wings, and chicken patties, trying to keep her mind on the road ahead. A wind roared through just as she passed, bringing a gush of loose feathers blowing across and into the van. Both her front windows were half open.

Spitting feathers and gagging from the stench, Cecile hit the gas pedal hard. Finally she was safe.

Ten minutes later she slowed down and was marveling at the rolling, beautiful landscape, the fields of growing grain, the sky, almost dark now, and the soft air blowing in the open windows, when the chicken truck stormed up on her tail, shifted quickly to the left lane, and passed her in a gush of stench and feathers, then cut back in front of her. Suddenly the huge truck slowed unexpectedly and made a fast right into a chicken processing plant.

Cecile gaped in wonder; the only thing keeping her mouth from opening in awe was the fear of feathers. She made careful note of the factory. "Never eat that brand," she said. "Never."

"Never take Route 13," she said an hour later, stuck in traffic at a bridge. It was, she supposed, a lovely bridge with beautiful scenic vistas of Chesapeake Bay, the Potomac, and the Atlantic Ocean. Unfortunately it was dark and all the nun could see were headlights of cars behind her, taillights of cars ahead of her. Traffic stopped. She finally stepped out of the car and stood on the bridge and watched the currents below. The water swirled in cyclonic circles, dark, deep water, reminding her of the tides of hell. The traffic on the bridge didn't move.

Two hours later she found a motel on the outskirts of Newport News and tucked in for the night. Before she turned out the lights she called Sister Raphael. "I'm somewhere," she said.

"No problems?" Raphael asked. "That killer hasn't showed up?"

Cecile laughed lightly. "No. Thank God. We really fooled him. Paul rented a blue van, then we switched to a white van, so by the time he figured out I didn't take the airplane and was probably in a blue van, I was well out of there."

"Clever," Sister Raphael said.

"We thought so."

"Get some sleep. Where will you stop tomorrow?"

"Probably Georgia. I'll call you. I'll be stopping near Orlando, by the way, at Pearla Cruz's place. I've arranged to see her."

"When?"

"Day after tomorrow, around noon. How's Leonie doing?"

"Fine. Very quiet. I think she's annoyed with you for putting yourself in danger. You know how she is."

"Tell her I'm fine." Cecile paused. "Tell her I love her."

"I will. Good night, Cecile."

"Good night, Raphael."

Sister Raphael delivered the message to Leonie as soon as she hung up. Leonie was swimming in the dark, and pulled out of the pool when she heard Cecile had called.

"What's she doing going to Orlando?" Leonie asked. She sounded argumentative.

"Visiting Pearla Cruz. Mrs. Cruz is hoping to hire Cecile to find John. Or maybe it's Juan, as she calls him."

"Will she go to Epcot?"

"No."

"Sea World?"

"No."

"There's a lot of stuff in Orlando," Leonie said. "I'd like to go there. Why doesn't she take me there? I've never been there."

"Someday," Raphael said. "The Cruz place isn't in Orlando, anyway. It's thirty miles out somewhere."

"Where?"

"Minneola is the post box. It's a ranch. John Cruz raises cows."

"No kidding. What's the name of the ranch?" Leonie asked. She was out of the pool now, sitting on a lounge chair with her knees drawn up to her chest, entirely wrapped in a large towel. She didn't seem annoyed anymore, just inquisitive. She was always inquisitive.

"It's called Rancho Del Sol. Pearla told me that."

"Wow. Very romantic."

Raphael smiled at Leonie's idea of romance. So young, so much life ahead of her, the old nun thought. They should take her to Orlando one of these days. The child had been in Miami for a long time now and hadn't been there yet. "You'll be in Japan with your father in no time. I suppose that's first. Do you need to do any shopping?"

"I'd rather go to Orlando. Maybe Dad can come back with me and we can go. Good idea?"

"That would be nice."

"When will Cecile be at the Cruzes?" Leonie asked.

174

"Day after tomorrow, around noon. And then she'll come home."

"Okay."

Cloud was still on the road. He had thought back to every aspect of his travels and realized that the locator button had probably been left behind at the last rest stop. He pictured the scene, the blond woman in the blue van, the redhead in the white van. He thought about the redhead. Same size as Cecile, same features. He had a picture of Sister Cecile in a folder on the front seat and he took it out and studied it again. Nice face. Put some red hair on this person, and bingo, you had the woman in the white van. Shit.

Where was she now?

Probably almost in Virginia, he decided, and cursed a few more times. He would have to drive all night, because she was bound to stop somewhere. He would keep driving. He would lie in wait at some point ahead on the road.

While Sister Cecile slept the night away in Newport News, Jeffrey Cloud drove. At six in the morning he stopped for a two-hour nap in Rocky Mount, North Carolina, then continued, finally pulling off the road near Lumberton to plan his strategy. He sat in the car along the side of the highway and polished his gun for a few minutes. If he were really smart he would have stayed in Providence, flown down to Miami, and taken the good sister out right there. Everyone got shot in Miami. But there was one problem. He had already reported the nun dead. In fact, he had read the obituary in the *Miami Herald* himself. It would do his career no good at all if it came out that the nun hadn't really died. Business would go to hell. Word spread much too fast in his industry. A failure was like a death blow.

So he had to get the nun before she returned.

Police lights came up from behind. Cloud slipped his gun under the front seat and pulled out his road map. A North Carolina State Trooper car pulled up behind him, lights flashing. A cautious, uniformed man emerged and approached Cloud's window, hand resting gently on his gun. Cloud rolled down the window.

"Having some trouble?" the officer asked.

175

"Checking my map, sir," Cloud answered respectfully.

"Where you headed?"

"Well, I have a cousin in Purvis, down the road here." Cloud pointed on the map. "But I was thinking of picking him up something at South of the Border for a present. It's a little early to drop in on Harry."

"Purvis? What's your cousin's name?"

"Harry Moore," Cloud said, grabbing at a name.

"Harry Moore? What's he do?"

"Harry? Hell, he's a cop, just like you," Cloud said, hoping to get on the officer's good side. "I've been seeing these damn South of the Border signs for so long, I feel like if I don't stop there, I've done something wrong."

"They're counting on that," the policeman said. "Well, have a good visit."

"Thanks."

The officer walked slowly back to his flashing car, pausing just long enough to make a note of Jeffrey Cloud's license plate. In fact, the state trooper just happened to be from Purvis, North Carolina, and he knew every cop in that town. There was no cop named Harry Moore. The trooper made a call to headquarters to have a check run on the Rhode Island plate. Then he called his buddy in the South Carolina troopers.

By the time Jeffrey Cloud was eating a Mexiburger at South of the Border, the troopers in South Carolina were aware that a suspected hit man had arrived. An unmarked car pulled in to "Pedro's" and two state troopers, dressed in civilian clothes, slid out, ready to spend the day making sure the peace was kept in the border town.

176

27

" 'You never sausage a place,' " Sister Cecile read. Then, " 'Top Banana,' " a huge road sign that showed a twenty foot banana and a Mexican hat. " 'Pedro says,' " she read further. By the time Cecile had passed her fourteenth sign advertising Pedro's South of the Border, she decided she must stop. She could pick something up for Leonie.

Finally she spotted the huge caricature of a Mexican wearing a giant sombrero and the sign that said, "Keep yelling, kids." She was there.

Sister Cecile pulled onto the exit ramp, shot around and under I-95 and slowed down, driving the streets that wandered among South of the Border's playground, or whatever it was. Cecile wished desperately for Leonie to be with her. The girl would love this crazy place. Meanwhile she would just have to look around at all the possibilities, restaurants, rest rooms, and shops for herself.

Cloud spotted her the moment she parked the van. He was waiting outside the African Shop beside a couple of huge fake zebras. He had been there for some time, first sipping a drink, then standing and watching. When Cloud saw the white van pull in, he stepped back behind the giraffe. Two undercover state policemen standing and smoking by the Hot Taco Palace caught his sudden movement and went on alert.

Sister Cecile headed for the ladies' room. Cloud fell in behind. The troopers followed, joking softly about a group of large fake bulls.

Cloud knew that too many people were around for a good hit. He paused and stared into a shop window, inspecting dancing puppets. Cecile would have seen his reflection in the glass if she had looked.

The troopers climbed on the oversized plastic bulls.

Cloud felt under his jacket, a sport jacket that looked way too hot in the 87 degree temperature.

The troopers nodded to each other at the familiar motion. Their man had a gun. "The target has to be that redhead," the first trooper said. "He jumped the minute she walked by." The trooper sat tall on the black bull. He *was* tall, dark, and looked good sitting up there. His partner was short and light and balanced precariously on the other fake animal. The second trooper gave an almost invisible thumbs-up sign. Hands on their guns, they were ready.

Cecile came out of the rest room and looked around. So many places, so much sucker bait. She went into a large building that sold everything from postcards to Mexican bullwhips. Cloud started to follow, but stopped when a group of parents and children stepped in between him and Cecile. The troopers began to make vague cowboy noises from on top of the fake bulls.

"Yippie ki-yi!" the tall one chortled. His hand was wet on the gun.

"I'm a lone cowboy," the short one sang. They both kept their eyes on Cloud.

Sister Cecile couldn't believe all the stuff she could buy. Finally she purchased ten Mexican woven mats for Sister Germaine to put hot serving dishes on. She bought Sister Raphael some maracas, and for Leonie she chose a long, black bullwhip. Sister Cecile gave the whip a few practice cracks and discovered it worked just fine. Leonie would love it. For all the rest of the nuns she bought a large number of scented pods for them to put in their dresser drawers to make things smell nice. Everything cost less than forty dollars.

Sister Cecile emerged, immensely pleased with her purchases, her bags in hand. Leonie was going to love the bullwhip, something just dreadful enough to appeal to her twelve-year-old sensibilities. The nun looked around, wondering where to go next. Food would be good, preferably something Mexican, or maybe just a hot dog from the restaurant that showed a fifteen-foot-long hot dog out front.

Mexican, she decided, her hands reaching into her bag of purchases. The leather bullwhip had a softness that was extraordinary. Hopefully it wouldn't fall apart in a week. Leonie

178

would appreciate something verging on the dangerous. She put her hand around the end of it, pretending she was a cattle driver, like Leonie would.

Cloud pulled out his gun. He was only twenty feet away. Such an easy shot. He whistled, a bad habit he had, and the nun looked up.

Cloud.

The taller trooper had his gun out and aimed. "Don't shoot," the state trooper called, and Cloud swung around. Even the air stood still.

One shot from Cloud's mauser and the tall trooper toppled from the bull, crashing to the ground, blood pouring from his chest. Cloud was ready to take the second man when the leather whip streaked through the air and the slender black tip wrapped around his wrist. No cracking whiplash sound like Cecile had expected, but enough energy to send the deadly handgun spinning across the pavement.

The second trooper jumped down off the bull, panicked at seeing his partner fallen. He looked up, down, up again. He let off a wild shot at Cloud. Then another shot, sure Cloud was hit. The smaller trooper knelt beside his partner and watched the blood pool darkly on the cement.

Jeffrey Cloud ran. He knew better than to stay when the odds slipped out of his favor. Within fifteen seconds he was out of sight somewhere behind the bingo palace across the street. Within minutes he was in a T-shirt shop. He picked up a couple of shirts, put the red Donald Duck T-shirt on over his blue shirt, and donned a sombrero off the racks. He strolled out, being sure to pay for the hat, the shirt, and what was in his hand as he left. Five minutes later he drove sedately away in his black Honda. Nobody had seen the red blood drip from his left forearm where the trooper's bullet had gone through the fleshy part. Cloud had clamped his hand around it, then wrapped the second T-shirt tightly over the wound.

The young trooper, whose partner lay dying, had already completed a call for aid. Leaving Sister Cecile beside his partner, he raced from building to building, gun drawn, sending tourists into a flurry. He never saw Cloud. The trooper finally returned to Cecile and sank down beside her and his partner.

Cecile waited with him for an ambulance and backup. She

knelt beside the man and repeated the Our Father loudly and firmly with hopes that the dying man would somehow hear and join her in the words of praise, petition, and reparation. ". . . lead us not into temptation, but deliver us from evil. Amen," she said more softly.

"Why?" the young trooper beside her choked. "Why was he after you?"

"He was hired to kill me," Cecile said quietly. "It's a long story. I'm so sorry. So terribly sorry."

"Jeffrey Cloud," the small trooper said. "They made him on the interstate. He was waiting along the road."

"He's the one." Sister Cecile nodded, her hand wrapped around the wrist of the dying man. "Where's the ambulance?"

"I'll get him," the trooper said. "I'll get Cloud if it's the last thing I do."

"I think he's going to Miami," Cecile said.

"We'll need a statement from you," the trooper said grimly. His partner lay dying.

"I'll wait."

The wounded man died on the way to the hospital. His partner's name was Buddy Dilts. He spent a long time talking to Sister Cecile that afternoon. "I'm coming to Miami. I've got two weeks' leave coming," Buddy said firmly. "I'll get the bastard."

Sister Cecile studied the young man, so much in his element here in the South where his drawling accent matched the Spanish moss draped on the huge oak beside the state police barracks. Slow, mellow, too easily shocked by the unseen terror of a man like Cloud, Buddy Dilts had the soft sweet look of a man who wasn't old enough to see his partner die. Barely old enough to leave home. "Buddy, you could stay with my community. We have rooms we rent out sometimes. I don't think any of the sisters would mind too much."

"Community?" Buddy said, stretching the word halfway across the county. "Sisters?"

Cecile reached up and felt the stiff, unreal, red-haired wig she was still wearing. "The thing is, Buddy, I'm in charge of a home for retired nuns, the Sisters of Our Lady of Good Counsel. I'm a nun. I'm in disguise."

Buddy's pale blue eyes opened wide. He spoke slowly and deliberately. "You mean you are one of them Catholics?"

Sister Cecile spoke very seriously. "I'm one of them," she said.

"That's why you was praying," Buddy said in awe.

"I might have prayed anyway."

Buddy Dilts took a long, deep breath. "Well. I might just come and stay there anyway."

"Good," Cecile said. "We have a very good cook."

Jeffrey Cloud went south on the interstate and got off at the next exit. He knew an APB would be out on his black Honda wearing a Rhode Island license plate. Damn, but this blew everything. Now he was a wanted man, a cop killer; he could never get back to the wife and kids. The whole country would be after him now. The family was a bore, anyway. He'd had it with domestic life. He had money stashed. Those troopers had taken the numbers from his license plate, traced them. Jeffrey Cloud was history. There was no going back.

He drove down the road toward Dillon, South Carolina, and pulled over at a small shopping center. He removed the license plate from his Honda and tossed it into the car trunk, then strolled behind the buildings and saw a car that looked like it wasn't going anywhere for a while. He unscrewed the South Carolina license plate, moved back to his own car and put on the stolen plate. With a little luck it would be good until at least five o'clock, when the owner emerged from the auto parts store it was parked behind.

From his small bag beside him, Cloud pulled out a wig. The nun wasn't the only one with hairpieces, he thought wryly. He took off the red Donald Duck T-shirt, stuffed it under his blue button-down shirt, and shaped it into two immodest lumps, held in place by his undershirt. Thirty-six B, he thought, and slid on the fluffy blond wig, applied glossy pink lipstick, and drove back in the direction of the interstate. He wasn't about to quit. That nun was history. If she kept walking around, alive, he'd never get another job.

Cecile was ready to go. She and Buddy Dilts had completed the paperwork and sat in the lobby of the local police station

181

sipping black, sugarless coffee. The bitterness tasted good to Cecile.

"You could drive to Atlanta, then back around through the Panhandle," Buddy said to the nun. "It would be safe, but sure as heck take a lot longer."

"I have to be in Orlando by noon tomorrow," Cecile said. "I think I'll take my chances. I don't think Cloud's going to be hanging around the interstate. Not with what happened here today."

"You better believe it. Someone shoots a trooper, you know every cop from here to Miami's gonna be out on the road. Nobody's out there they won't see."

"Exactly," Cecile said. "So I think I'll head straight down."

"Pick up a different rental," Buddy suggested.

"No, I have this organ. I have to deliver it."

"I don't want you to get hurt." Buddy stared at the nun, his pale blue eyes sorrowful. Cecile had seen him cry when his partner lay dying. She held him, patted him on the back like a mother comforting a child.

"You're my good friend now, Buddy," Cecile said. "We've been through something, you and I. We're in this death together, and we'll find that man."

Buddy nodded. "I'll be in Miami in a couple days. I'm taking a leave of absence. I'll be there. Save that bastard for me."

"I'll do my best, Buddy." She was right, he had forgotten she was a nun again. He'd cleaned his language up briefly, but emotions were strong. His best friend had died. "I'm heading out now. You have my address, the telephone number, all that. I'll have a room ready for you at the community."

They shook hands solemnly and Cecile left, driving directly to a gas station to fill the van's tank.

Five minutes later she was back on I-95, driving south.

28

LEONIE called up the bus terminal and discovered it was possible to travel from Miami to Orlando by bus, but that she would have to arrange her own transportation to the bus terminal. That would require an expensive cab ride at a very early hour of the morning. The nuns were sure to figure out that she was up to something, because old nuns never slept. They prayed, they walked the community hallways all night, they ate, they watched television. She could never escape unseen.

Leonie approached Sister Raphael. "Can I stay at Zoe's tonight? She asked me to. We have a lot to talk about, because I'll be leaving soon."

Raphael was on the computer again, checking some stock prices. "You know how Sister Cecile feels about sleep-overs. You know what you did last time. Cecile was furious."

"I'm leaving for the whole summer! I have to see Zoe. Just this once? Please? This is really important, and she's gone. I mean, Cecile is gone. So why not?"

"I suppose," Raphael said. "You'll go directly to school with Zoe, then? Don't forget your uniform."

"Thanks, Raphael. I'll go exactly where I'm supposed to be." Leonie smiled innocently, bending her conscience freely. She was supposed to be with Sister Cecile in Orlando. That's where she was supposed to be, and that was where she was going to be. She had the address of the Cruzes' ranch, she had the bus route, she had quite a bit of money, because her dad always sent too much and Leonie had a tendency to hoard money, keeping it in a hollowed-out book in her shorts drawer.

Leonie showed up at Zoe Cabrall's with a small duffel bag

packed with what she would need for a trip to Sea World: a water bottle, a camera, a change of clothes, toothbrush, and so on. Zoe was surprised to see her friend at seven in the evening packed to stay for the night.

"How come?" Zoe asked.

"I have to leave here at four o'clock in the morning. The nuns never sleep. I figure your mom won't know because she leaves for work early and you don't usually see her. Right?"

"Well, sometimes. You'll have to leave a dummy in the spare bed. Something like you." Zoe paused and grinned. "Get it?"

"Isn't funny. How many times have you been to Orlando?"

"I don't know. Lots."

"Disney, Epcot, Universal Studios, Sea World, and there's a ton of other stuff too. You've seen everything, right?"

"Uh, yes. Are you sure you want to go? I mean, Disney World?"

"Sea World. Killer whales. Dolphins. I want to see all that. And Old Key West."

Zoe shook her head. "You really think Cecile will greet you with joy and take you where you want to go? I mean, she might just be furious."

"Then I'll go by myself," Leonie said stubbornly. "I have five hundred dollars."

"Okay, fine. I think you're crazy."

"I think I'm smart. We'll have to go to bed early so I can get up."

"That's really crazy," Zoe affirmed.

The twelve-year-old girls made it to bed by ten o'clock, giggled until eleven and drifted off to sleep. When Zoe's mom peeked in to check on them before she went to her job at Bell South early the following morning, she saw Zoe sleeping peacefully and a well-covered lump on the spare bed. She wondered how Leonie could sleep all covered up like that, but didn't want to wake them, so she tiptoed away.

When Zoe's mom tiptoed from her daughter's room, Leonie was on the bus for Orlando, sleeping peacefully in the semi-reclining seat as the huge air-conditioned machine rumbled its way up the road.

Sister Cecile was on the road as well. She had spent an uneasy and very short night in a motel near Jacksonville, then hit the road with one eye on the rearview mirror, another on the cars ahead. Buddy Dilts had described Cloud's black Honda to her, but neither of them expected that Cloud would still be driving it.

In fact he was, but now it wore a Florida plate stolen from a car in Orangedale. Cloud was still dressed as a woman, and no one had even appeared to notice the pale stubble on his face. The only human reaction he had received in his disguise was from a gas station employee somewhere near St. Augustine, who winked.

Cloud had no plans to stop in Orlando and see the sights, nor would he stop anywhere else. He would appear on Miami Beach and shoot the nun. It would be a very public execution, because after all this she deserved to go out with a big bang. And public executions were in. Then he would disappear, his reputation intact.

Jeffrey Cloud was so engrossed in his plan he didn't stop to think that he was losing his professionalism.

Leonie arrived in Orlando at nine-thirty in the morning. She gazed around the streets, wondering why the bus terminal wasn't just a little bit nicer. She stepped along, found a small diner and went in. Everyone spoke Spanish. She felt right at home, ordered ham and eggs in Spanish, and then asked the waiter how to get to Minneola.

It wasn't too difficult. A particular bus to the end of the line, another bus, and then she would be in Minneola.

Leonie's Mickey Mouse watch read eleven o'clock by the time she reached downtown Minneola, which, she decided immediately, was not a very exciting place to be. Leonie walked up to the first approachable human being that she saw, an elderly woman, at least elderly in Leonie's eyes. The woman was in her middle fifties.

"Could you tell me how to get to the Rancho Del Sol?"

"That's the Cruz place?"

"Right. John Cruz."

"Well, it's maybe ten miles down the road. You a friend of Carlito's?

Carlito? Who was that? Leonie wondered. "Yeah. I have to

get out there." She stood in the hot sun, her blond hair mussed and stringy. It had been growing and was long past her shoulders. Her blue eyes had circles under them because sleeping on a bus wasn't very restful. "How can I get out there?"

The woman looked thoughtful. "You're alone?"

"I came on a bus. I have to get there."

The woman looked puzzled, then worried. "I'm driving past the ranch. I could drop you off, maybe stop and see Pearla. I could give you a ride."

Leonie drew herself up straight. "I would appreciate that very much."

"I have to pick up some milk. Wait over there by that Buick, dear. I'll be right along."

Leonie waited by the Buick. She had lucked out, gotten a ride right to where Sister Cecile would be. Now all she had to do was face Sister Cecile and convince her to go to Sea World.

Leonie stood and watched the small town go by. Not too many cars, people who all looked vaguely familiar, nice small town people. What if Cecile should drive this way? Leonie edged around behind the Buick and for the first time had a thought that maybe this whole expedition wasn't such a good idea. She could be back in Miami by suppertime.

No. She would see it through. It wasn't just Sea World, or any of that stuff in Orlando. This trip was about Sister Cecile, her nun. Someone was trying to kill Cecile, and she wanted to prevent that. Somehow.

A half hour later Mrs. Bricklier, as she introduced herself, turned off the main road and headed down the half-mile drive to the ranch. Leonie gazed wide-eyed at the small cattle that grazed alongside the road.

"Spots," she said. "Cows with spots. Aren't they cute?"

"Cute, yes. John developed an entirely new breed that apparently is revolutionizing the capabilities of the less prosperous farmers. These little cows can live anywhere."

Leonie nodded and clenched her fists in excitement. She was getting closer and closer.

Before they pulled up to the classic white farmhouse surrounded by big live oaks, Mrs. Bricklier stopped the car.

"There's Carlito. I'll drop you off and go see Pearla for a few minutes."

"Fine. Thanks an awful lot. I really appreciate this." Leonie jumped out of the car and stared in the direction Mrs. Bricklier had indicated. Carlito was a boy about her own size. A boy? Why couldn't he be a girl? Girls understood things.

"Carlito!" she called, crossing her fingers.

The boy looked up. He was slim and tawny-skinned, slightly taller than she was. Cute, Leonie thought as she drew near, but not cute the way those cows were. Not that kind of cute at all. Really cute.

Leonie came closer. "I'm supposed to be your friend," she said.

"Like, you're really my enemy?" He eyed her disdainfully, but he was curious.

Leonie dropped her bag on the dusty earth. "Well, Sister Cecile is coming here today, and I had to see her. I've never been in Orlando."

The boy stepped closer. He didn't know what this was about, but he did know his dad was gone and his mother was going crazy. "My name is Carl," he said. "And this is about my father, isn't it?"

Leonie nodded. "I guess it is."

"Where is he?"

"We don't know, but someone's trying to kill Cecile. Is it him?"

Carl suddenly looked frightened. "They said that. My father never killed anyone. He told me that. He wouldn't kill this nun either."

"What did he tell you? Why?" Leonie felt a thump in her chest, like she had just discovered something new. "Carl, we have to talk. My name is Leonie."

Carl looked at Leonie, then hesitantly he put out his hand and they shook like adults. "Come with me to the barn. We can talk."

From the steps of the big white farmhouse Pearla Cruz and Jane Bricklier watched the two children walking toward the barn. Their heads were down and they were talking earnestly. Carl was carrying Leonie's bag.

"I guess they do know each other," Pearla said. "I never knew. Do you suppose Carlito has a girlfriend?"

"He's twelve? That's when it all begins." Jane sighed.

"Oh, my God, what am I going to do? She's very pretty. Very blond."

"You tell John it's time for a man-to-man talk with that son of his, that's all," Jane said.

Pearla's worried looked became even more intense. She swallowed hard. "Yes, that's a good idea."

"Well, I've got to run. I have some milk in the car. Just wanted to make sure she wasn't some problem child."

"No, I'm sure everything is fine. Thanks, Jane."

Carl and Leonie hadn't emerged from the barn when Sister Cecile pulled in. They didn't see the big Chevy van, or Sister Cecile, dressed in the white habit of her order and with hair that was her own.

After a long talk about everything, Carl wanted to show Leonie what was new in cattle breeding, and Leonie really wanted to see. "Your father figured out that smaller was better?" she asked.

"Not exactly, but for certain purposes, yes. These little cows give a huge amount of milk fat, and they can survive on crummy stuff like vines. A lot of countries with small farmers have been buying them to help the independent small farmers have better lives." Carl was proud and knowledgeable. Leonie was impressed.

"I'd like a cow," Leonie said. "But my dad is never in one place for very long. I have to go to Japan and meet him very soon. I'll be there all summer."

"That's really cool."

"You think?"

"I'd die to go there," Carl said. "Wanna see my very own cow?"

"You really have a cow?"

"Come on."

Meanwhile, Sister Cecile and Pearla sat in John's study and talked.

"He said or did nothing to indicate why he was leaving?" Cecile asked.

"Nothing at all." Pearla fingered the paperweight on John's desk; a glass orb with daisies inside. "Of course the letter, I showed you the letter he sent me." She held it up, a wrinkled piece of paper that she had cried over enough to smudge the ink. "He says a problem came up. A misunderstanding, something he didn't do. So why should he leave? What could have made him go? I didn't do anything. Nothing is different."

"No death threats," Cecile mused, thinking of her own problems.

"Unless he kept it all a secret. He's like that. There was something in the past, before I met him. And he changed his name."

"He did. What was it?"

"Juan Calderon."

"Not Juan Caldo?"

Pearla looked up. "You mentioned that name to me before. Who's that?"

"It's the reason your husband hired me in the first place. He wanted to clear this man. Caldo was a convicted murderer, apparently innocent, at least according to your husband. I've been looking into it." Cecile examined the woman across from her. Pearla looked haggard from lack of sleep, but was still quite beautiful. Cecile didn't know that the woman hadn't eaten more than a nibble since her husband had vanished, nor that she had lost fifteen pounds. Cecile's problem was whether she should take on John Cruz's wife's case. Would it be a conflict of interest? She had already breached the confidentiality of the case by mentioning Juan Caldo at all. And now it seemed highly possible that Juan Caldo was in fact John Cruz. Should she tell Pearla?

"I will pay you to find Juan," Pearla said firmly. "I will pay anything."

"Your husband sent me a packet of money to continue his own case. He said he would send more."

"From where?" A light of hope entered Pearla's eyes.

"Postmarked Atlanta. That's no help."

"No. I will pay you more to find him."

"I'll look, but Pearla, your husband has first claim on my time. I feel I'm close to solving the case he hired me for. I've

189

unearthed a whole can of worms and have to see it through. I could begin working for you when this is over. If your interests combine, I can still only charge one of you for my time."

"Whatever. I have the cashier's check already here for you." Pearla pushed it across the desk. "Take it. Cash it. Do what you can. I have a packet of everything that could help, Juan's credit card numbers, things like that. Even some photographs."

"All right," Cecile agreed. "And if he should come back, I'll return the money."

Pearla smiled. "That's acceptable."

"Is there anything," Cecile said, fingering the cashier's check absently, "any unusual thing you noticed that might give me a clue as to where he went? Think of the character of this man. What was outstanding about him that is unusual? Something, perhaps, so strong he can't hide it."

Pearla Cruz pushed some papers back and forth on the desk, then swiveled her chair around and stared out the window. A small group of cattle was just visible across a distant pasture. "The animals, of course. No man ever loved animals like my Juan." Pearla turned her chair back. "Something new. He was reading about pigs."

"Pigs?"

"I noticed when I looked through his things. Articles on pigs, the wild pigs, the domestic pigs. He never read about those before."

"I'll keep that in mind," Cecile said. "And before I go I'll make a list of ways you can begin to trace him yourself. So much is public record these days. Maybe you can find out if he took a plane from Atlanta. We know he was in Atlanta. Maybe you can discover if he booked a flight from there. I'll explain how to begin the trace. Then we won't lose time while I'm working on clearing his name."

"I'll do anything."

Cecile's eyes drifted out the window to where cattle grazed. Cecile saw a boy and a girl walking across a stretch of green. A blond girl and a dark-haired boy. The boy was swinging a duffel bag around in circles. "You have children?"

"Oh yes, three," Pearla said proudly. "My oldest stayed home from school today. He's concerned about his father, but he claimed it was a stomachache. His friend arrived today. I think he has a girlfriend. He must have met her in Orlando." Pearla sound vaguely shocked at the implication. "Out there." She gestured out the window.

"That girl," Cecile said, staring at the slender blonde, "looks very familiar. Who is she?"

"I don't know," Pearla said helplessly. "I really don't know where he met her. She just arrived out of nowhere."

Sister Cecile rose from her chair and hurried to the window. "I think I know that girl. I know exactly where she came from."

29

Leonie and Carl came into the big farmhouse, grinning. They had similar grins, perfect white teeth, the exact amount of smile showing, the same crinkle to the eyes. Brown eyes and blue eyes. They both looked very happy.

Sister Cecile came out of the office first and saw them in the big hall. "Hello, Leonie."

"Oh, hi, Cecile. This is my friend, Carl."

Cecile stared at the boy. He looked stubborn, the way Paul had looked at that age, and vaguely protective of the blonde at his side. Somehow Leonie and this boy had established a relationship that meant something. It was like the first time she had gone to the vegetable garden with Paul and talked about something so incredibly important, which she couldn't to this day remember. "Hello, Carl," Cecile said.

Pearla stepped out. Carl spoke. "Hi, Mom, this is my friend, Leonie."

Pearla nodded. Nobody spoke for a moment.

"I took a bus down," Leonie said. "And Carl and I figured out why his dad split."

Carl spoke quickly, quietly. "Some people at the breeders' conference thought Dad was a killer. They thought he was someone else."

"Or maybe he was the man, but he was never the killer." Leonie shuffled her feet. "Because Carl's dad has to be the man he hired you to prove innocent, Cecile. That man must be him. So that means he's really innocent. There are two Juans."

"But that he really escaped from jail," Carl put in. "Dad broke out of jail," he said proudly.

Carl's mother looked confused. "What in the world are you two talking about?"

"Let's sit down and sort this out," Cecile said. She knew exactly what the twelve-year-olds were saying. It didn't solve anything, it just explained why John Cruz had vanished.

They all sat in the front parlor, a well-decorated room that was rarely used. It held clean furniture and western art, a Remington copy and some western landscape watercolors. "Now, Carl, you say someone knew your father was a killer?" Cecile asked.

"I heard them talking," Carl said. "They thought Dad looked exactly like this man, Juan Caldo."

"His brother, maybe?" Pearla asked hopefully.

Cecile shook her head. "John hired me to clear this man. He said he was innocent. He. Himself or Juan Caldo, or whoever he is. He would not have hired me if he had been guilty."

Meanwhile the two little girls showed Leonie how to build block towers, a skill she already possessed. Carl joined in the massive construction, sending his little sisters into squeals of laughter, while Cecile told Pearla everything about Juan Caldo, John Cruz, and the missing convicted murderer.

"So, you must prove him innocent, and then find him," Pearla said.

"Yes."

They sat in the parlor, looking at each other, then stared outside through the lacy curtains at the fields beyond. "Juan will miss this place. He must be so unhappy." Pearla made a move to stand. "You will join us for dinner."

They ate a delicious supper of grilled beef, potatoes, and a huge salad. Pearla ate next to nothing. "I can't eat," she informed Cecile. "Until Juan is home."

"I understand," Cecile said. "I'll do my best. I think I'm very close."

"We have spare rooms. You can stay here tonight," Pearla said.

"No. Leonie and I have business, things to discuss. We have to go."

"Carl wants to come to Miami Beach with us," Leonie said. "Can I, Mom?"

"You have school. One week left," his mother said.

"And, you, Leonie, have the same. Then you're going to Japan." Cecile looked stern.

"I'm being transported to the penal colonies," Leonie said very quietly.

"You're going to be with your father," Cecile reminded her.

Leonie looked at Carl and made a face, a "Didn't I tell you?" sort of face. "I do want to see Dad," she said piously. "Can Carl come up at the end of summer?"

"Please, Ma? I've never been to Miami."

Pearla looked bemused. "Maybe," she said.

"That means yes," Carl said to Leonie.

"Yes," Leonie said triumphantly, and Carl's two little sisters giggled.

"Meanwhile, Leonie, we have some talking to do," Sister Cecile said with a glint in her eye.

Leonie and Sister Cecile left shortly after dinner with promises to keep in touch. Sister Cecile pulled the van slowly down the long driveway and made a left, heading back toward Minneola. Leonie didn't say a word.

"Tell me," Cecile said.

"Carl is very smart. He knew why his father left, but he didn't want to tell his mom because he didn't want to hurt her."

"I see."

"Smart, right?"

"Leonie, how did you get here? *Why* did you come here?"

Leonie looked out the van window at the vast fields that ended somewhere in the evening light where the earth met the sky. "Cows are really neat. Carl has his own cow."

"Answer me."

"I was afraid," Leonie said. "You almost got killed again. I had to be there. So I came. I took buses. I stayed at Zoe's last night and left really early this morning. I got up at four-thirty."

Sister Cecile felt a surge of affection, no, more than that, it was like a tidal wave of love for this girl who had taken her into her young life, who actually got up really, really early to protect her from the demons. "God takes care of me, Leonie," she choked out. "I pray. I have faith. I'm fine."

"Right," Leonie mumbled. "Besides, I really want to see Sea World."

"Oh."

"Can we? Stay in Orlando tonight, go tomorrow? Please?"

"I should be mad at you, Leonie. You should be punished. You can't just run off and do things on your own. It isn't safe. It isn't right!"

"Can Carl come with us?"

"We have to find a motel, and I'll call Raphael right away so she won't worry," Cecile said. It was hopeless, this motherhood business. Impossible.

Carl took another day off from school and went to Sea World with Leonie and Sister Cecile. They stood in long lines and saw Wild Arctic, they watched Shamu, were splashed by the amazing killer whales, and stumbled their way through Pacific Point, marveling at the sea lions and the seals. "I want a manatee," Leonie said.

"When we grow up we can get a place along one of those big canals and maybe have one as a pet," Carl said.

We? Did that young man say *we*? Sister Cecile asked herself. What was he talking about?

"But I still want to raise animals like my dad," Carl continued. "Maybe pigs. Dad was talking a lot about pigs lately."

"Let's do Key West," Leonie said, giving Cecile another jolt, but Key West was here, the nun realized, another bit of fantasy made better than the real thing. Except it really wasn't better.

"My feet hurt," Cecile said finally. "Let's quit. Are you guys ready? We have a long drive ahead of us."

"How about we stay another night and go to Universal Studios tomorrow," Leonie said.

"It's cool," Carl said.

"No." Sister Cecile felt good. No one had tried to kill her all day. The children were wonderful, but enough was enough. It was time to return to real life, and the children both heard the firmness in her "No."

Leonie shrugged. "I guess that's it."

They ate supper in one of the junk food emporiums, then Cecile delivered Carl to his home. She backed out quickly.

195

"We have a long drive to Miami. I'll call you as soon as I know anything," she told Pearla, and they left.

Cecile pushed the van to a fast seventy miles an hour once they got back on the highway. Leonie slid the seat back and was sound asleep within moments of their getting on the big road. It had been a long day. They were both still alive. Sister Cecile began to hum.

30

MARIE, the community housekeeper, called her husband and several of his friends to help unload the organ and move it into the small nuns' chapel. This was all accomplished while Sister Cecile and the other nuns attended Mass at St. Patrick's on the Beach. All the nuns offered their Mass for the repose of Sister Linda's soul.

Cecile was very circumspect about the tragedy because, like the folks she had left behind in Providence, she figured the less said the better. Sister Linda's death was explained to be from natural causes, because, as Cecile rationalized to herself afterward, it was very natural for Jimmy Gigliardi to shoot people. She didn't mention how a state trooper had died in her arms. The old nuns lived close enough to death as it was. Sister Cecile prayed alone for Buddy Dilts's partner.

After a breakfast of blueberry pancakes, Sister Raphael took the Ford Explorer and accompanied Sister Cecile to the car rental agency where she returned the white van she had driven from Providence. Raphael was unnaturally quiet all morning, but finally she spoke when the two nuns were together in the Explorer, with Cecile driving them back from the car agency on Le Jeune Road.

"Linda's death," Raphael began. "Tell me about it."

"You don't want to know."

"That bad?"

"Her family was Family," Cecile said.

"I know."

They were at a long red light, and Cecile took a moment to stare out at Miami. Through the tinted windows and the crisp air-conditioning, the city resembled a garden with rows of flowering trees, palms, circling sea birds. The temperature outside was 87 degrees, and the humidity was seventy percent. "Providence is air-conditioned outside," Cecile said. "Paul claims the town is a dump. I liked it. Except for a few problems."

"I miss the Northeast," Raphael agreed. "But I love it here. Did anyone try to kill you there too?"

Cecile nodded and drove through the green light. "Twice."

"I prayed all the time you were gone. And then Leonie took off. Of course, nobody knew she was gone. She was supposed to be at Zoe's."

"The prayers worked. I guess we'd better find the real killer. Then find Juan, or John. Whoever he is."

"And hope Cloud doesn't find you first."

"Keep praying, Raphael."

"Adoremus Te Domine," Sister Raphael said, and blessed herself.

Jeffrey Cloud was no more. The black Honda was gone, left behind at a motel near Bunnell, Florida, not far from Daytona Beach. The blond floozie he had been rented a room, and emerged the following morning as a young man named Davis West. Cloud, now Davis, had bleached, platinum hair and wore heavy sunglasses. He caught a bus to Daytona to distance himself from the Honda.

From Daytona the blond man carrying a driver's license in the name of Davis West took a bus to Miami. Cloud was too smart to steal another car right where he left his old one. He could wait. Buses were cool. Besides, in Miami cars were stolen every day and loaded on boats bound for points south. He could pick up a car when he needed one. It didn't much matter, because he had a lot of money in an account located in a bank in Barbados. The wife he had left behind in Providence would be happy to see the last of him. No more beatings, no more fear for that woman, who, in fact, was not his wife at all. And he had left her some money in their joint account, enough to see her through the year. Cloud smirked as he thought of her pleasure that he was gone. When the police came to his house with a warrant for his arrest, she would laugh and know he was history.

Cloud registered at the New Glasgow Hotel on Miami

Beach under his new persona. He spent the first day buying some clothes and strolling on the beach. He thought he looked cool as a blond, but he missed the ponytail. Now he needed a deep tan.

He figured the nun was back in Miami by now. Rumors that she was alive would be circulating all too soon. He needed to get in touch with the person who hired him before the rumors jeopardized his future employability, and to explain a few things, in particular why the woman he'd been hired to kill, and had been paid to kill, was still alive.

Then he would kill Sister Cecile.

Sister Cecile was back on the job Monday morning, poring over her notes, running through ideas about all the people who had known Juan Caldo, people she had contacted. Ron Dubaker, the notary whose wife, she noted carefully, was named Graciella; then Nestor Lezo, who was killed too, leaving his widow, Mirtha, and that beautiful daughter, Rita Lezo. Then there was the Reverend Rubin Gonzalez, called Ruby, his cigar-selling wife Daisy, and their stunning daughter. Those were the only people she had talked with. It didn't take many brains to conclude that one of them hired Cloud. These were the players.

All the men wanted Victor Torres dead. That made sense. He was a Romeo who went after all the women. What about the women? Several women had been made pregnant, Cecile recalled, and she thought back to the people involved. Two beautiful daughters born close to the same time, shortly after the time of the killing. Cecile pictured Mirtha's daughter Rita in her mind, then thought of the photograph Daisy had showed her of the Gonzalez daughter. Two dark-haired beauties with brilliant smiles. They could be sisters.

Well, maybe half sisters.

Now that was an interesting thought.

What if, Cecile asked herself, Mirtha and Daisy had both been pregnant, and Victor Torres had been the man involved? The girls really did look alike. That would have meant two husbands would both have a motive for murder, Nestor Lezo and Ruby Gonzalez. Victor Torres got around, that was an established fact.

Today, Cecile decided, she would revisit the Reverend Ruby Gonzalez. He would be busy with his school, but maybe he could give her a few moments. Maybe she could catch him thinking she was dead, shock him, or shock something out of him.

Of course, she would wear that vest. It had worked twice and was showing some dents, little pockmarks in the amazing fabric. She would have to call Jim and thank him one more time. She would do that later. He wouldn't be too happy about the latest attempts on her life.

The drive to West Dade was hot and monotonous. Even with good air-conditioning the car felt uncomfortable, although when she stepped outside and met the blast of reality in the schoolyard where Reverend Ruby presided, it felt like a descent into hell.

Once again Cecile walked into the small office building, and once again the reverend sat behind a pile of books. He was alone.

"Good morning," Cecile said.

Ruby looked up with a start. He definitely looked surprised, but was that abnormal? He must have heard she was dead, because she had supposedly died not far from his wife's business.

"Praise the Lord!" Ruby jumped out of his chair and came forward, grabbing Cecile's fingers with both of his hands. "God be praised!"

Ruby stared into her eyes, speechless except for invocations to the Lord. Cecile answered in kind. "God was good to me. I'm alive."

"Sit down, sit down. Tell me. My wife was sure you had gone to your eternal reward. I can't believe this! The Lord in all His glory has been good to you!"

"He certainly has." Cecile sat down, grinning. Ruby appeared to be truly happy that she was alive. It was one mark in his favor. He slipped to number two on Cecile's list of suspects. "Your wife was so kind to me, and you too, Reverend. I came back to go over a few things."

"Daisy swore you were dead." Ruby shook his head and wiped a bead of sweat from his chin. The cluttered office was warm in spite of the clanking air conditioner struggling from a hole in the wall.

"It was close, but here I am. I'm still investigating. There were some points that needed clarification."

"I'll help you. You, dear Sister, have God's favor resting on you, a woman with the true resiliency of Lazarus. I'll tell you everything you want to know."

Cecile had doubts about that. "I thought I'd start with your wife."

Ruby paled ever so slightly. "A good woman," he said as though he had said it a few times too many.

"Lovely woman. I saw a picture of your beautiful daughter. What's her name?"

"Liliana. We call her Lilly. She's a third year student in college. Very bright."

"Your wife was pregnant at the time of Victor Torres's death. So was Mirtha Lezo. I thought that was an interesting coincidence."

"My wife was three months ahead of Mirtha," Ruby said slowly, his eyes half closed. He wasn't so eager to talk, suddenly.

"She was a good wife to you, then?"

"My wife is wonderful. She runs her own business. Without Daisy's support this school couldn't make it."

Could she ask Ruby if Victor was the father of his child? No. How about asking him if he beat his wife? No. "Could you tell me about her business?"

"You should ask her."

"Cigars. Very profitable, right?"

"Extremely."

Sister Cecile pulled out the cigar band she had borrowed from Leonie early that morning. "This is one of hers?"

Ruby took the band with the beautiful gold design. "Perhaps. I don't know for sure."

"Now, I don't really care about cigars," Cecile said, "but I believe this band is generally found on a Cuban cigar. It occurred to me that either Daisy was using Cuban bands for her cigars, or selling authentic Cuban cigars."

"Not legal, either way," Ruby said.

"Not legal."

201

"Or is it illegal for our government to forbid trade of an innocuous item?" Ruby asked.

"Depending on whom you ask," Cecile said. "Some people feel cigars are rather noxious." She didn't smile; she was deadly serious. Cigars smuggled from Cuba could be worth more on the black market than drugs.

"What do you care? Who pays you?" Ruby asked.

"I don't care, really. I won't pursue this point, Ruby."

"What is your point, then?" He sat back in his chair and folded his arms in a defensive posture.

"It seemed the least difficult of my thoughts," Cecile said quietly.

"I see." He pushed his chair back farther. "You're thinking murder, of course. What motive would she have?"

"Daisy? I was thinking about you." Cecile mimicked his posture, folding her arms over her chest, feeling the heavy security of the Kevlar vest.

"Well, no more motive than most." He smiled grimly. "Why don't you go away, leave us alone. We've been happy. We have a life of love and peace in the Lord now. I'm done with my anger. The Lord has been my salvation. Praise the Lord."

"There's another family out there, a very sad family who lives in injustice."

"I have nothing to say beyond the fact that I didn't kill Victor. I deal with my family, my children." He spread his hands to encompass the school grounds and all they meant. "Leave us alone. Go away."

"Nothing more?" Cecile asked. "You can't tell me anything else?"

"No."

Cecile thanked him and walked out the door. He didn't try to kill her. He didn't pull a shotgun from behind that messy desk and blast her from the back. Maybe Ruby was not the killer. Or maybe he was just waiting for Cloud to do it.

Cecile climbed into the Explorer and turned on the ignition. She drummed her fingers on the steering wheel and kept an eye open for any movement in the bushes. She could go talk to Daisy, she could find the *notario*, Ron Dubaker, or she could go back to Mirtha Lezo's for a visit.

Dubaker. He had the gun collection and she wanted to see it, wanted very much to see the gun, at least the twin of the gun, that had killed Victor Torres.

Sister Cecile drove to the mall where Dubaker had his office. She dialed his number from a pay phone as she stood on the simmering sidewalk, watching crows in the air, bubble gum puddling on the sidewalk, and the stunning people who lived in West Dade, home to more Cubans than Havana held, more Colombians than in Calle, perhaps more Nicaraguans than in half that country.

Cecile heard Olga say, *"Dubaker Notario, un momento, por favor."*

"It's Sister Cecile," Cecile said, but she was already on hold. She stood in the sunlight that streaked in sideways, cooking her well until Olga's voice came back.

"Diga me."

"It's Sister Cecile. I wanted to speak to Mr. Dubaker about seeing his gun collection."

"Hold please."

"Sister Cecile!" The bubbling voice sounded glad to hear from her, unsurprised that she was alive. Perhaps Ron had never known she was dead. Could this be an innocent man? "You want to see the guns? Tonight. I have to call my wife and confirm, but maybe you could stop by later this evening. How's everything going? Any luck with the missing murderer?"

He sounded too ebullient to be true. Cecile answered simply, showing little emotion. "Not much progress, I'm sorry to say. But I would like to see the gun. Tonight would be fine. Should I call you back to confirm?"

"Why don't I give you a ring. You're in your office?"

Cecile looked around the vast mall parking lot. "No. Can I call you back?"

"Give me half an hour to reach my wife."

"I'll do that. Thanks, Ron."

Cecile went back to the car and headed for Miami Beach. She had paperwork to deal with, the organ to inspect, the air-conditioning problem to confront. And maybe a killer to avoid. After all, she had just spread the word that Cloud failed.

The worst thing, she realized, not for the first time, as she

203

joined the traffic heading back toward the center of Miami, was the fact that she had gone all the way to Providence, Rhode Island, to find out who had hired Cloud to kill her, and had done nothing but stir up a hornets' nest and send Sister Linda off to her eternal reward. And poor Buddy's partner. Somewhere along the congested road to Miami Beach, Sister Cecile began to cry for the loss of two good people. She sniffled and wiped her eyes, but the tears didn't stop. Sometimes it was good to be stuck in traffic. There was so little time to mourn.

31

JUAN Calderon landed in Mexico City. He bought a second-hand truck. It was easy. He had an American passport and a lot of cash and Spanish was his native language. He spoke slowly, trying to hide the Cuban accent. Not that it mattered. He was an American citizen as far as the Mexicans were concerned. Most Americans rented cars, but he had no difficulty buying one. He was able to register it properly and even get it insured for a modest sum. He wanted to have a life here, properly establish himself, and maybe, in a while, when things settled down, he could call for his wife to come to Mexico. Dear Pearla and the children could have a good life here. But first he had to make that life happen.

The roads leading away from Mexico City were tortuous and steep. Juan headed down from the high altitude to the lowlands along the west coast. The roads got worse, then better. He studied the terrain, looking, feeling, getting a sense of the land, looking for the perfect parcel. He wanted ten or twenty acres, enough land to raise pigs, to begin the experimental breeding program that he had been thinking about, plus he needed space to breathe. His plan was to develop small pigs, not the big, hungry porkers that the American farmers mass-produced, but a small breed that would do well in a small farmer's backyard, supplying good nutrition, bacon and ribs and barbecues for festivals.

Juan found his land near the town of Las Cañas. It was close to the Rio Balsas, a place where the vast river spread for miles before it dumped into the Pacific Ocean. The land was high, so when floods came, the pigs wouldn't drown. Electricity didn't extend that far into the hills, but the small house with a wood-burning stove had a well for water and an electric generator that ran on gasoline to provide all the power he needed. The owner, an old man who lived alone down the road, said it had been rented and farmed for a few years by marijuana planters, and much good furniture and comforts had been brought in. "The *policia* removed the renters and the place has been empty two years now," he said.

The owner's name was Manuel Vargas. He not only agreed to sell John Cruz, now Juan Calderon, the land for the sum of fifteen thousand dollars, but also agreed to help him with the animals.

Juan arranged the purchase in Las Cañas, utilizing a Mexican lawyer to make things go smoothly. He paid a substantial bribe to the town clerk to avoid unnecessary paperwork, and within a week was the owner of twenty acres and a small house. He put the property in his wife's name, Pearla Cruz.

Juan began scouring the countryside to assess the native pigs. He planned to crossbreed the best of the local swine with a Vietnamese potbellied pig, a small animal used as a house pet in some Miami homes. Later he could try other combinations that he had studied, perhaps one of the big American porkers with a smaller Mexican hog. Each night he returned to the tiny farm and the equally small house, which he named Casa Linda. He framed a picture of his wife and children and set it on the dresser. Each night before he went to bed he wrote a letter to Pearla that he never mailed. He collected the letters in an empty cigar box he found in the living room. Someday she would read them all.

Pearla thought about Juan every night as well. She had done all she could by hiring that private detective. Following Sister Cecile's advice and instructions, she even checked into information available from the airport in Atlanta. She discovered that a Juan Calderon had flown to Chicago on a minor airline, but at that point she lost the trail. Juan could have gone anywhere.

Pearla was ecstatic that she had traced her husband as far as Chicago. He was running under the name of Juan Calderon. That meant he was alive and living somewhere. She had done something else, not suggested by the nun. Very carefully she went about the house and barns with bottles of spray cleaner and rough rags. She wiped clean every surface that Juan might

206

have touched. She polished all his colognes, his shaving cream, everything from the inside of the bathroom medicine cabinet to the jar of Bag Balm in the barn. There was not to be a single fingerprint left in the entire place that could be traced to a convicted murderer who had escaped from jail almost twenty years ago.

The last thing she cleaned was a gas can in the garage. Mike Baxter, Juan's partner, now running everything, saw her walking across the broad front yard, spray cleaner and rag in hand. "What's going on?" he asked.

Pearla looked at the young man. "You've done so well, Mike. I should tell you what this is about."

"I wish you would." He looked tired, a little bit annoyed. The farm was bringing in record profits. Mike had just completed a deal begun by Juan a month before. Pearla could see how he wanted to share the victory with Juan.

"Come on, we will have coffee. I will tell you."

They sat in the kitchen and Pearla told Mike the entire story. Mike slammed his fist down on the table, spilling coffee in a dark puddle. "John is no killer."

"No," Pearla said. "But he's gone."

"What can I do?" Mike asked.

"We continue our life. I have hired a private detective. Juan already hired her to clear his name, so she is doing that first. Then she will find him and he can come home and be free of the past. Meanwhile she has told me how to begin to trace him. Listen to what I know."

Sister Cecile joined the community for dinner. Sister Germaine served a concoction of chicken strips layered with finely chopped veggies and mild green chilies inside of soft tortillas. They were covered with a bubbling hot cheese sauce. A huge green salad dominated the center of the table. The community devoured massive amounts of the food. Sister Germaine had managed to integrate her French cooking style well with the South Florida cuisine, and everyone applauded her. Tomorrow, however, was Wednesday, and most of the community looked forward to the fast. The Order of Our Lady of Good Counsel taught that God should be praised both in plenty and restraint.

"*Alors, merci. Après la, nous avons tres leches* for dessert."
Sister Germaine smiled, managing to combine three languages into one sentence as well as she combined the ways to praise God.

"*Tres leches* is the greatest dessert yet," Leonie said. "I had that at Zoe's." Leonie was clearly happy today. She had spoken with Carl on the telephone and they had made big plans for the future. He was definitely coming to Miami at the end of August, and they had discovered they were both online. They had already sent their first e-mail to each other.

Sister Cecile began eating the dessert, a soft, moist sponge cake layered with cream topped with whipped cream and a cherry. "I have to go out, Leonie," she said. "I have an appointment to go to someone's house. You know you have to stay in and do your homework."

"Can I come?"

"No. I'm going to look at Nestor Lezo's gun collection. You'd be bored. And don't you have homework?"

"No. I did it all in school. Did you know that I love gun collections?"

"Well, it might be dangerous. Ron Dubaker is a suspect."

From the distance a telephone rang. Sister Raphael got up from her chair and went in to pick up on the kitchen phone. She came back a moment later. "Cecile, it's for you. Vincent Mascapone."

"Oh!" Cecile jumped up and ran for the kitchen. Raphael took her seat on the other side of Leonie.

"Who?" Leonie asked.

"Sister Linda's brother," Raphael said, taking a bite of *tres leches*.

In the kitchen, Sister Cecile swallowed her bite of dessert, then said, "Hello."

Vinny's rough voice came through as though he were right there in the nuns' kitchen. "Aye, Sister, I talked with some people here. I got you some information."

"That's wonderful, Vinny," Cecile said. "What is it?"

"I talked to the wife, or whatever, Cloud's woman. He's gone for good, cops come around with a warrant. I heard all about it. So I went over to see the wife. She was glad the man was gone. Told me some stories you don't wanna hear."

"I'm sure."

"So when the call came in to hire him—she thinks it was the call, anyway—it was a woman. This was after the answering service, see. They make the first contact, then it's the real thing."

"I understand. A woman who hired Cloud." Cecile felt a chill. "How does the wife know?"

"There was a couple of calls. One before he left for the South, like a couple weeks ago, another call later on. The wife always answers the telephone from the service, see. And these calls came in after this business was in hand. He didn't have any male calls except from the Custom Suits Company."

"So she's sure it was a woman."

"Yeah. That gonna be a help?"

"I think so."

"How's that organ? You sisters playing it? Don't it sound real good?"

"It's wonderful, Vinny. Absolutely beautiful. Everyone loves it. Thank you so much."

"I got a plaque getting engraved. I'll send it along. You make sure it goes right on that organ someplace."

"I certainly will, Vinny. It will be a wonderful memorial to dear Sister Linda."

"Yeah. And I'm gonna take out that Cloud if he sets foot in this town. That's the other memorial."

Sister Cecile thought carefully before speaking. "The law will take care of him, Vinny. And later he'll face God's justice."

"That's right, Sister, God's justice is gonna come real quick. You take care of that organ, now."

"I certainly will."

Cecile returned to the table and finished her dessert. Some of the nuns were still there, some had already excused themselves to watch television. They would all gather to pray in half an hour. Cecile would say her evening prayers in the car on her way out to Dubaker's. It was allowed. "Well, isn't this a good dessert," Cecile said.

"I'll be very good," Leonie said. "Quiet as a mouse. I love gun collections. I saw some in Washington with my dad. He always brought me along."

"He did?" Cecile had forgotten all about Leonie's request.

209

"What harm?" Leonie asked.

Cecile took a final bite of dessert. It looked smaller than when she had left to answer the telephone. Maybe Leonie had eaten some. "It's a woman," she said thoughtfully. "So maybe it will be safe. Of course, Ron Dubaker has a wife, but on the other hand, she hasn't really been part of this investigation. Unless Ron had her make the call. That seems really unlikely."

"Who is Ron and who would his wife call?" Sister Raphael asked.

"Ron owns the gun collection. I suppose it would be all right if Leonie came along to see it. What do you think, Raphael?"

"Could I come too?" the old nun asked.

"That might be too many. Besides, Leonie is just a kid who's interested in old guns. Right, Leonie? It might help me ask questions more casually. People say the most revealing things to Leonie."

"Right." Leonie smiled a big triumphant grin.

"And who am I?" Raphael asked sourly. "I really have been a part of this case, Cecile."

"You're my muse," Cecile said.

"Me? A muse?" Raphael scraped up a tiny crumb of *tres leches* residue from her plate and licked the fork carefully. "I like that," she said. "A muse."

"Good. Come on, Leonie, we should head out. It's a fairly long drive. I feel safe so far, here in town. No sign of Cloud. He's got to be hiding out. Every trooper from here to Rhode Island has his description."

Cecile and Leonie left shortly after. The Dubakers lived in North Miami Beach, which is not on the beach at all but a crowded section inland where rows of pleasant homes are inhabited by people from all over the fifty states and the countries of Central and South America.

"I have to say vespers as we go, Leonie. Will you read from the Bible passages for me as I drive?"

"It's too dark."

"No it isn't."

"It's bad to read in a moving vehicle. You always tell me that."

"This is praying."

"Well, you know I don't do that."

"Ever?" Cecile asked. She pulled out of the parking lot and headed for the causeway.

"Very rare occasions, and only when it's really important." Leonie folded her hands and ignored the Bible that was on the floor of the car.

"I have a marker in the page where I want you to begin reading. Just read the words and I'll listen. I really need to pray now. It's part of the Rule."

"Reading is not praying," Leonie said firmly.

"Praying is lifting your mind and heart to God. That's all. Read. I marked the Psalms."

Reluctantly, Leonie picked up the big book and opened to the Thirty-ninth Psalm. She began slowly, her voice hesitant, stubborn, refusing to hear what she read. Then she became interested. " 'Tell me, Yahweh, when my end will be, how many days are allowed me, show me how frail I am.' " She paused, swallowed, and continued for a few more verses to the end. " 'Look away, let me draw breath, before I go away and am no more.' "

She looked up at the passing houses, then at Sister Cecile. "That's really cool."

32

LEONIE read all the way to the Dubakers. Cecile pulled into the driveway of the long, low home and turned off the ignition. "Wait in the car, Leonie. I want to check things out."

The nun emerged to find herself surrounded by massive bougainvillea and Alexander palms, traveler's palms and a large live oak. It was beginning to get dark and floodlights lit every part of the house, leaving some flowering hibiscus bushes in shadows. Cecile looked down at the pink brick driveway, then through the car window at Leonie.

It was then she realized how totally crazy it was to bring Leonie along. The hit man could be in the bushes behind any shadow. It would be so easy to just pluck her out of life with one shot. What was she thinking? She wasn't even wearing the vest.

She whispered into the half-open window. "Leonie, just in case, I want you to lay low in the car for a few minutes while I make sure it's okay. The car windows have a dark tint. Nobody can see you, so scrunch down. If I get shot, you'll be alive."

"Fine, just walk out and get killed. Now you tell me."

"You know about the hit man."

"Big deal. He keeps missing."

Cecile let out a long breath. "Not exactly. Wait in the car, roll up the windows. I'll be back."

Sister Cecile slipped away and went up to a big oak door with beveled glass inserts and rang the bell. Nobody let off a shot from the hedges; there was no sound but the music of a mockingbird. Cecile looked around and back at the car. Nothing. Even the car looked empty.

Ron Dubaker came to the door. "Sister Cecile. Good to see you, come right in."

He seemed surprisingly amiable. Maybe it was the glass he held, or what was in it, or what was in him. A drink can do wonders for a man's disposition, Cecile knew. And the house seemed safe. She could see the wife in the background, smiling, not holding a gun.

"I brought a friend. Do you mind?" Cecile asked. "She's quite interested in gun collections."

Ron looked out and around. "Invisible?"

"No, no, she's in the car. I'll go get her."

Cecile went back to the car and opened the door. "Things look fine. Come on."

Leonie was frightened. Cecile could see it in her wide blue eyes, in the slight trembling of her hands. The nun gave her a quick hug. "No problem. They're smiling, no guns."

"I don't want you to die, Cecile," Leonie said. "Every so often I remember."

"I won't die. Nothing will happen to me. Like you said, the killer keeps missing."

"Yeah," Leonie said. "Maybe we can buy a gun. I think that would be a very good idea."

"Well, I don't."

The house had an open floor plan, done in white tile with a scattering of Oriental rugs. The light cane furniture held fluffy flower print cushions. A piano occupied one corner, a huge dining room table with eight chairs filled the open space on the right. It was a typically beautiful Florida decorating scheme.

"My wife, Graciella," Ron said. Cecile introduced Leonie.

Graciella offered drinks, and then went to get lemonades for Leonie and Cecile. She was short and dark with a wide smile and bright eyes; not the sort of person at all that Cecile had envisioned for Dubaker's wife. Somehow, in Cecile's mind, she had pictured Dubaker's taste would run to the svelte Venezuelan rich-girl types that she ran across from time to time in Miami.

Graciella Dubaker rejoined them in a moment. She not only carried the lemonade but also balanced a tray of coconut cookies for Leonie. "Our children love these," she said. "We

213

have three boys and two girls, all scattered in their rooms or the family room. They'll probably peek out."

"Well, shall we see the gun room?" Ron asked. "This way. I have a little private room left for myself. Not much space allowed for me in this madhouse."

Somehow the evil *notario* didn't seem so evil after all. He had become a benevolent, busy father, although the crocodile grin was still intact. So much for that character reading, Cecile thought, and followed him as he unlocked a door and led them into a small study with a five-tier gun rack situated above a tiny fireplace. The room resembled a miniature hunting lodge. A large stuffed marlin hung on an opposing wall, several Audubon prints gathered dust over a cluttered desk. Someone had stacked up wooden boxes on one side of the room, and a glass cabinet on the other side exhibited half a dozen shelves of small, old-fashioned pistols. A soft chair piled with hunting and fishing magazines looked comfortable but inaccessible, and several fishing rods leaned crookedly in one corner. The couch was covered with a hairy polar bear skin, real or fake. Leonie headed for it, balancing cookies and lemonade. She didn't look afraid anymore; she appeared to be entranced.

"Well," Cecile said, "I'm really honored to be invited into your inner sanctum."

"I love this room," Ron confided. "I let one kid in at a time. It makes a special place for them. A treat, or a private talk."

"He won't let me touch it," Graciella said. "And I'm going to back out. Call me if anyone wants anything."

"We're fine, Graciella. Thanks," her husband said. He produced another key and opened the glass gun cabinet. He pulled out a beautiful old-fashioned dueling pistol. "This is the gun's twin. Fine example of an early derringer. Feel it."

Cecile set her drink down on a clear space on the desk and took the gun. The carved stock fit neatly in her hand. She held it up and sighted at the marlin. "Nicely weighted," she said.

"He made a good gun."

"It looks fake," Leonie said. "Like something from a pirate movie."

"It's real," Dubaker assured her. He pulled out another gun, similar but with a double barrel. "Hold this. It's not light. No toy, this one."

Leonie put out a hand. "Heavy."

"Is it loaded?" Cecile asked.

"No. Pull down the trigger and check the barrels. Easiest thing in the world to do. Just don't look in the barrel from the front." He laughed. "Blow your head off that way."

Leonie turned the gun and checked the barrel from the trigger end. "It's solid," she said. "It's beautiful. You just stuff a bullet in, and some gunpowder, and shoot?"

"Something like that. See these balls? This is what it shoots." He pointed to a glass jar full of metal balls. "I keep the room locked because of the kids," Ron said. "Although I make a point of teaching them gun safety and the dangers of firearms. Half the kids in Miami have guns, and probably a third of those use the guns. I let my kids learn the right way, at a firing range under adult supervision."

"My dad let me use his gun once," Leonie said. "I was at a firing range."

"Where was that?" Ron asked.

Leonie licked her lower lip. "I'm not supposed to say, you know?"

Ron raised his eyebrows. "Secret places. I thought you handled that gun well. Now, the one Sister Cecile has is quite a nice specimen." He took the derringer from Cecile's hand and traded Leonie for the double-barreled one the girl held. "This derringer is a good example of the particular model, but if we ever found its mate, it would be worth a fortune because it's in such perfect condition. By itself it's just a curiosity."

Leonie held up the gun and sited on the telephone on the desk. "Pow," she murmured. "This is really a cool gun. I love the way it looks."

"Like I said, it's the twin of the murder weapon, and it needs its mate to be worth anything. I even have the velvet-lined box," Ron said, and went over to a bookshelf. He pulled out a small wooden box and handed it to Leonie. "See how the gun fits right in there?"

"Cool," Leonie whispered.

Sister Cecile couldn't see how this was helping her case. "To actually use this gun, what would you need?"

"The gun, one of those round balls." Ron pointed to the glass jar on the cluttered desk. "Actually those in that ashtray." He pointed to an ashtray full of lead balls. "Those are the right size. Of course you need a propellant. That's gunpowder, then a special cup. You set it all in and shoot. The question of where the murderer got the gunpowder has never been answered. I guess you could pick it up anywhere. People still load their own bullets even now. There's a specially designed little packet, rather like a cap but holds more gunpowder than you're supposed to use for the derringer. It keeps the powder in place. The police theorized at the time that Juan Caldo packed it himself. Juan was taking a chance because the gun could blow up if it isn't done properly. A little metal cup sends the explosion in the right direction. Kind of a precursor to the modern bullet."

"If it was Juan," Cecile said.

Ron Dubaker settled down on the white animal hide on his couch, opposite Leonie, who was still holding the gun, carefully pointing it away from everyone. "I think you may have a case," he said. "I've been doing a lot of thinking. Juan wasn't the type. Question is, who was?"

Cecile sat on a stool, actually a large elephant footstool. Away from his office and his dubious but profitable employment, Ron Dubaker was being very polite, cooperative, downright friendly. His alligator smile was suddenly charming. It couldn't be an act. Couldn't be. She decided to push it. "I think it was a woman. Which woman would have been most likely to kill Victor?"

"Now, there you have me. Women still confuse me with their loves and their motives. We could ask Graciella."

"Your wife?"

"She was there, just arrived, knew all the same people. Leonie, could you run outside and ask Mrs. Dubaker to come in? Then maybe you could scare up one of my kids to show you the family room while the grown-ups talk."

Leonie looked nonplussed to be ordered around so diplomatically, but she was a polite child by nature and found herself without argument. It was obvious Ron didn't want to discuss sexual matters before a twelve-year-old girl. Leonie put the gun back in the case and placed it on a pile of papers on the desk, then did as she was told.

Graciella returned, alone. "Leonie went off with Sarah, said you needed me."

"What can you tell the sister about women and Victor Torres? Would any of them want to kill him?"

Graciella sat down on the couch beside her husband and put her hand in his. "You know what I thought of that man, Ronnie. He was a disgusting creature, thought he could get every woman in town."

"Did he?" Cecile asked.

"Not me. I don't like men like that. But there were some."

"What about Mirtha Lezo and Daisy Gonzales?" Cecile asked.

Graciella smiled softly. "Yes."

"Their daughters look like sisters."

"Don't they? The rule is that children tend to look more like their father than their mother. Most of ours do."

Ron Dubaker watched silently as the women talked. At his wife's last remark he interrupted. "You never told me this, Graciella."

Graciella picked up his hand and brought it to her lips. "You're too young, Ronnie."

"Which one would have killed him?" Cecile asked.

Graciella chewed on her husband's knuckles thoughtfully. "Honestly, I can't see either of them killing him. Victor had the knack of being able to make all the women happy. The men, now that's another situation."

Ron retrieved his hand. "I would have killed him if he touched you, Graciella."

"I know."

"Any husband would have. And that's why Juan Caldo was convicted. Because his woman was there with Victor that night." Ron Dubaker's mouth came out like a pouch at the bottom, as though trying to catch the killer with excess lip.

Cecile stood up and walked about the small room, the floor barely big enough to pace. "That leaves me at the same old impasse. But I know it's someone I've contacted."

"Anything you haven't told me, Graciella?" Ron asked.

"Other than being pregnant again?" Graciella returned.

"What!"

"Just kidding. Actually, I was kind of hoping . . ."

"Later," Ron said, eyeing his wife.

Sister Cecile picked up the gun from its velvet lined case and stroked it. "The real weapon was never found," she said, moving back to business.

"Apparently not," Ron agreed.

"It vanished from the scene. Now, when Nestor Lezo was killed for his gun collection, how did that happen? Do you remember?"

"Sure, I wanted to buy his collection, even back then. I had my eye on it. Nestor was home in the afternoon, his wife, Mirtha, was shopping. She arrived home with groceries, Nestor was shot through the heart and the collection was gone. The house was messed up, some other small items were reported missing, as I recall." Ron frowned, trying to remember. "The cause of death was gunshot to the heart. It was done by another gun in the collection, an old Colt Walker revolver. That's what the police said. I remember that gun. It was the only one missing when we recovered the collection, and according to Mirtha, it had bullets with it. Amazing weapon, built in the mid-1800s, it had the potency of a .357 Magnum. Powerful, accurate thing. I wish it had stayed in the collection."

"Nasty guns," his wife said. "Ronnie's just fascinated by those old things." She waved scornfully at the glass cabinet full of antique pistols.

Cecile put the derringer back and sat down on the elephant stool again. "So, someone walked into Nestor's house and picked him off with one of his own guns. How could a stranger have done that? It doesn't make sense."

"He lived in a house down by the river. Anyone could have come in there," Graciella said. "Back then people didn't lock their homes quite so carefully."

A knocking sounded on the door and a small voice squeaked. "Can I come in?"

"Come in, Ella," Graciella said, and a small girl of about eight skipped into the room.

"Can we watch a video?" Ella asked.

"The big kids put you up to that. No. It's the last week of school. Everyone needs to study," her mother said.

Leonie appeared at the door, saw Ella in the room and came in too, making quite a crowd. Cecile looked around. This was a busy place, busy family. She should leave them in peace. "We have to go," the nun said, and got up from the elephant stool. "You both have been very helpful. I have some ideas, some new thoughts. I really appreciate this. Things are becoming clearer to me."

The Dubakers rose from the couch together. Ron spoke. "I'd like to see justice. Sure, if Juan was innocent, he should be cleared."

"Absolutely," Graciella agreed. Her soft Spanish accent became noticeable only when she used long words. She became slightly tangled in the ending. Then her bright eyes seemed to laugh at her own mistakes. "Well, you must come back and tell us the truth. Very soon."

"I hope I can," Cecile said.

Ron looked at the roomful of women, then at the single dueling pistol on the desk. He went over and took the pistol. "Keep this. Perhaps it will point you to the killer." He held the case up for Cecile.

"No, I couldn't, really. I don't have guns."

"Leonie? To start your collection? It's not worth anything to me without its partner."

Leonie grabbed for the gun.

"Oh no!" Cecile said. "It's dangerous!"

"It isn't," Ron said. "The bullets are totally unavailable. This thing couldn't even fire a cork."

"Please?" Leonie's wide blue eyes pleaded. "It's no big deal. Like he said, every kid has a gun these days. Besides, this is hardly real."

"Hardly," Cecile said dryly. "Its twin killed a man. No, Leonie."

"Please? Dad told me I could have a gun someday. He's already taken me shooting," Leonie said.

Everyone stared at Sister Cecile as if she were some great villain depriving this child of an innocent toy. This was not the case. This was a valuable pistol that could kill. Of course without bullets it was strictly ornamental. Cecile heard herself speak against her own good sense. "I'll keep if for you until your father gets back, then he can work things out with you, Leonie. How's that?" Then she turned to Ron Dubaker. "Are you sure? This is a valuable antique."

Ron smiled the crocodile smile again, but this time it was quite pleasant. "It's not a good addition to my collection. Take it."

"Thank you!" Leonie said. "I'll take really good care of it. I'm going to have my own collection someday. You'll see, Cecile."

"I'm afraid I will."

Five minutes later they were in the car heading back to the beach. Leonie had the wooden gun box clutched tightly between her hands, stroking the old pine as though it were made of gold. "They were so nice," Leonie said.

"They were," Sister Cecile agreed. "Too nice. I was surprised."

"Did you learn anything?"

"Yes."

33

PAUL Dorys never let his love for Sister Cecile interrupt his social life. He was not a nun. As one of Boston's premier and perennial bachelors, he enjoyed the company of a steady stream of women who invited him to parties and places. Maybe, he told himself from time to time, he would fall in love with someone else, marry, have a family. He really should. He should face the facts. Cecile was a nun, and she wasn't going to quit the order.

In the meantime Paul didn't deprive the world of his company. In fact, shortly after Cecile arrived safely back in Miami Beach, he went to a gathering in Boston's Back Bay neighborhood in a ten room condo with a fine view of the Charles River. The penthouse belonged to an old friend, Jacob Barr.

Paul arrived with Maggie Dunlop, an attractive divorcée, and they both began to do the things people do at such affairs: eat, drink, and talk. Paul finally found Jacob alone for a moment and they moved over to the huge window overlooking the river. Paul pulled out two cigars and offered one to his friend.

"Good Cuban," his friend murmured and accepted Paul's light.

Paul lit his own and began to puff. "Some question about that. We weren't sure if these were the real thing, or just came with the right cigar band."

They both smoked for a moment, tasting, testing, breathing in the deep aroma. "What do you think? Real?" Paul asked.

"Smelly." Maggie wrinkled her nose. "I'll be on the other side of the room." She walked away, leaving the men to their cigar talk.

"If not real Cuban, then damn close," Jacob Barr said. "What'd you pay for these things?"

"A present from a friend. She brought me a box."

"People pay a grand for a box of these."

Paul nodded. "Or more."

"Early CIA plot was to blow up Castro with a cigar. Ever hear about that?" Jacob asked.

"Yep. Tough to turn down a good cigar."

"I have a cigar," Jacob mused. "A Cohiba, supposedly, in one of those little individual tubes. I think it may be a real Cohiba, and I've been dying to try it. I've had the damn thing for a year."

"So, what's keeping you?" Paul asked.

"It's an exploding cigar. Three good puffs and then blooey!"

"The perfect murder weapon."

"Not deadly. It shoots tear gas, enough to incapacitate the smoker and anyone within ten feet. It's one of those government deals used in spy circles. Expensive but useless in the ordinary course of the world. I've been wanting to take the first two puffs and let it go out, but I'm not that much of a gambler."

"Why not?" Paul laughed.

"Want it?" Jacob asked. "You deal with crooks, right?"

"Sometimes," Paul said. "Sure. I could find a use for it."

"It's in my office. Come on." Jacob took Paul through the murmuring groups of Boston social life, folks talking and drinking and listening to some good jazz. They went into a small, paneled room with Piranesi prints on the wall. Jacob opened a lower drawer of his desk and pulled out the cigar tube. He handed it to Paul. "It's a perfect forgery of the real thing," Jacob said proudly.

Paul held it carefully. "It won't just blow up?" he asked.

"Safe as sin," Jacob confirmed.

"That does not instill confidence."

"Three puffs, then ka-pow. Really. Carefully tested."

Paul placed the cigar in his sport coat pocket. "This could come in handy," he said. "Thanks, Jacob."

The next morning Paul carefully wrapped the exploding cigar along with a note and mailed it, overnight mail, to Sister

222

Cecile. He was worried about her, and worried doubly because she did so little to protect herself offensively. No guns. Just a bulletproof vest. So far the nun had been lucky.

Early the following morning Sister Raphael brought the mail in to Sister Cecile. "Package from Paul," she said.

"Really? I wonder what."

"And a letter for Leonie from her dad. And one for you. What do you bet she's not going to Japan after all. She's due to leave in a week."

"Well, we'll find out." Cecile proceeded to shuffle the mail like a deck of cards while Sister Raphael waited. It was a game they played sometimes. Raphael always wanted to see if the mail held anything new and exciting. Cecile liked to open her private mail privately. Finally, Sister Raphael sat down in the client's chair and began to study her nails.

"Don't you have anything to do?" Cecile asked.

"Actually I've been doing something rather important. I've been outside several times this morning looking for Jeffrey Cloud. I have a method," the old nun said. "I pull out my rosary beads, the longest ones I own, they're huge, really, and I walk very slowly up and down the sidewalk in front of this place, and I pray. Most of the time I keep my head down, but once in a while I look up. That's when I check for that hit man."

Cecile looked up from the mail abruptly. She had no idea the old nun was out there guarding the fort, so to speak. She looked at Sister Raphael intently. "You haven't seen him, have you?"

"That's why I brought the mail in. I saw the mailman."

"Thanks," Cecile said.

"And I saw him."

"Cloud?" Cecile felt a spasm somewhere in her stomach.

"Yes."

"You're sure?"

"Quite sure. Last night he was out there while you and Leonie were visiting that man. I saw him parked in a small green Fiat. He doesn't look anything like you described him. I wasn't sure, because I haven't been introduced, but you described him enough times. On the other hand, he's not stupid, so he's changed his appearance. I called Jim Cypress, and he sent three Miami Beach patrol cars. I saw them drive by. They would have picked him up but the man must have a sixth sense because he was gone by the time the cars arrived."

Sister Cecile spoke very slowly. "Why didn't you tell me?"

"I went to bed early last night. As soon as it was safe for you. You and Leonie came home late."

"And he's out there now?"

"A man about five eleven, platinum-blond hair, sunburned, on Rollerblades."

"Cloud was a very gray man with a dark ponytail. I doubt he can skate."

"Don't delude yourself. He's gone blond, gotten some sun."

"Gun?"

"Not that I could see. Skimpy shorts, no shirt. One of those ugly tummy packs. A cool dude," Raphael said proudly. "I'm sure it's him. He kept looking at the front door."

"Should we call Jim again?"

"No. He skated away when the mailman came. I think he was just trying to catch your movements. He'll be back. Besides, Jim had some doubts it was him. He doesn't trust me the way you do."

"This has got to end," Cecile muttered. "I don't like it. I'll have to keep wearing that vest. I can't be seen with Leonie again. Maybe we should keep her in." She ripped open the package from Paul. The small encased cigar fell out along with a note. She read it silently, grinned, and tossed the note to Raphael while she picked up the cigar tube and shook it gently. "My father had things like this."

Sister Raphael read the note aloud. " 'Danger, exploding cigar. Contains enough tear gas to wipe out people standing within a ten foot radius. Cigar detonates on the third puff. Hey, Cecile, think you might be able to use this? Give it to the bad guy and watch him blow up. Love, Paul.' "

"Her," Cecile said. "It's a her."

"Who?" Raphael asked.

"The bad guy. Bad person. I've got it figured out. It's Mirtha Lezo."

"Mirtha? Her husband was killed shortly after the first man died, right? Why her?"

"Well, because she was carrying his child."

"Whose child?"

"The way I see it, both Daisy and Mirtha were pregnant by Victor Torres. I figure Mirtha wanted to marry Victor and he said no. So she killed him. Does that sound good?"

Sister Raphael shook her head. "Half good. Hard to prove. Why not Daisy?"

Sister Cecile picked up the exploding cigar and sniffed. "Well, maybe it's her." She tossed the cigar into her purse, which was on her desk.

"And what about Nestor Lezo, Mirtha's husband?" Raphael asked. "I think he did it. He found out his wife was pregnant and he killed Victor."

"That makes the most sense, really, but then who's left to hire a hit man? Why care? Nestor's been dead twenty years. So has Victor."

Raphael rose very slowly from the big brown chair and walked over to the window that looked out on the swimming pool. The mid-morning light was brilliant on the water. A palm frond floated in the pool. "It's a puzzle," she said.

"How about this," Cecile began. "The husband kills Victor Torres, the wife freaks out and kills the husband. That works. I mean, that really works! It explains everything."

"So Mirtha hired the hit man to keep you from unraveling everything."

"Exactly."

"Sounds good. How can you prove it?"

"I can't."

"Well, you need a recorded confession. We've done that before, remember?"

"More or less. Of course then I die, right? Nobody's going to confess and let me walk away."

"That's what the killer thinks will happen. You need to buy a tape recorder, highly sensitive. Maybe one of those things they have on television when they say a person is wired," Sister Raphael said.

"I'll do that. Wear a wire, a Kevlar vest, carry an exploding cigar. Maybe I could pack a gun." Cecile felt sick for a moment. This was the world she lived in, a world adopted from television. "Some days I just want to pray. That's why I became a nun. I want to stay in the community."

"And hide. I don't blame you." Raphael fingered the cross around her neck. "But this is your job. Our mother superior, Mère Sulpicia, agreed that you could do this to support the order. Now you're stuck with it."

"Strange how the vow of obedience works, isn't it," Cecile mused. "Well, I guess I'll get on with it. Did you say gun?"

Sister Raphael laughed. "You'll never carry a gun."

"You're right."

The conversation was interrupted by a knock on the door. Sister Emma peeked in. "Someone's here for you, Sister Cecile. He said he had a room booked here. A young man. I'm afraid he's mistaken."

Sister Cecile jumped up. "Buddy Dilts! Come on, Raphael. He's just the one I need to tie this up. We're working together."

"Buddy Dilts?"

"He's a South Carolina State Trooper. Cloud killed his partner. He's come to help!"

Five minutes later Sister Cecile and Buddy Dilts were in the kitchen looking for a late breakfast for Buddy. He had been driving since the night before and had a heavy beard, red eyes, and bad breath. He needed food and a few hours' sleep. Sister Cecile cooked him a plate of scrambled eggs and some fried ham from last night's dinner. "Coffee?"

"Sure. Then I could use a couple hours' sleep. After that we can get to work. You find out anything?" Buddy's eyes were half closed, his plaid shirt and khaki pants wrinkled. He was wearing civilian clothes, and not acting in his official capacity. He was on vacation.

"Sister Raphael has identified Cloud in the neighborhood. He's now a platinum-blond, wears bright, tight clothes, uses in-line skates. He drives a small green Fiat."

"Sister Raphael's that elderly nun?" Buddy asked, digging into the eggs while Cecile buttered him some toast. "She recognized him?"

"Yes. She's very good." Cecile didn't bother explaining that Raphael had never actually seen Jeffrey Cloud. Buddy wouldn't understand.

226

"An elderly nun." Buddy looked around the community kitchen, noting the spotlessly clean surfaces and the large brass crucifix over the stove. "I'm staying here?" he asked himself.

"There's a room all ready. We have a spare for visiting priests, but it's empty now. It's for you."

Buddy visibly shuddered, then shoveled in a pile of ham. "Catholics. Regular bed? Not nails or anything in it?"

"A very good mattress," Cecile promised. "It's in the secular part of the building. We have a few people here who aren't religious. I'll have someone give the door a knock in time for lunch if you want to eat with the community, or maybe you'd rather eat alone later?"

Buddy chewed madly for a moment, then put his hands on his hips and tilted his head back to look up at the nun, who was still dithering around the kitchen. "I'll get up. I give myself three days to get my partner's killer. Three days."

"That should be enough," Cecile agreed, and poured some coffee. "I've worked out an agenda."

34

SISTER Cecile was elusive. Either that or she was a master of disguise. Jeffrey Cloud hadn't seen her since he returned to Miami Beach and began watching the old motel with the sign, carved on wood, reading, MARIA CONCILIA RETIREMENT COMMUNITY. He had no desire to blow away the wrong nun and bring out the full force of the Miami Beach Police Department before he hit the right nun. He needed to pop Sister Cecile the first time. Zero tolerance for mistakes. Of course, the Miami cops were already on to him, but nobody had seen him, nobody could even identify him.

Cloud observed the elderly nun with rosary beads wandering back and forth in front of the retirement community. In fact, he was sure she had spotted him. Certainly the old blue eyes had focused on him at least twice as he rolled by on the skates. The old bag was admiring him. Women loved this new man. He cut quite a picture, although his skating really wasn't all that smooth yet. His incredible tan, in fact a glowing sunburn, the hair, the snazzy clothes. He'd even started working out at the exercise club at the beach hotel where he was staying.

He could get into this beach stuff, Cloud realized, staring into his bedroom mirror later that day, flexing his trapezius muscles under his sunburnt skin. When this job was complete, he might emerge in California as a surfer dude, a health food nut, a man who lived on the wild side. Enough of the conservative hit man lifestyle he'd lived that had passed for a life in the dismal Northeast.

He picked up his .357 Magnum Ruger from the dresser top. The gun was loaded and ready. Where was the nun? Perhaps he could telephone for an appointment. That would require a trip to somewhere else. Everyone had Caller ID these days and he didn't want anything traceable back to this hotel. He slipped the gun back into his luggage and pushed it into the closet.

Jeffrey Cloud called the retirement community number from a pay telephone near the fruit drink bar on the beach. Lunch was over, and as Cloud quickly discovered, Sister Cecile was out.

"When will she be back?" Cloud asked.

"Who's calling, please?" Sister Raphael asked.

"A friend. I want to surprise her."

Sister Raphael didn't answer for just a hair too long. "If you could give me your name, I'll have her call you."

"I'll try later." Cloud slammed down the receiver. That didn't take long; he was blown. The nun knew exactly who he was. He could tell by that hesitation, by the faint edge in her voice. He would just have to hang out near the convent, blow her away, then split.

Unfortunately, to linger on that street wasn't all that easy. The sun was hot, for one thing, and skating shirtless yesterday had been a mistake. All that gray skin was blistering red. Cloud returned to the hotel and looked through his new wardrobe. He pulled off the fifty percent polyester, fifty percent cotton, button-down shirt that he had worn to the telephone booth. It was part of his old self. Besides that, polyester was hot. He was a hundred percent cotton T-shirt man now. A cool dude. He wiggled carefully into a large, green tee, covering up those admirable, red muscles. He slathered his face and arms with sunscreen, put on sunglasses and his Miami Dolphins hat, stuffed the Ruger into a tummy pack, and then poked the pack down into one of the skates, tossed the skates over his shoulder and almost screamed at the pain.

Maybe the desk clerk could recommend something for sunburn.

An hour later Cloud strolled by the retirement community. He didn't know that Cecile had left an hour ago with Buddy Dilts. He saw a police car rolling by, slowly, but he was walking, his blond hair covered by the hat. He wasn't the same man Sister Raphael had called in about two nights before. The policeman kept right on driving.

Cloud would not quit, would not leave. He had discovered the secret of Miami Beach. To be unobtrusive was to be obtrusive. The more noticeable one's outfit and demeanor was, the less people looked. Or maybe the more they looked, the less they remembered. Miami Beach was like that. Jeffrey Cloud felt invisible in the lime-green T-shirt and the spandex shorts.

He spent the better part of the day within spitting distance of the community. First he walked the blocks, swinging his skates beside him. Later he put on the skates and skated, wearing the gun in the tummy pack around his waist. He cut a good picture. Women stared at him, men stared at him. Nobody really saw him. The chameleon was back.

What he didn't know was that Sister Raphael saw him too. Unfortunately, Sister Raphael couldn't get in touch with Sister Cecile. Cecile had slipped out the back door with Buddy Dilts a long time ago.

Sister Cecile and Buddy Dilts were following the nun's agenda. It was simple. "I want to visit Mirtha Lezo. I think she's the killer," Cecile said.

"Just walk right in? You got two of them Kevlar vests?"

"No, but I want to have a good tape recorder. With the two of us, both taping, it should work. We need to watch out for the hit man, get the confession, then we go after the hit man. I want to call my friend on the Miami Beach police force. He's good. Sister Raphael's been in touch, but Jim's skeptical about Sister Raphael. He still thinks she's too old to be effective."

"Isn't she?" Buddy asked.

"Sister Raphael is very sharp. Let's stop and call my friend on the force. Cloud is out there. I don't like to admit it, Buddy, but I'm afraid of that man."

Buddy shook his head. "Wait. Give me a day. I want to get that . . ." Buddy paused, looking for a euphemism for "bastard" that he could use in front of a nun. "I want to get the creep myself," he said. "Then call in the locals. Once we get him we can find out who hired him."

"Jim's good," Cecile said. But she understood Buddy Dilts's need. "Today is yours. Tomorrow I'll call Jim. We may need help. I don't think we can take Cloud alive. But we must. I certainly won't kill him myself. In fact I don't want to kill anyone, but you're armed to the teeth, Buddy. Be careful."

"Sure will." Buddy patted his gun. Cecile winced.

"I have a feeling Cloud won't tell us who hired him, but we really need him alive just in case he decides to squeal," Cecile said firmly. "Not dead. On the other hand, I think we have to go from the first killer to the second. Not Cloud first, but the one who hired him. I know you don't care about my case," she continued, "my twenty-year-old murder mystery. But I do. To me that comes first, not Cloud."

"Okay," Buddy agreed. He was her guest, and a fine southern gentleman. That he was. Her killer first, then his.

"I'm glad you see it my way," Cecile said. "Now, I suppose we should go to one of the police stores. I know a good one on Calle Ocho and Red Road. They have everything." Cecile had compromised and agreed to ride in Buddy's truck, a tan, three-year-old Dodge Daytona pickup. For this southerner to have a woman drive him was too humiliating. That she was a nun would have made it unbearable for him, so Cecile settled in to the surprisingly comfortable seat and gave directions.

At the police store they picked up another bulletproof vest, at Cecile's insistence. The store didn't stock the recording device that Cecile wanted, but suggested a small, private supplier. The owner gave a call through to pave the way, "because what you're looking for isn't strictly legal in every sense of the word, and we sell nothing but the best in legal equipment, but this here fellow knows the importance of the recorded word in the style you're looking for." He had an accent similar to Buddy's and wore army fatigues.

Cecile listened with half an ear, letting Buddy do all the arrangements because this was a guy place. She simply stared at the racks of gunslinger equipment, the incredible pistols in glass cases, the gold badges, costumes, and gun racks, and prayed. She pulled out her credit card when the cash register began to blink. She insisted on paying.

"I'm on an expense account," Cecile said when Buddy objected. "This is paid for."

They walked out with a pile of equipment, then drove several blocks to the address the proprietor had given Buddy. A small door with a sign advertising AUDIO SALES opened up to a miniature showroom. The owner was another Buddy clone, but the Hispanic variety, rosy-faced, slick hair, eager, smart. He explained how the equipment worked, how to wear it for most effective recording, and how to play it back. After some conversation, he apparently accepted Buddy and Sister Cecile as legitimate customers, and proceeded to show them a variety of bugs and wiring devices.

"I think all we need is something for recording. Several things," Cecile said.

Buddy purchased a number of other items. "Personal use," he said to Cecile.

"Right," Cecile agreed, and pulled out the credit card again. Surveillance equipment didn't come cheap. It felt good to use some of her amassed trust fund for something to help the world become a safer place.

They clambered back into the truck and began to wire up. "I don't want to waste time," Cecile said. "We should stop for a sandwich somewhere and I could slip this sound business on in the ladies' room."

"Let's go for a coffee," Buddy said. "Do it there."

By 3:45 that afternoon Buddy and Cecile were on the way to Mirtha Lezo's. It was crazy to go there, they both agreed. They might get shot, but they might walk away with what they needed.

"Sure is pretty here," Buddy said as he drove through the little neighborhood bordering the river. "Goes from real crummy to strange to downright Caribbean. Like the way the palms grow, and the bushes, and all."

"It's an old section of Miami," Cecile explained. "The river holds a lot of the smaller boats from the islands, and people live along it as it heads up. Now, there's the Lezo's place. See, back in all those trees? Miami's a relatively new city, but along here the homes go back in Florida history."

Buddy pulled into the yard. He turned off the ignition and hopped out. Cecile followed. "Low-key," Cecile said. "I'll just start her talking, then we dig for the truth. And don't worry when she comes to the door with a shotgun. It's a rough part of town."

Cecile and Buddy passed the shotgun test. They found themselves in Mirtha's cool living room drinking small cups of Cuban coffee and chatting with Mirtha. She appeared happy to see them. Two tiny tape recorders rolled, taking down a great many useless words. Nothing was happening.

Finally Sister Cecile became tired of pussyfooting around. "Mirtha, I think it was a woman who killed Victor Torres. I'm quite certain, actually."

Mirtha looked up from the table where she had been watching a small bunch of flowers, as though the flowers could do something. "No, that's not true. It was a man."

Cecile and Buddy Dilts exchanged looks. "No, I think it had to be a woman," Cecile said.

"A man," Mirtha repeated more firmly this time.

"But not Juan Caldo," Cecile said hopefully. "He's a good man with a wife and three children, a man suffering because of a murder he didn't commit."

"No. But, you understand, Juan had no family then, nothing to lose. The rest of us had so much. Children coming, families, husbands." She sighed. "I couldn't hurt my baby, my unborn baby. She never knew. Now it should be made right. I've been thinking all the time about this. Ever since you came the first time. I really do have a conscience."

"Yes," Cecile dared to whisper, dared to hope Mirtha really did have a conscience. "Who?"

Buddy sat so still, barely breathing, that Cecile had almost forgotten his presence until she saw his hand move very slowly to his hip where a gun waited in a holster, hidden by an oversized blue shirt.

"My husband killed Victor Torres. Nestor did it. I was there. Nestor took me by the arm, dragged me into that apartment, and we saw the man unconscious. We came in very quietly. Juan was standing there staring at Victor, unconscious on the floor, Nestor hit Juan on the head from behind. Such a fool. It was so simple. Nestor picked up the gun and shot Victor dead in front of my very eyes for revenge on me. Nestor was so angry with me, I thought he would kill me too. There was nothing I could do then. *Nada.* I would not raise my child thinking her father was a murderer."

Tears flowed slowly down Mirtha's solid face as she talked.

"I loved Victor. He would have married me if he could have. I believe that, even now."

"He's Rita's father? Your daughter, Rita?" Cecile asked.

"Yes."

"Would you swear that your husband shot and killed Victor Lezo?" Cecile asked. She tried to make her voice very clear for the tape she wore, just in case something went wrong here.

"It's time," Mirtha said. "It's time. My daughter is grown now, she should know the truth. Yes, I would swear to that."

"An affidavit," Cecile said. "I could get some papers, an attorney, a notary, would that be all right? We could clear Juan Caldo."

Mirtha nodded.

Buddy had relaxed, but his mind hadn't shut down. He finally interrupted Cecile's taping session. "Mrs. Lezo, there's a problem here. Someone went and hired a gun to kill Sister Cecile. Why the heck is someone going to all this trouble to cover up the fact that a dead man committed murder twenty years ago? Could your kid have done that? I mean, why would anyone? You didn't go and pop your husband after he killed this guy, did you?" Buddy's hand was wrapped around his service automatic, ready. Cecile saw the movement and flinched. She didn't want her witness dead before she obtained the affidavit.

Mirtha turned very slowly and faced the trooper. "I wasn't the only one who loved Victor Torres. I wasn't the only one who carried that man's baby. I don't kill, you understand. I love. I want life for my child. The other one," she spat, "that one killed for her child. Twice."

"What?" Cecile started to jump from the couch, then forced herself back down. "Daisy?"

"Big businesswoman. Important. Best cigars." Mirtha scoffed, then tossed down another hair-raising tiny Cuban coffee. "How do you think she gets to own a business like that? How do you think Carlos Zaruda died? Good man like that. Daisy killed Zaruda. Daisy killed my husband."

"Why didn't you do something?" Buddy asked. He looked revolted by the scenario, women killing men. Men weren't used to that, not in his world.

"She did me a favor. Nestor killed the man I loved too."

234

Mirtha rose from her chair and paced the room. "Why should I object?"

"Did the husbands know about the babies not being theirs?" Cecile asked.

"Not mine. Ruby Gonzalez is a fool. He thinks his wife is a saint because she supports his mission. His school is his life."

"So it's Daisy who did it, Daisy still trying to cover up," Cecile mused. "The only way to prove Juan Caldo is innocent is to prove Nestor killed Victor, and then it would open things up to who killed Nestor," Cecile continued. "So Daisy hired a hit man. She's probably selling cigars all over the country, and would know about hit men."

Buddy looked confused. Maybe it was the Hispanic names. He wasn't used to things not southern. "She doesn't sound too smart," he said. "I mean, why eliminate you?"

"Maybe she thought I was getting close. Well, Daisy was right. I'm very close."

"Shall we go see this Daisy?" Buddy asked. "Bring her in?"

"She's the one who hired Cloud, no doubt about that." Cecile turned to Mirtha, who was standing in front of the old fireplace, clenching and unclenching her hands.

"I'll make this right," Mirtha said. "I'll swear what happened. Your man will be free. I can't live this way anymore."

"We need a notary," Cecile murmured.

"Ron Dubaker," Mirtha said in a low voice. "He always helped us. Charged a lot, but a good man."

"I'll call him," Cecile said. "Thank you, Mirtha. You've done the right thing. I'll take care of the notary. The *notario*. Ron is a good man after all."

35

LEONIE couldn't find Sister Cecile when she got home from school. Sister Raphael was out visiting a nun who had to be taken to the hospital. The elderly nun had left Leonie a message taped on the refrigerator. "Took Sister Mary Pat to the hospital. Don't go out. Love, Raphael." There was nobody else in the community, except Sister Germaine, whom Leonie considered worth talking to. But even Sister Germaine was out buying groceries.

Leonie didn't like that. Someone should be here. It was two-thirty and a long afternoon stretched ahead of her. Raphael said "don't go out." Well, maybe she should just go out.

Finally Leonie went into her bedroom and saw the letter from her father that had arrived earlier that day. Cecile had placed it on her pillow. Leonie ripped it open and read.

Dear Leonie,
    I've pushed the trip back a week. No big deal, but I'm tied up here with something, so you get one week of vacation in Miami before you head out . . .

"Darn," Leonie said, and finished reading the letter from her father. That meant she wouldn't leave for Japan right away, as planned. She wondered if Cecile had heard from her father as well. Probably.

Leonie tossed the letter down and went to Sister Cecile's room. She knocked, then walked right in. No nun.

As usual, Leonie was impressed with the bareness of Sister Cecile's bedroom. A cross on one wall, a wooden chair, a battered old dresser and the bed. Not even a very comfortable bed. And a very uncomfortable chair.

Leonie pulled the chair up to the dresser and started pulling out drawers. Cecile must have the derringer in here somewhere.

Sure enough, the wooden case was in a drawer full of some worn underwear. Leonie took the gun out of the case, then put the empty case back under the underwear. Cecile would never know the gun was missing. Besides, this gun didn't belong to Cecile. It belonged to her.

Leonie stuffed the derringer under her belt and strolled casually back to her room. She took out the bottle corks she had obtained from the kitchen. Sister Germaine always cooked with wine, and there was a drawer full of old corks that Germaine saved for God knows what. Leonie was ready to load the gun exactly as it had been done in the duel she read about. Bottle corks could be shot out of this gun, just like the case of Magruder and the seconds; the duel where the pistols had been loaded with bottle corks and nobody died.

The girl put on some music, sat down at her desk and proceeded to remove gunpowder from the fireworks Zoe had brought to school that morning in response to Leonie's urgent late night telephone call. Leonie held the little powder clip that she had retrieved from the gun box earlier and collected the gunpowder in it.

How much powder?

She filled the clip, added a little extra powder because it didn't look like enough. She took out several corks and found one that fit into the barrel, and put it on the little clip, mushing it into the gunpowder. She fit everything carefully into the derringer.

The gun was loaded. Now she had protection.

Leonie had an agenda too. She knew the hit man was out there waiting for Sister Cecile. She had heard Sister Raphael describing the bleached-blond dude in the green Fiat, and Leonie had seen the man for herself when she sauntered home from school at a slow, almost teenage pace. She spotted the skater in the lime-green T-shirt two blocks from the community and knew who it was. Definitely the creep who had talked to her on the beach. Of course he didn't recognize her, dressed in schoolgirl plaids, slouching, her hair pulled up high in an attempt at sophistication. She and Zoe had been working out new hairdos all week.

Maybe that was why Raphael had said not to leave. Leonie furrowed her brow. Maybe if she pretended she hadn't seen the note, she could leave. Maybe she should just be disobedient and admit to herself that she had read the note, and leave anyway. She had too many ideas to sit around all afternoon in an empty building and wonder what was going on. Somehow Leonie knew she had to neutralize the hit man. She had to get the person who hired him, and she definitely had to save Sister Cecile's life.

She dressed in cutoff blue jeans and a huge, floppy shirt, stuffed the gun in her belt and wondered if she might shoot off her foot with a cork. No, the gun needed to be cocked, and besides, it was only a cork in there. Nothing could happen. She would be the only one who knew the gun wasn't lethal. It was the perfect weapon.

Wearing the gun was awkward, but it was relatively safe and accessible tucked in her belt. She emerged from her room and scribbled a note for Sister Cecile. "I have serious research at the library," she wrote. "See you later." Then Leonie signed her name. The note was the literal truth. She did have serious work due, but she didn't actually say she was doing it or that she was actually going to the library. She left the note on the front desk with one of the very old nuns who guarded the telephone and generally slept away the afternoon. Sister Lulu was snoring softly as Leonie tiptoed by.

In her pocket, Leonie had thirty dollars in one dollar bills. She always had too much money. She had a stash. Money was never a problem. She would take a cab. It was late afternoon, past four-thirty. There wasn't time to take buses all over the place to get where she wanted to go.

Leonie strolled out of the convent and looked up and down the street. Cloud was gone. Good. She was safe. Cloud wasn't so smart, anyway, Leonie felt, with that ugly bleached hair. Plus the fact that he was a lousy skater. The man had no skill. It never occurred to her to call Jim Cypress.

Leonie walked down the street, and at the first pay telephone she called a cab. Ten minutes later she was on the way to the

238

Zaruda Cigar Company. Leonie had instincts about that woman. Daisy had been too nice. All she had to do, Leonie thought, was to get the woman to slip up. It was easy to slip up in front of a kid. Leonie knew how most adults regarded people her age. Dumb, dumb, dumb. It didn't occur to her that in this case they would be right.

Cloud saw Leonie leave the old motel from where he looked out from behind a parked truck. He saw her go to the telephone booth, and he saw the cab pull up. His Fiat was parked half a block away, but the skates were fast. He was developing skill. He jumped in the car, fired up the engine and hit the gas, catching up with the cab within two blocks. The kid was going to lead him to the nun. Cloud patted the tummy pack digging into his ribs. The Ruger was ready.

The only hard part was driving the damn Fiat wearing Rollerblades.

Calle Ocho thronged with people. Folks were shopping, strolling, living a life they had brought with them from Havana. Even the smells were from the island; the mangos being eaten on the street, the scent of strong coffee served in tiny paper cups from outdoor cafés, the domino players intent on winning, men who reeked of male cologne and the smoke of strong cigars.

Leonie paid the cabbie, tipping him two dollars. "Thanks," she said, and strolled down the street in the direction of the Zaruda cigar factory. Now that she was here, she was having second thoughts. Just what was she going to do, anyway? What could she do? She paused by the dingy window and looked in at the long tables of tobacco, at the women rolling cigars by hand, carefully twisting the broad leaves around the filling. Leonie looked down at her watch. It was almost five-thirty. The day had fled. Maybe all these workers would be leaving soon, leaving the place empty. Maybe she should wait for Daisy on the street, by the front door.

That was a good idea. It was much safer.

Leonie stationed herself near the door and began to watch the people on Calle Ocho, or Eighth Street. Everyone spoke Spanish. She understood about a quarter of it, which wasn't

239

fair considering all her practice with Zoe, and all the verbs she had memorized under her Spanish teacher's tutelage, but then, this was Cuban Spanish, a fast version with numerous peculiarities. Zoe had told her that nobody understood Cuban Spanish, not even the Cubans.

Leonie was daydreaming in the hum of the late afternoon when Jeffrey Cloud skated up, still wearing Rollerblades. She saw him coming, but he was moving too fast for her to do anything. In fact he was slightly out of control as he shimmered up in the thick sunlight, just enough out of control for him to be off balance. His hand was ready to pull out the gun to force Leonie into the shop, but instead he grabbed her with two heavy hands, ready to bring them both down on the spittle-stained sidewalk.

He held her by both arms. "Inside," he whispered, using her slender body to steady himself.

His hands felt like two vise grips. Leonie struggled to keep from falling. Cloud was not a huge man, but the skates added several inches to his height, and he was heavy.

"Move it," he said. His soft, too soft voice, sent chills down Leonie's spine. "Open the door, walk in. I'm right behind you."

Leonie had no choice. She couldn't move away from him, in any case, as the man propelled her along in front of him, almost lifting her off the ground now that he had regained his equilibrium, using her as a counterweight.

The cigar-making women barely glanced up at the garish man on skates and the twelve-year-old girl. Tourists took on many guises. These people appeared to be quite normal, and Leonie knew it. Even if she screamed, struggled, kicked, she doubted if these women would care, because most of them came from Castro's Cuba, where such events were best ignored.

They entered the back room where Daisy Gonzalez was hard at work checking shipping orders and sipping a rum and Coke. She looked up, her face creased in annoyance. "What's this? Who are you? Get out of my office!"

"Cool it, Daisy. It's Cloud."

Leonie struggled in his arms but couldn't budge. Slowly

240

she managed to inch a hand to her belt where the gun waited. It was her only chance.

"What's the kid here for? What's going on?" Daisy stood up, her black eyes flashing.

"She was snooping outside, ready to blow in. I think we can use her effectively," Cloud said, his voice fluid, casual, his hands hard, bruising Leonie's arms.

"You're not the man I expected you to be, Cloud. This should all have been taken care of by now. I should have done it myself." Daisy was the disdainful feminist looking up at Cloud, who currently stood high above the Cigar Mistress.

Cloud chuckled softly. "I'll give the nun a call, she'll come to Papa. I suppose a good place to do it is out by the river. Near your friend's house. See, I'll have her little friend call her and tell her where we should meet. That'll make the nun come running."

Leonie didn't struggle. She stood limp, waiting for the right moment to pull out the gun and escape. She wiggled a half an inch and Cloud didn't notice. Quickly, she took a step away and pulled out the derringer. She pointed it directly at Cloud's head.

"Don't move," she said, her voice surprisingly strong. "I'll kill you. I will." Her voice started to shake just enough to make it sound real. She took a step back. "Move over next to Daisy. Hurry up, or I'll shoot."

"It's the murder weapon," Daisy said. She sounded delighted. "How did you ever get my gun? Sneaky little brat must have come into my office. I keep it in a desk drawer, all loaded but locked in. How'd you get it, little girl?"

Leonie didn't answer. She was busy edging toward the door, ready for a fast getaway.

Cloud watched her through half-closed eyes. He pushed off on his skates, one simple roll forward, and grabbed the gun from Leonie's hand, twisting her arm behind her back.

Leonie closed her eyes in pain. It was more than pain, it was the realization that she really *was* stupid, and all for nothing. Now the question was, should she just let Cloud kill her, or make the call to Cecile and get them both killed.

She thought about the cork in the gun.

"Where'd you get my gun, kid?" Daisy asked.

Leonie's voice came out surly, angry. "It isn't yours. It's Ron Dubaker's. He gave it to me. I loaded it."

With that revelation hanging in the air, Cloud jammed the gun hard into Leonie's ribs. "How?" he asked.

"He had the lead balls. I got the gunpowder." But I used a cork, she added in her mind. "It's loaded."

36

SISTER Cecile and Buddy Dilts drove through the late afternoon traffic. Buddy parked in a no-parking zone and put a Police Business sign in the front window of the Dodge pickup. He slammed the door and looked warily up and down the crowded street. This was not North Carolina.

"This is Little Havana," Cecile explained, urging him forward "It's more like Cuba than Cuba, they say. Some of the cafeterias are fabulous. You should come down some morning for a real Cuban breakfast before you leave."

Buddy's eyes roamed back and forth from people to businesses, his ears straining at the foreign words. This was not a Buddy Dilts kind of place, he realized, but neither was this nun a Buddy Dilts kind of person. He could handle it.

"Up there's Zaruda's cigar factory," Cecile said.

They stopped at the door, then stepped inside. They both automatically took long, deep breaths to get their fill of the sweet aroma. Not smoke, not cancer-causing yet, just the scent of sun-drenched tobacco fields, the cured leaves, and a lingering whiff of rum.

Buddy's blue eyes were wide as saucers, but he still rested one hand on the gun under his shirt.

"Come on," Cecile said quietly, stepping toward the back of the shop. She could see the door to Daisy's office was ajar.

The cigar makers continued rolling cigars; the day apparently hadn't ended yet, although it was going on six o'clock in the evening. The workers kept working as Buddy and Sister Cecile walked to the office door, a door partially opened to reveal Leonie's stark white face, Daisy's sneer, and Cloud's expressionless gaze.

243

Buddy saw it first. "Whoops." His hand slid down on his gun as he pushed into the room.

Cloud saw Buddy walking into the office. He stepped back, drawing Leonie with him. Cecile walked in next, her face frozen. It was too late to back off.

"I've got a gun on this little girl," Cloud said, his eyes on Buddy's hand. "You got a gun there, I suggest you toss it on the ground, slowly. With one finger."

Buddy's eyes focused on the derringer stuck in Leonie's side. Very slowly he removed his service revolver from his belt and let it drop gently to the floor.

"You, nun, toss your bag on the desk. Daisy, go through it. Look for weapons."

Cloud's calm, impersonal voice took over the office, everyone doing what he directed as though it were a performance, a last performance. Buddy stood with his hands flat out. Cecile tossed her bag on the desk, then mimicked Buddy's position, her eyes staring at Leonie's face. Leonie, for some inexplicable reason, winked.

Daisy dumped Cecile's nun purse out on the desk. Sunscreen, a comb, sunglasses, huge black rosary beads, a glossy holy card showing a picture of St. Sebastian, wallet with credit cards and money, and the cigar in its small, expensive case, upon which was the name Montecristo embossed in fine letters. "No weapon," Daisy said as she picked up the cigar case and twisted it open. "Not one of mine," she murmured. "Real?" She smiled very slightly.

"Try it." Cecile shrugged.

"Magruder," Leonie said abruptly. "Remember Magruder?"

Everyone stared at the girl. She was supposed to be trembling with fear, a gun jammed in her side. She wasn't. Buddy's mouth dropped a quarter of an inch. He closed it carefully. He wanted to yell, stamp his feet, do something. Miami was crazy, even the kids here were nuts. He was totally defenseless, his gun on the ground at his feet, a beautiful woman standing in front of him lighting a cigar, a child babbling about Magruder. Who the hell was Magruder?

"Pick up your gun, Buddy," Cecile said firmly.

"You want a dead kid?" Cloud asked.

Daisy struck a match and took a long puff on the cigar. "It's real," she said. "Stale, but real."

"Pick up the gun, Buddy."

"I'll kill this kid."

Daisy took another big puff on the cigar. The room was filling with tobacco smoke.

"Pick up the gun, Buddy," Cecile said a third time. "Now."

Buddy slowly bent over to retrieve his gun. This was against all reason, but the nun had rare, desperate authority in her voice.

Cloud pushed Leonie to the side and took aim at Buddy Dilts just as Daisy Gonzalez took a third puff on the cigar.

Buddy was really frightened. He knew the dueling pistol was aimed at him, at the top of his head, to be exact, but he found himself doing exactly what Sister Cecile ordered. Just as his hand wrapped tightly around his gun, Buddy heard the derringer go off. He felt a stinging on his head and at the same instant heard a huge explosion as the gun blew up in Cloud's hand. A split second later the cigar exploded. Cecile grabbed for Leonie, took Buddy Dilts by the arm and dragged them both to the door. The three of them made it through the passage, then Cecile slammed the door shut.

"I'm not dead," Buddy said, reaching for his head with one hand, fingering his gun with the other. "What the hell was that?"

"A cork," Leonie and Cecile said in unison.

"And an exploding cigar," Cecile added. "I'll go call for the police if you can take care of those two in there. They'll be blind for a half an hour or so from that stuff. Potent tear gas. And it looked like the gun blew up. I don't think Cloud's going to be using his trigger finger for a while."

"I think I used too much powder in the gun," Leonie said quietly.

"I think you're right," Buddy said. He was quick. "Don't you two ladies worry about a thing, now. I can take care of everything from here on."

"Thanks, Buddy." Cecile turned to Leonie. "Could you tell all the women working here to go home? In Spanish?"

Leonie nodded. "I'll try."

"And then you come with me, Leonie Drail. I'm never

letting you out of my sight again." Sister Cecile grabbed Leonie by the hand. She was too relieved, too shaken, to yell at Leonie the way the girl deserved to be yelled at. That would come later. "My purse is in there. Got a quarter so I can call?"

Buddy produced a quarter. "You go ahead." He fingered his gun. "Everything's under control."

EPILOGUE

LEONIE was grounded until the day she was to leave for Japan. She went to school, returned directly home, and did her homework. She also swam in the pool and talked to Carl Cruz on IRC, the Internet Relay Chat. Sister Cecile spoke at length with Leonie, delivering an extensive lecture about acting foolishly and endangering her life. Leonie agreed that she had, indeed, been stupid, foolish, arrogant—just about all the things that Sister Cecile accused her of being. She apologized profusely and promised to behave herself for the rest of her life.

Sister Cecile realized this was an impossible promise, but accepted the apology and the promise in good faith, with a large grain of salt and a long prayer of thanksgiving that they had all walked out of the Zaruda Cigar Shop alive.

"The case is closed," Cecile said on Wednesday evening a week later. She had been fasting on bread and water all day and felt slightly giddy. Fasting had changed from a requirement of the order to an option, a way to offer private sacrifice in honor of Our Lord's passion and death on the cross. Personal sacrifice in an age of too much materialism made sense to Cecile and the other nuns. Only the very old, and Leonie, and the secular elders who lived in the community appeared at the dinner table on most Wednesday nights. Cecile was in her office.

Sister Raphael also fasted, but she handled it better. She sipped slowly from a glass of clear water. "Buddy's gone home," she said to Cecile. "I miss him. He sang in church on Sunday. Such a nice voice."

"A returning hero. He put the man who killed his partner behind bars."

247

"With your help."

"I couldn't have done it without Buddy." Cecile closed her eyes and settled back in her chair; she kept talking. "Of course, Mirtha gave a great affidavit. Daisy Gonzalez is in jail for two murders: that of Nestor Lezo, and that poor man she inherited the cigar shop from. He had curable cancer, but he died of something she slipped him in the hospital. Juan Caldo is clear, John Cruz is clear. He ran away for no reason." Her eyes were still closed. She tilted her office chair back another two inches and appeared to fall asleep.

"John ran for a good reason," Raphael objected. "He would have been brought in for questioning. Pearla did call to tell us how the police showed up at the cattle farm and wanted to talk to him—actually tried to take fingerprints."

"By running, John avoided bringing scandal on his family," Cecile agreed. "In a week or so his case will be cleared from the books. I talked to Paul and he helped me set everything in motion with the legal matters. John's innocence will be a matter of record. He could come home now."

Sister Raphael stared at Sister Cecile, who still appeared to be asleep. "You really must find him, Cecile," Raphael said.

"He vanished after leaving Atlanta for Chicago. He said he would call me. I don't think he ever will. He wants to protect his family. I suspect he left the country. Canada, maybe. He could just walk across the border into Canada. Canada has a lot of empty land. I think John would like that."

"How will he know he's been found innocent?" Raphael asked. "How will he live without his family? Canada is so cold, too."

"I'm thinking," Cecile replied. "I'm thinking of something I saw on the Internet. Leonie's been hogging the computer lately, you know, since I grounded her. She talks to Carl, wanders the Net. I told her to look up animal breeding. She gave me a couple of sites, and I checked them out just a while ago. I want you to look at this article. Tell me if I should call Pearla."

Cecile's eyes finally opened and she sat up. She turned her chair to the computer that had its own place to the left of her desk. She began to push buttons. "I found this," Cecile said as she located the article she was looking for. "It's from Mexico. Read it."

Cecile rose from her chair and let Sister Raphael sit in front of the computer. The article was in Spanish.

"Cerdos Miniaturos, Una Revolución en México," Sister Raphael read in badly pronounced Spanish. "I don't understand this, Cecile."

"Well, I thought maybe your Spanish was better than mine. Where's Marie?"

Raphael glanced at the wall clock. "She goes home in fifteen minutes. Usually she helps Germaine clean up the kitchen."

"Stay here," Cecile said. "I'll go find her."

Raphael nodded and continued to try to read the Spanish article. *"Un hombre que,"* she began. "A man who raises miniature *cerdos*. What's that? What's a *cerdos*?"

Marie walked in as Sister Raphael spoke. "That is the word for pig," Marie said. "What is it you read?"

"Here, Marie. Raphael, let her sit down. She shouldn't be standing anyway. When is the baby due?" Sister Cecile asked.

"Three months. Long time. I am fine. Now I will read this in English for you."

Marie began to translate the article slowly in soft, accented English. " 'Miniature Pigs, A Revolution in Mexico. A man who plans to breed a new type of pig has taken up residence near the town of Las Cañas . . .' "

She read the entire article, then stopped. "Is that good? Was it clear?"

"Wonderful, Marie. Thank you. But they didn't mention the man's name, did they? How could we find out?" Cecile asked.

"Well, in Mexico, in a small town, you just ask. People will know," Marie said.

The two nuns nodded. "Marie, thank you. You are such a help."

"You're welcome," Marie said and left as quietly as she had arrived.

"I'll call Pearla. I think this man in Mexico is John, or Juan. What do you think, Raphael?"

"Call her right now."

An hour later Pearla Cruz and her son Carl turned off the computer in their home office. "It's Dad," Carl said. "Who else would do that? Mini-pigs!"

Pearla's eyes were wet with tears. "Get ready. We're leaving for Mexico immediately."

Pearla booked a flight from Miami to Mexico for early the next morning. It was quicker than flying from Chicago, as Juan had apparently done.

The entire family packed. Pearla, Carl, Pearlita, and Beatriz traveled without incident to Mexico City, then were able to take a bus to within fifty miles of their destination. They rented a car and drove steadily until they reached the town of Las Cañas. Pearla was a determined woman. The children didn't fight during the long day, even into the night when she refused to stop and kept driving over the winding, bumpy roads. They found a place to stay late that night in Las Cañas.

The following morning Pearla questioned everyone she saw. The Las Cañas police had never heard of a man who raised pigs. Everyone raised at least one pig, they said. This was Mexico.

Finally she located a grain supply store on the outskirts of town.

"Oh sure, Cerdito, we call him. Little pig." The proprietor laughed. "This man is mad about pigs, I think he never sleeps. He is driven. I tell you what. Take this road maybe six kilometers, take a left on a little road you'll see next to an old church. Drive up the hill and there's the farm. Nice spot. Manuel Vargas owned that land. He's still around someplace." The man looked at the sleepy children behind Pearla. "His family?"

Pearla nodded. *"Gracias."* She was gone.

Juan Caldo, John Cruz, now Juan Calderon, had risen early that morning. He knew what he was doing was not scientific. He should be doing genetic engineering, developing pigs the way it was being done in the scientific centers of the world. Who was he? A madman on a small speck of dirt out in the backwoods of a third world country. Yet what he was doing was how the world had developed and bred animals over

250

thousands of years. Breeding a better animal had always been done this way. By seeing the good traits, putting them together, checking, remembering, letting nature provide the changes in a real environment where there was real weather, real life, food gleaned from native plants; that was the way it had always been. He had ten pigs now. Seven were bred.

In several months he would have his first litter of new pigs. A modest-sized pink barrow that was supposedly a descendent of a European wild boar, a small Vietnamese potbelly pig for the father. He couldn't wait to see what developed. Pig gestation was three months, three weeks, three days.

Outside, he walked to the barn and tossed in some food for the animals. He had chickens too, for eggs, for a good chicken dinner now and then, for company. He was very lonesome. His stack of letters to Pearla was growing. He would give anything to see Carlito. No, Carl. His son was a man now, the man of the family. His daughters, what he wouldn't give to see his darlings. Beatriz, Pearlita. His wife, Pearla.

Juan felt an arrow pierce his heart.

He saw dust rising down the road. A car was coming. Travelers never came this way, only Manuel Vargas now and then, and Manuel drove an old truck that made as much noise as dust. This car was low, a Toyota perhaps. Probably a lost tourist. Juan went out to see, his hunger for human companionship stronger than his fear of being discovered. He stood by the road, a tall Hispanic man dressed in dungarees and a worn blue T-shirt. On his head was an old straw hat he had found in the house.

Juan saw the thin woman and the boy in the front seat, then the two little faces peering over the backseat. It looked like his family. His heart lurched, almost tore open in his chest with the desire for his wife, his children. He stood mute as the car pulled up and stopped. The doors all seemed to open simultaneously and Pearla was in his arms. Pearlita and Beatriz wrapped around his legs and Carlito stood to one side, almost as tall as a man, with tears running down his cheeks.

*　*　*

They roasted a chicken for lunch. Pearla used the woodstove, Carl pumped water from the well, Pearlita and Beatriz played with the chickens and wandered among the pigs in awe. The warm Mexican sun beat down until some high clouds moved in off the Pacific Ocean. A wind picked up and they gathered inside the house, sitting on an old green couch in a row, hugging each other.

"I'm free," Juan said. He kept repeating it, disbelief in his voice. "That nun," he said.

"And she found you here." Pearla's face was clean now; she had washed away the tears. They all had.

"My pigs," Juan said. "I wonder if I can bring them back to Florida."

"This is a beautiful piece of land," Pearla said. "Maybe we can spend the summer."

"Yes," Juan said, his voice quivering. "And it will be ours forever."

"And mine," Carl said.

"Carl has two more days of school. We will go home, come back next week," Pearla said, already planning their life.

Carl frowned. His father patted him on the back. "Yes, Carl. Do your life right."

That night the Cruz family slept in a small house in Mexico. Outside, chickens clucked softly, an occasional grunting noise came from a pig. A gentle breeze stirred the trees.

A week later Sister Cecile received a check for twenty thousand dollars and a note from Pearla. "We are so happy," the note read. "Our family is complete again, we are free."

Leonie sent a last e-mail to Carl. "Leaving for Japan tomorrow. Glad you're on-line in Mexico. Next time I write, it will be from Tokyo!"

The retirement community had a new air-conditioning system installed by the end of July. A bronze plaque commemorating Sister Linda arrived and Marie's husband mounted it on the side of the organ. That week, a memorial Mass was held for the repose of Sister Linda's soul and suitable music was played by Sister Emma, one of the retired nuns.